zero To HERO

HARMONY A. HAUN

ISBN: 979-8-9868359-9-0 Paperback
ISBN: 979-8-9868359-8-3 e-book
ISBN: 978-1-961040-90-8 Hardback

First edition

Author Contact: harmonyahaunauthor@gmail.com
IG: Harmonya.haun_author
TT: @authorharmonyahaun
www.harmonyahaunauthor.com

zero To HERO

Playlist on _Spotify_

Click the Spotify link above or scan the QR Code

Preface & Triggers

As an author, I am constantly aware and extremely nervous about writing something that could potentially offend someone. Please know that it is NEVER my intent. That being said, I am human and I do make mistakes. I do not know everything, I am not the most educated person, and we all live lives that give us experiences no one else will understand or relate to. So, in the event that something I write EVER makes you feel uncomfortable or attacked in any way, please reach out to me. My Instagram DMs and/or email are always open, and I genuinely care about my readers' experiences and feelings.

Now, please keep in mind this is a work of FICTION. I am trying to do my best to write authentically and to give real-life scenarios justice.

POTENTIAL TRIGGERS: Adult language and content, trauma, abandonment, suggested child abuse, suggested sexual assault, blood/gore, physical violence, murder, loss of parent/friends.

Dedication

To those who feel alone. Unseen. Unimportant. To those who feel
like zeros and could never fathom being a HERO.
I promise you; you are seen. You are important.
You are already someone's HERO.
Just. The. Way. You. Are.

zero To HERO

Prologue

Long Ago... by Disney Hercules Soundtrack

Many eons ago, back when the world was first created, Earth wasn't what it is today. Humans lived alongside the Mageía, a beautiful and magical race of otherworldly beings. Most of the Mageía were friendly and peaceful. However, within this race of magical beings, one group stood above all others.

The Titans.

There was no one powerful enough who could control them. They had no rules and no goals other than doing what they wanted when they wanted. And what desires were at the heart of most?

Power, above all else.

Love.

And if love wasn't an option, fear would do.

Unable to defend themselves against the Titans, humans were on the verge of extinction before they ever had a chance to flourish. Until a desperate prayer shot up like a beacon into the sky, pleading for someone, *anyone*, to help save them. The prayer was heard by Zeus, God of Mount Olympus, and it zapped like his own lightning bolts across his skin. It settled deep in his bones, thrumming like electricity, intensifying his power.

Curious and intrigued, he descended his throne on Mount Olympus to seek out the source of such a power. It shocked him to find only a simple woman. A woman desperate for help, not only for her own life but for the world.

Zeus thought she was one of the most beautiful things he'd ever seen. Or maybe it was just the power of her prayers that made

Zeus wild with the need for more.

The need for *her*.

He seduced her and promised to help under one condition; that she not only keep praying but recruit others to join her. And not just any praying but specifically praying to *him*. Of course, once the people saw Zeus's strength and realized he was their savior, prayers flowed easily from mouths across the world.

Zeus fought the Titans, forcing them into an underground prison of his design known as The Underworld, and sent his brother to oversee it. But The Underworld didn't just become a prison for the Titans, it was tethered to *all* with magic, pulling the entire race of Mageía into its depths. Knowing most Mageía were harmless, Zeus designed another option for them. The Underworld was one small step away from the mortal realm, separated by a hidden portal that allowed the Mageía to come and go as they pleased.

But there was a catch.

The portal out of The Underworld took away that which made them...them. They could only walk Earth as human versions of themselves. And just as Earth was restricted so, too, was the portal into The Underworld. Humans could not cross over without an invitation from someone on the other side, and once they were in The Underworld, all protection was gone.

Enter at your own risk.

And risk it was. Because even worse than the Titans was their new ruler, Hades. He only wanted power, to hell with love, and would do anything to maintain it. He was known for his devious and often one-sided deals and gods-awful ruthlessness. If there was one person in The Underworld you did not want to cross, for any reason, it was Hades. And he now has his eyes set on ruling Earth.

As a god, Hades could feel the power of the once-strong prayers fading. With no magic of any kind left to be witnessed on Earth, gods and goddesses had slowly been forgotten. All tales of the Mageía, Titans, and Zeus had fallen into myth and legend. But unlike Zeus, Hades had never received his power from prayers. His power came from death, the *one* certainty life had to offer. So, he bid his time, growing stronger with every soul he added to The Pit of Souls. Meanwhile, the portal is ever so slowly weakening. But Hades was patient. Afterall, what was time to an immortal god?

Though nothing was ever quite that simple. There were whispers of a prophecy, of a *hero*. A boy that had been born from Zeus's visits to the human woman he'd selfishly kept alive all that time. And that boy, that hero, was the only one with the power to stop Hades from taking control of the human world.

His name was Hercules.

While Zeus had kept his human lover hidden and safe, his power faded along with the prayers, and Hades watched Zeus's every move closely. He was determined to find the boy and stop the prophecy before it had any chance of coming true.

The only hope for the world was Hercules. He would become the people's champion. He would keep Hades from ruling over and destroying Earth. He would finally set the Mageía free of Hades' cruel reign and release them from their underground prison.

IF he fought.

IF he survived.

Chapter one

Lonely by Onlap, Halocene

As soon as I step out onto the open sidewalk, I close my eyes and inhale deeply, savoring the fresh night air that fills my lungs. Even though most people would think I'm crazy for enjoying polluted air, it's still a million times better than down there. Besides, it's so much more than that to me. This world may not be nice or pretty in most cases, but it's free. It's freedom in a way I've never been afforded but have craved as far back as I can remember.

Only a few seconds pass, but I don't dare linger. Not here. There's too much of a chance I'll be seen, so I move swiftly and quietly down the sidewalk, sticking to the shadows. I pull my jacket tighter around my body, trying to stave off the frigid air, but I don't mind it all that much. I like how the seasons change up here because things *never* change down there.

I don't have any particular destination in mind, I just want to walk aimlessly and carelessly through the night. Well, that's not entirely true. I've always felt a pull to be topside. Something in my gut that I can't quite describe. In the hopeful, quiet corners of my mind, I tell myself it's my connection to *her*. A bond stronger than anything else. But those are just whispered thoughts on lonely nights. Nothing more than the broken fragments that remain of a hopeful child's dream. Besides, I wouldn't know her even if I did see her. Or would I?

As much as I try to let go, to be at ease and just enjoy the open sky above me, again it's not something I've been afforded. So, even out here, alone, I can't completely relax. I can't be careless. Ever. The consequences are too great.

Coming here is careless.

And yet, I can't stop. Well, I can but I don't want to. It's the only time I truly feel even the slightest bit of life stirring inside me. As if this polluted night air is the only thing that can stoke the dying embers in my chest. That slight feeling of *something* aching to catch fire and burn brightly inside me is the only reason I continue to come here. The feeling that I haven't been snuffed out completely…not quite. Still, defying him even this much, without really doing anything deliberately bad, is terrifying.

Terrifying or exhilarating?

Honestly, sometimes I can't tell the difference. But these small escapes, these moments of pretend peace and feigned freedom, are all that keep me going these days.

The sound of a familiar voice coming from the alley just ahead of me has me plastering my body up against the brick wall, hoping the deep shadows of the building will hide me. Coming here is always a risk and this is *not* someone I want to find me. It's amazing how quickly one's heart can start to race out of control. I take a few long, deep breaths, steadying my nerves. Controlling my emotions is something I had to learn at a young age, but there are still times when they rebel, and I have to fight to rein them in.

Tiberius is the worst of them, and that's saying something considering they're all dangerous. They're strong, powerful, and loved by pretty much everyone. No one loves them more than Raymond though. Mainly because they make him a shit ton of money and have no qualms about doing all of his dirty deeds. No doubt Tiberius is out here now because he's on one of Raymond's errands. Or he's just out to have a good time amongst the mostly oblivious humans. Compared to what most people consider a good time, his is drastically different.

My curiosity, the calamitous bitch, has me inching my way along the wall, getting closer to the alley. Perhaps I can catch Tiberius doing something he's not supposed to be doing. Perhaps I can get some dirt on him.

But then what, Meg?

It's not like Raymond gives two shits about anything that happens unless it's losing him money. And if Tiberius is up to no good, which he probably is, that will just gain him *more* favor. I swear, it's such a fucked-up world. A world most of us have no choice but to endure and simply hope to survive.

I slowly peek around the corner of the building, grateful for the tall chain link fence that blocks off the alley. It's not *really* a barrier, not to Tiberius, but it makes me feel slightly better and less exposed. He towers over a boy who doesn't look to be any older than sixteen and is practically the size of one of Tiberius's arms.

A vicious backhand across his face makes the boy cry out as he's thrown to the ground with the force of it. "I swear! It wasn't my fault," the boy pleads.

"Wasn't your fault? That's cute." Tiberius's voice rattles deep with excitement.

His humorless laugh sends shivers running down my spine. He loves this. Toying with people. Tormenting them. Terrifying them. He's no different in the ring either. He loves to put on a show, even when there's no crowd to cheer him on.

"Did you or did you not take the product?"

"I did but—"

"Did you or did you not know the responsibility of taking on this task?" Before the kid can answer, he continues. "Did you or did you not know the consequences?"

"It wasn't my fault! I was jumped and my backpack was—"

"And now you have no product *and* no money, and the one thing my boss doesn't tolerate is loss of any kind. You cost him money, Joey. A lot of money. Do you know what happens to people who cost him even one fucking penny?"

"Please! I can get money! I can pay him back. I can—"

"Get up!" Tiberius yells the order so fiercely even I jump.

No sooner does the boy stand before a closed fist cracks against his cheek, sending him crashing to the ground again.

"You wanted to play with the big boys. Now you're going to take this beating like one. Get up."

The boy is crying now, shaking his head, and begging for it to stop. The pure desperation in his voice tugs at my heart but I'm powerless to help him and that awful reality makes tears prick behind my eyes.

"I said get up!"

I don't know which option would be worse; to do as Tiberius says and get to his feet or to stay down. Once again, the boy pushes shakily to his feet and, once again, he's knocked back down. Hard. I squeeze my eyes shut against the brutality of it. I don't have the option to do it when I'm in *his* presence, watching the fights, but I do it now, trying to save myself new visions for my nightmares.

I'm about to turn away and head back when another voice joins the fight.

"Hey! You fucking piece of shit! Why don't you pick on someone your own size."

Blinking away my tears, my eyes focus on the tidal wave of anger heading right for Tiberius. He looks like a beautiful shining beacon of hope. A golden glow on the horizon from a lighthouse leading a ship out of the storm. Except he has no idea what kind of storm Tiberius is. Even if he doesn't have all his strength here, he's still a massive wall of hard-earned muscles, and centuries worth of honed fighting skills. This poor guy, no matter how heroic he might seem to be, has no gods-damned chance in hell.

"Walk away," Tiberius warns. "This has nothing to do with you. And trust me, you don't want to fight me." His tone is mocking, accentuated by a mischievous smirk as he looks the newcomer up and down, unimpressed.

However, I am a little impressed. Once he gets close to Tiberius, I can see he's not that much smaller than him. Alas, his size will do him no good here.

"Oh, but I really, really do," the new guy taunts. "I'll even give you the first swing."

I swallow down the anxiety that's snuck its way into my throat. "Get out of there, you fool. Walk away while you still can," I whisper into the shadows, hoping by some miracle he hears me. Of course, he doesn't.

The kid uses the guys' focus on one another to scramble out of the way. Smart kid. I just wish he had been smart enough to never get involved with Tiberius.

That low, deep chuckle I've heard one too many times pulls my attention back to the men standing off.

"How generous of you. If you can even stand after one hit, you're going to regret it because I'm not going to stop until you're dead."

I watch, wide-eyed, my breath caught in my throat, as Tiberius pulls his massive arm back and lets it fly with all his weight behind it. The sound of his fist connecting with the other man's cheek sounds like a crack of thunder booming and echoing through the alley. My eyes burn from not blinking, not wanting to miss a single second of what's unfolding in front of me. And I think they may be failing me because the newcomer staggers slightly, but quickly regains his footing, appearing entirely unaffected by the hit.

The devious smirk that pulls at his lips and the deadly gleam in his eyes make me draw in a deep, shaky breath. I know dangerous when I see it, after all I've been surrounded by it my entire life, and this man is definitely dangerous. I thought he looked like a hero when he first walked up, but boy, looks can be deceiving.

"My turn," he says cooly. And then...he unleashes fucking hell.

Chapter two

Natural Born Killer by Highly Suspect

I've always been quick to fight. Quick to inflict the pain I feel inside onto others. Something about seeing the blood, the internal pain escaping the body, helps me feel less isolated in my own. I've hurt plenty of people, but I've never killed before.

Not until tonight.

To be honest, I didn't mean to kill him. I've always had this ungodly amount of strength. Even as a child, when I had no business being so strong, I was. It made me equally fascinating and terrifying to others. For a young kid, just trying to make friends, it was confusing. I didn't understand why I was so different. I didn't understand why people seemed to want to watch me from afar but were always afraid to get too close. I was like a walking, talking, living car wreck and everyone else was the passersby, slowing down to see the destruction, but not daring to stop and help.

Talk about giving a kid a complex.

But there's always someone who stand out from the crowd. Someone who doesn't follow along with the other sheep. Someone brave. My friendship with Jonah was new and exciting. He wasn't scared of me and treated me like I was normal, even though we both knew I wasn't. He was my one and only friend, and when the time came to use my strength to fight and protect him, I failed.

Luckily, I had a mother and father that were the best parents a kid could have. They were loving and understanding. They didn't ignore my unique gift and, most importantly, didn't lie to me. They didn't coddle and they didn't push. They were always just...there; for whatever I needed. Even when I didn't know what that need was, they *did*. They were the best fucking things in my life until they were taken from me too.

Too young to understand everything that was happening, I didn't ask questions. I didn't fight. I just let them whisk me away and turn my entire life, everything I ever knew, upside down literally overnight. Needless to say, I've learned to survive on my own since then. I've used my pain to keep going instead of succumbing to it like so many others I've seen living on the streets. But the most important lesson I've learned?

To fucking fight.

It's always served me well. Until tonight. I don't know what happened. Maybe it's this city. Maybe being back here reminds me that I don't even know who the fuck I am. Or maybe I do care about others after all. All I know is when I saw the young boy getting beaten by someone four times his size, it was Jonah all over again and I snapped. All I saw was red. I let him hit me first, desperate to feel the sting of pain, only to be disappointed. Angered even more by that, I smashed my fist into his face until the red behind my eyes became tangible and flowed down his skin.

Even when he was no longer fighting, I didn't stop.

I couldn't hear my fist cracking bone with every brutal punch. I couldn't hear the nearby traffic on the street. I couldn't hear the boy yelling that we needed to go. All I could hear was a deafening silence. Utterly...peaceful...fucking...silence. The only time my mind isn't a constant riot of noise is when I'm fighting. When I see blood.

An empty beer bottle hitting the side of my face finally

managed to shake me from my stupor. The poor kid looked terrified as I snarled at him, finally acknowledging his presence. Even if he was scared of me, he was still brave enough to stick around and save me from being caught. Picking my backpack off the ground, I followed him over the chain link fence at the back of the alley only to run through more darkened and rundown alleys, turning this way and that way until the streets started to get slightly cleaner and more illuminated.

The boy slowed to a walk, and I followed suit. I had no idea where he was taking me but what else was I going to do? If I got even the slightest hint he was taking me somewhere I didn't want to be, no one would be able to stop me from leaving short of putting a bullet through my heart or head. Hell, I'm doubtful even that could stop me.

I was surprised when we turned onto a main sidewalk, slightly busier than where we had just been, and he walked casually into a gym. Before blindly following him inside, I took some time to look around. Not the best part of town but not the worst either. It didn't seem like anyone was following us or paying us any mind whatsoever, so I finally followed the boy inside.

That's where I'm now sitting, on a hard bench in a locker room that smells like sweat, piss, and desperate dreams, staring at my blood-stained hands. Flexing my fingers, I clench and unclench my fists slowly. No broken skin. No bruises. No pain. The fact that I don't feel anything physically or emotionally when I fight makes it all too easy to keep doing it.

I keep waiting for shock or guilt or fucking *something* to overcome me, but nothing happens.

I killed a man.

In cold blood.

With my fucking bare hands.

And I still feel empty inside. Maybe my first foster mother was right. I am the goddamn devil. Evil to my core at the very least.

Heartless. Emotionless. Soulless. All the *lesses*.

A throat clears near me, getting my attention. A short, older man stands just inside the doorway, arms crossed, staring at me with brown eyes as cold as I feel. His dark sideburns run into a full beard, no mustache, and he's started to go bald. Only the sides of his head are covered in slightly graying brown hair. He has the build of someone who used to be in shape, probably packed with muscle, but has gone soft in his older age. I don't doubt he still has some of that strength though. It's there. I can see it in his eyes and in his confident stance. And he is definitely sizing me up.

After a long stare-off, he finally speaks. "I'm Phil and this here is my gym. I won't be having any trouble brought here."

"Then you should have that discussion with the boy who brought me here."

"I've already had a talk with Joey, and we'll be having an even sterner discussion if he plans to keep coming here, but that ain't your business." He pauses. I'm not sure if he's waiting for me to argue, but I won't. "He tells me you saved him."

I cock an eyebrow, amused by the idea of me saving anyone while the life of another still coats my hands. "That all he tell you?"

"He told me enough. Your hands and clothes tell me more."

"Look, I don't know why he brought me here and, honestly, I'm not sure why I even followed. I don't want trouble any more than you do, but trouble always seems to find me anyway." I push to my feet, towering over the small man, but he doesn't cower before me. "If I can just wash up, I'd be grateful, and then I'll be out of your...," my eyes move to his shining head, "hair."

I know he hears me, but he doesn't answer the way I'm expecting. "That man that was beatin' on Joey, he ain't a good man, and I ain't sorry 'bout what happened to him one bit, but it ain't the police that's gonna come looking for ya. He was real important to a very dangerous man. You got a safe place to lay low?"

I shake my head. "I just got to town, but trust me, I'll be fine."

It's his turn to shake his head. "Follow me."

I'm not usually one to follow orders from anyone, but for the second time tonight, I find myself following. I'm in an unfamiliar town and I don't know these streets the way I knew the streets where I grew up. I don't have connections here. As much as I prefer to be a loner, I'm not stupid. You can't survive on the streets being careless. I understand the importance of knowing when to punch and when to block. I guess being careless is one of the few *lesses* I'm not.

Killing a man was careless.

I take it back. Is that my guilty conscience speaking up finally? No, it's simple truth. It *was* careless. Lucky for me, I also know when to dwell on something and when to move the fuck on. And I very rarely dwell on anything. What's done is done. What good is it going to do to feel bad about it now?

I follow Phil around the edge of the main gym floor. It's a small space, only allowing for one boxing ring in the middle, surrounded by workout equipment along the far wall, a couple punching bags along one side, and open space for the rest. It's not much but there are people everywhere. Mainly young boys but I see a few older men. Men who look like they actually train to fight. All the training in the world and they still wouldn't be prepared for me.

At six foot five inches, packed with my own hard-earned muscle, I tower over most of them. All eyes are on me and a hushed-quiet falls over the room as Phil leads me to the far end of the gym. I can feel their fear, curiosity, and uncertainty hanging in the air like humidity. By now I'm sure every single person here knows what took place tonight. If not, one look at my blood-stained hands and clothes should reveal the story easily enough. Phil starts climbing a staircase at the back corner of the room and I continue to follow. As soon as we're out of sight, the whispers start.

"He's huge!"

"Did you hear? He killed Tiberius."

"Who is he?"

"He saved Joey."

"He's dangerous."

"Is Phil gonna train him?"

The whispers fade as I climb to the landing and focus on my new surroundings. A hallway stretches out in front of me with two doors opposite each other and one directly in front of me at the end.

Phil walks to the door on the right and pushes it open before stepping aside and motioning me forward.

"It ain't much but I reckon it's more than you've got. Make do with it what you will."

Walking slowly toward the open door, I stop next to him to peer inside. It's a tiny room with only a bed and one nightstand to fill the space. There's a small nook in one of the walls which I'm assuming is supposed to be the closet, though there's no door on it.

"The bathroom is through that door there," he gestures to the door at the end of the hall. "You can get washed up and stay here 'til you're on your feet," he says, before nodding once then walking back down the hall the way we came.

"Why offer me this when you know what I've done?"

He turns to face me. "Regardless of *how* you saved one of my boys I ain't gonna return that act of...well, never mind what kind of act it was. I ain't gonna kick you while you're down."

I stare at him, trying to understand him as I mull over his words. They're not necessarily kind words, but the gesture is. He doesn't want trouble brought here, that was the first thing out of his mouth, yet he's willing to tempt that fate by allowing me to stay. I haven't come across many kind people in my life, so I'm not sure what to do or even what to say.

Apparently, I take too long figuring out a response. He grunts and starts to walk away again.

"I can't pay you," I call after him.

"Then you'll work for it," he yells back, before disappearing around the corner and I hear his footsteps descending the stairs.

It's my turn to grunt. *Work for it.* For the second time tonight I find myself thinking, *what else am I going to do?*

The room feels even smaller once I'm inside. I toss my backpack on a bed no wider than a full-size mattress, but it's longer than normal. It might actually fit my large body and that's good enough for me. As far as accommodations go, it's not nearly the worst I've dealt with. It's clean, it's private, and it's warm. If the water is warm, too, which I suspect it will be, that's the icing on the cake.

Rummaging through my pack, I take out my toothpaste and toothbrush, along with a clean pair of underwear. I won't need anything else to sleep in, not that I have much. The shirt I'm wearing is past the point of no return, leaving me with only three shirts to rotate through. Same goes for socks and underwear. Luckily, the jeans seem to have been spared any blood, nothing a cycle through a washing machine can't fix. Thank fuck. Shirts I can come by easily enough on the streets, especially with all these kids dressing in clothing five times too big for them. However, finding jeans that fit is more of a struggle. Plus, who has fifty bucks to spend on jeans? And that's on the cheap side. Most people do, I guess, but I certainly don't.

The bathroom isn't much to look at either. It's old and smells a bit musty, but it has a toilet, a sink, and a shower. What more is there to need? The shower is bigger than I'd have guessed. The showerhead is installed surprisingly higher than normal, which means I'll barely have to duck underneath it. I suppose if this has always been a gym, it makes sense that things like the bed and shower would be made to accommodate bigger bodies. Or Phil did his own custom renovations. Whatever the reason, I'm grateful.

Turning the handles, water rushes out immediately, the pressure strong and forceful. Fucking hell, did I actually somehow end up in Heaven? Pulling the ruined shirt over my head, I toss it in the trash bin by the toilet, then fold my jeans, wrapping my briefs and socks inside, keeping them safe and secure for the next round of washing. My black sneakers look clean enough as I set them next to my pile of dirty clothes and finally get into the shower.

The water is blissfully hot as I step under the spray, placing my hands against the cool tile, ducking my head to let the water cascade down my back. I don't know what it is about showers, but they've always been soothing to me. Maybe it's the simple fact that you appreciate things more when they're not everyday pleasures. A shower shouldn't be a pleasure. It's a necessity. But we don't all live a charmed life. Still, even when you think you have it bad, there's always someone who has it worse. Always.

Speaking of having it worse, the white suds from the soap turn red as I start to lather it in my hands. Yeah, he definitely had a worse night than me, whoever this Tiberius guy was. Even if he was a piece of shit that this world is better off without, the possibility that he's like me, completely alone in the world, is unlikely. He was still someone's son, possibly a father or brother. Someone will miss him. Someone will come looking. Phil said as much.

The thought should scare me. At the very least it should worry me. It doesn't. Not because I'm cocky and think no one can best me, but because I just don't give a fuck. I'm not scared of pain, and I'm not scared of death. I don't necessarily want to die. I will fight like hell against anyone who threatens me, but I don't fear the consequences of losing. This truth only makes me more dangerous.

I wash my hands until all traces of blood are gone. Then, and only then, do I wash the rest of my body and move on to my hair. Every fiber of my being wants to stand under the water and relish every second until there's no hot water left, but I don't. Stepping out of the shower, I scan the room for a clean towel but don't see any. There's a small cabinet next to the sink. I walk over to it and open the door to find a small storage closet with towels on one shelf.

Once I'm dry, I pull on my clean pair of briefs then begin to brush my teeth, careful not to look in the mirror. I try to avoid them as often as possible. It's not that I'm ugly or anything, quite the opposite actually, but I never recognize the man looking back at me. It's an odd feeling, not fully knowing yourself. Every time I come face to face with my reflection it just reminds me that I have no idea who I am. Not really. I sure as hell don't fit the image I see. The image the world sees.

With eyes downcast, I manage to leave the bathroom unscathed and slip back into the bedroom, closing the door softly behind me. I sigh quietly as my head hits the pillow and my body slowly relaxes. This is better than I've had in a long time. Too bad I know it won't last.

Looking up, I see a skylight in the middle of the room. A detail I hadn't noticed earlier since it's night and no light filters through it. Now, I stare out into the darkness though it's not complete darkness. There's never complete darkness in cities like this. There's always the faintest glow of lights from the streets and buildings. And stars? Good luck seeing those through the smog and pollution. I suppose that's the only thing I miss from my time in the country. The sky and the clean air.

Even though it's not late, probably no later than 9 p.m., it is late for a gym to be to be open. The soft murmur of voices and the clanking of weights and machines filter up through the floor. Instead of irritating me or keeping me from sleeping, the sounds only comfort me further. I focus on them, trying to quiet my mind, but like always it doesn't do any good.

I'm finally here. Back in the place I was born. Back in the city that I would have grown up in had my life not been taken from me. How different would my life have been had my parents not died? What kind of man would I have become with their love and guidance?

What if?

What if?

What if?

A fool's question.

Who I might have become is a fantasy. What life I might have lived is a dream. Who I hoped to become by coming back here? Fuck if I know. There's no past here for me to grab onto. I'm no different here than I would be anywhere else. But I needed to come back. I don't know why, but I needed to come back. Something about this city called to me like no other place I've been. It's not home but it's...*something*.

Considering I've been here for mere hours and already killed a man, it might just be the place that destroys me not saves me. Maybe it's some kind of fucked up destiny that I die where my parents did. Maybe it's for the best. There's nothing worth saving anyway.

"Give me your worst, Chicago. I'm up for the fight."

Chapter three

O.K? by Picturesque

It wasn't the sound of knocking that woke me. I very rarely sleep, and when I do, it's not for long. Even though I didn't sleep, the fact that I wasn't on the street and I could actually relax, is a huge benefit. And despite the night I had, I feel pretty decent this morning. I pump out five more pushups before pushing to my feet to open the door.

Phil stands in the hallway with his hands on his hips. "This ain't no hotel, sleepin' until noon and being a bum kinda deal. If ya wanna stay here, you're gonna be up at 5 a.m. helping me with this place. You don't like my rules you know where the door is. Now, get dressed and meet me downstairs."

"Good morning to you, too, old man."

He grunts and walks away, muttering under his breath, "Old man. These dang kids today ain't got no respect."

I like him. I don't know him well, but I get the sense that he tackles life like he tackles fights. There's no dancing around the ring, throwing jabs to test your opponent. No, this old man goes straight for the knockout. He speaks his truth and leaves no room for assuming, second guessing or questioning. You'll always know exactly where you stand with him. In this world, with so many two-faced and selfish people always working some kind of angle, Phil is a breath of fresh air. Yeah, I like him.

I get dressed in my only remaining pair of dark jeans, a faded blue T-shirt, and my black sneakers. At the sink in the bathroom, I brush my teeth and splash cold water on my face, pushing my wet fingers through my hair, styling the long strands on top and then running my hands over the buzzed sides.

On my way here, I stumbled upon a quaint little village called Downers Grove where I swept a barbershop for an entire day in exchange for a haircut. The barber had asked what I wanted done and I told him to surprise me. He chose this faded mohawk look. Apparently, it's in style. Not that I've ever given a damn about style. Other than the name of the village being fitting to my life, the village itself was a bit too *friendly neighbor* for me. It was way too small, and too many eyes on me is never a good thing.

That had been the most recent I had looked in a mirror, to make the barber happy and reassure him that *"Yeah. I dig it, bro."* And honestly, I do. It looks good and it's easy to style. No fuss. Which is the name of my game since I don't always have access to grooming supplies.

Now, without looking in the mirror to confirm it still looks good, I head down the hallway and descend the stairs. I don't want to keep the old man waiting and potentially cause him to become even grumpier than he already is.

The gym is lit by only a few dim security lights that remain on overnight, but there's a bright light coming from an open doorway across the room. As I approach, I see a plaque on the door which reads *office*. Phil is inside, sitting at a desk that's a mess of papers, folders, and old disposable coffee cups.

I rap my knuckles on the door, alerting him to my presence.

"Just a second," he says as he shuffles some papers around, clearly looking for something in the mess on his desk.

Leaning against the doorframe, I cross my arms and feet while

I wait patiently. It takes him a couple of minutes, but he eventually finds what he's looking for.

"Ah, here we are. Alright then...," he finally looks up at me, "come fill this out." He pushes a piece of paper and a pen across the desk toward me

Pushing off the doorframe, I walk over and pick up the piece of paper. I lift an amused eyebrow and look over the top of it at Phil. "A liability form?"

"I ain't gonna have you walking around my gym without one. My luck, you get yourself hurt and I end up footin' the bill. I ain't got money for no medical bills and sure as hell not for no lawsuit. You sign it and stay, or you don't and you—"

"Know where the door is," I interrupt. "Yes, I know." I set the paper back down on the desk, pick up the pen and fill out what I can. "What's the date?"

"March twenty-sixth. I'm assuming you know the year?"

I don't respond as I add my signature and date to the form and then hand it over. "There might be people who get hurt in your gym, but I won't be one of them."

"Awfully arrogant one, aren't ya?"

I shrug. "It's just a fact."

He grunts and takes the paper. "Jett Stephens, twenty-two years old. No address. No phone number." He scoffs. "Not even an email address."

Since he didn't ask a question, I simply respond with, "I go by T."

Phil eyes me up and down, contemplating...*something*. I'm not sure what he's inspecting. My old, tattered clothes? The serpents snaking up my arms? My stylish haircut?

"You don't look twenty-two."

"Are you asking if I'm lying?"

"Why would you lie about your age?"

"I didn't."

"Exactly. Alls I'm saying is you don't look like most twenty-two-year-olds I see comin' in here lookin' for a trainer. Not your body and not what I see in your eyes. I imagine last night's events are common for you."

"No."

"No?" He raises his eyebrows, questioningly.

"The streets, the life, yeah. Some call it criminal; I call it survival. I'm a fighter. I fight to survive, but I'm not a killer."

He sets the paper down and leans his forearms on the desk, an accusatory look on his face. I feel my irritation and anger starting to surge. How many times have I been judged without ever speaking a word? How many times have people looked at me this same way without caring to understand?

"Look, if you don't want me here, I'll leave. I said as much last night. Give that back and I'll be on my way." I gesture to the paper under his arms.

Something in his expression changes but I don't know exactly what. He sighs and reaches into the back pocket of his jeans, pulling out his wallet. He opens it up and holds a five-dollar bill out to me.

"There's a coffee stand at the end of the street. Mike's his name. Tell him I sent ya. When you get back, you're going to clean up the gym and get it ready for the day. Rack the weights, sweep and mop the floor, take out the trash. You know the rest."

I hesitate for a second before finally taking the money out of his hand. He's allowing me to stay. Why? I have no damn clue but I'm not going to question it. It's not like I have anywhere else to go, and people generally aren't this kind to me. People generally aren't this kind, period. I'm not sure why he's extending his kindness and trust to me, but I'll take it. I'll stay for a couple of days, maybe a week, get my bearings in this new city, and then be on my way. Hopefully I don't bring any of the trouble that likes to follow me into Phil's life. I don't want to repay his kindness with stress.

There's still snow shoveled into the corners of the sidewalks and streets. My breath puffs out in white clouds as I breathe but I don't feel the bite of the freezing air in my lungs or on my skin. Just like I don't feel pain the way normal people do; weather doesn't affect me as easily. I don't know what it is about me. I don't know why I have this strength. And the only people who could have provided me with answers are dead.

Those thoughts are quickly dispelled as my attention is pulled to the only other man on the deserted sidewalk. He's huddled in a huge marshmallow looking jacket, sweatpants, slippers, with a beanie pulled low over his ears. He's holding a leash to a beautiful albino dog that looks like a mix of Great Dane and Doberman. Its coat is so white it looks almost silver in the early morning glow.

"I said go to the fucking bathroom! You stupid fucking bitch of a dog." He pulls his leg back and kicks the dog in the stomach. It whimpers and shrinks away from him, pulling at the leash in a futile attempt at escape.

Much like with the boy from the night before, I snap. If anything, I hate the senseless abuse of animals even more than that of humans. Humans, mostly, know what the fuck they're getting themselves into. Dogs are innocent. Period.

"Hey!" I yell.

My feet swiftly carry me towards the guy, who's still shouting at the dog. I have to raise my voice to be heard as I approach.

"Hey, you motherfucker…," I grab a fistful of his jacket and jerk him away from the dog, "I'm talking to you."

He never has a chance to see my fist before it's in his face. I swing three times, still holding on to his jacket with the other to keep

24

him from falling to the ground, holding him captive to the minimal amount of mercy I'm capable of. Unlike last night, I manage to rein in my anger, dropping him to the ground in a dazed heap at my feet.

"How do you like it? You piece of shit!" I spit in his face before picking up the leash. The poor dog cowers on the ground, its tail between its legs. I kneel and lower my voice, speaking softly. "It's alright, I'm not going to hurt you." I lean forward slowly and unhook the leash from the collar around its neck. The dog immediately senses its freedom, gets up and backs away, but seems unsure of the situation.

"Hey, what the fuck man! That's my dog!" the man bellows.

I turn to face him, all my anger rising back up to the surface. "Not any more it's not. Test me, motherfucker. I dare you," I say through clenched teeth.

His hard swallow is audible as he shakes his head and slowly climbs to his feet. I mirror his movement, wrapping the ends of the leash in my hands, ready to use it as a means to strangle the fucker if he tries anything. Lucky for him, he's smarter than he looks. He holds up his hands in surrender, his face bleeding and already swelling.

"You can have the dumb bitch. She's not worth it," he says quickly, then turns and runs.

I turn back to find the dog still standing a few feet away, head cocked to the side, studying me with clear curiosity and caution.

"You're free now. Go on." I make a slow shooing motion. She backs up a step but still refuses to run, clearly not a coward like her previous master. "Well, have it your way then but if that jackoff comes back and catches you, it's not my fault."

I continue down the sidewalk toward my initial destination, disposing the leash in a trash bin on my way. There's still no one in the area, not even grabbing a cup of coffee to start their day, so I walk directly up to the stand.

"Mornin'," the man behind the counter says. "What can I get

for you?"

"You Mike?"

He nods. "That's me."

"Phil sent me."

"Ahh." He places his palms on the counter and leans forward. "You must be one of his new fighters."

"No," I say curtly.

"No?" he asks, shocked. "You look like a fighter."

"Only when I have to be."

He appraises me for a few seconds before nodding again. "I'll get Phil's coffee. You want anything?"

"Large coffee, black."

"Two large black coffees coming right up."

Seconds later, he slides two paper cups across the counter, and I slide over the five-dollar bill Phil gave me. "That enough?"

"It is. Let me get your change."

"Keep it."

He nods again, ringing up the coffee on his register. "Tell Phil he's missing out on an opportunity if he doesn't train you."

I ignore the comment, grab the cups, and turn to leave. "Thanks for the coffee."

I'm almost back to Phil's when I hear the quiet click of claws on the sidewalk behind me.

"Nuh-uh. Just because I saved you doesn't mean I'm your new master. I can barely take care of myself much less you."

Again, she cocks her head to the side, listening intently. Staring into her powder-blue eyes, I see the intelligence in their gaze. Even if she doesn't understand my words exactly, she does understand the situation.

"Go on," I shoo again, trying not to spill the coffee. She dips her head at my gesture, tail slightly tucking, but she doesn't step back.

She holds her ground stubbornly. I sigh in frustration. "I don't have time for this."

The clicking of her claws echoes my steps as I head back to the gym. I pull the door open and step inside, never once looking back. What the fuck am I going to do with a damn dog? I have no place for her. Not physically and not in my heart either. Not like she deserves. So, I leave her to her fate. Freedom, even on the streets, is better than being at the hands of that piece of shit that was beating her. I can at least rest assured knowing that fact.

"I hope you don't mind; I got a coffee for myself as well. I'll earn it," I assure him as I place his cup on the desk.

In true Phil fashion, a grunt is all I get for a response as he waves his arm distractedly, dismissing me. How fitting. I'm being shooed away too. Looks like the dog and I are one and the same. Strays that nobody wants around.

I don't take his demeanor personally though. Besides, being dismissed is hardly the worst thing I've dealt with. I prefer to be left alone than plagued with incessant questions and stares. So, I happily take my hot cup of coffee and walk out into the gym, ready to start my new, flashy janitorial duties.

T
Chapter four

"Whoa! Add more, add more!" Joey screams, excitedly.

"This is the last of them," another boy says as he lifts a weighted plate onto the bar, leaving barely enough room to secure it from falling off the end.

"Ay! What's going on here?" Phil's voice is full of annoyance as he pushes through the crowd that's gathered around me.

"Coach, you gotta see this! T's the strongest man I've ever seen!" Despite the nasty purple bruising on half his face, Joey's eyes sparkle with excitement as they make their way to where I'm sitting on the bench. "Show him!"

Phil comes to a stand next to Joey, arms crossed over his chest as he looks at me expectantly. I wait, giving him a chance to object, but he doesn't. I lay back, grip the bar tightly, lift it off the rack, and proceed to lower the bar to my chest and pump out a few reps before gently placing the bar back onto the rack and sitting up.

All the boys start talking at once. Their excited energy buzzes around me, leaving me feeling both content and envious. It's such a different feeling having young boys rally around me instead of being scared to get too close, but it's also a clear reminder that we're nothing alike. I'm not much older than these boys in years, and yet, I'm a million times older when it comes to life experience. I never had the chance to be a happy, carefree kid.

"Alright, alright, that's enough show-boatin'. It's time to close up for the night. Let's go," Phil announces.

"But Coach, that's *a thousand pounds!* And he wasn't even struggling! I wanna see what else he can do!" Joey exclaims.

"This ain't a play zone, Joey. This is a professional training gym, and I don't need no one gettin' hurt."

"But—"

"No buts! Now go on."

Joey heaves a heavy sigh, hanging his head, but he doesn't argue. "Yes, sir."

The boys all drag their feet as they clear out, their excitement slowly dissipating. Phil hangs back, waiting for them to leave before he trains his attention back on me. I can't quite gauge his expression. I know he's angry but...how angry?

"What are you?" he asks, voice clipped.

His question takes me aback. I scoff. "What kind of question is that?"

"Exactly what it sounds like. What. Are. You?"

I'm silent for a few seconds, trying to process his words. What. Not who but *what* am I? "A freak, I suppose." I shrug. "Always have been."

"Don't play with me, kid. What are you? I know you're not a Titan considering you killed one. So, what are you? Who do you belong to? Did someone send you here?"

"I don't know what you mean. I don't know what the hell a Titan is. The man I killed was just that. *A man.* Are you...ok? Like, mentally?" I furrow my brows, studying his very serious face. "Are you the one messing with me?"

"Kid, I'll only ask you one more time and so help me if you lie to me. Are you saying you're human? *Just* human?"

"I'm sorry…," I rub my forehead, utterly confused, "but what else am I supposed to be? Seriously, are you ok?"

"Who are your parents?"

"What?" I ask, suddenly very alert and watching the old man closely. The mention of my parents catches me like a sucker punch to the gut.

"Their names. What are they?"

"Look, I don't know what you're trying to get at here or what in the hell this is all about, but I assure you, I'm no one important. The name of my parents is irrelevant."

The tension in the air between us is palpable. I don't know what to make of him or his questions and he clearly doesn't know what to make of me and my strength. We both have trust issues, understandable since we know shit about each other, and it appears that we're at an impasse.

Not wanting to make Phil any more nervous than he already is, I stand slowly. "Look, I don't know what's going on here, but I'll save us both the trouble and get my things. This clearly isn't going to work out."

"Now just hold on a second. Don't go gettin' all defensive and runnin' away. Seems like that's what you're used to doin'. Isn't it?"

I ignore him as I walk past, heading toward the staircase to gather my pack and be done with this place. He's known me a day and acts like he already knows who I am. Fuck that. He doesn't know shit about me.

"Don't you want answers? Or at the very least, don't you want to know…*more*?"

That stops me in my tracks.

"You've always been different, haven't you? And, if you ain't lyin' to me, that means you ain't got a clue as to why or how. I can help you."

Only a day and he *is* right about that. But what exactly *does* he know? He's insinuating that he knows *something* and that's a hell of a lot more than I know. I slowly turn to face him. "Are you saying you know who I am?"

He shakes his head regretfully. "No, kid. I ain't got a clue who or what you are, but I can help you find out. If you let me."

There's no reason why I should trust him. Hell, I *don't* trust him, but I've never heard anyone else talk the way he does, like he knows about...*things*. Strange things. And the one thing I've always been is strange. This may be the closest I've ever been to finding out why I am the way that I am. I have to trust in myself, in my own abilities, and take that first step toward my unknown opponent. Besides, when have I ever backed down from a fight?

I nod. "You have my attention."

He runs a hand back and forth over his trimmed beard in contemplation. I can see the internal battle warring in his eyes, but I have no idea what demons he's fighting, just that he is. After a long pause, he nods his head in return. "Alright. Let's lock up here and make a little trip. I'll explain more as we go."

Once all the boys are out, I follow Phil outside. The sun has long since set and the streetlights offer sporadic domes of light every few feet. I glance up to the sky but, of course, I can't see any of the stars I know are up there shining brightly. As I wait for Phil to lock the door behind us, something catches my eye.

I sigh. "Shit."

The beautiful white dog from earlier gets up from where she'd been lying next to the door and approaches me cautiously. She stops about a foot in front of me and sits down, waiting patiently, her head practically level with my hip. I hadn't really paid attention to just how large she was before or maybe I hadn't noticed her true size because she had been cowering.

"You didn't tell me you had a dog," Phil says as he turns around and sees me having a staring contest with the dog.

"She's not my dog," I respond coldly, narrowing my eyes in the dog's direction, letting her know that she is, in fact, not my problem.

He grunts and starts heading down the sidewalk without another word. I turn and follow him. The sound of claws clicking behind us is immediate. I quickly turn and face her.

"Go on!" I yell, throwing my arms out toward her. "Get out of here! Go follow someone else."

She plants her stubborn ass on the sidewalk again, not even flinching against my shouts and flailing arms.

I sigh, running my hand through my hair. "Fucking hell."

"Sure looks like your dog," Phil comments.

"She's not. I saw her owner beating her this morning when I went out to get your damn coffee. I liberated her and now she seems to think that means I'm her new master." I fix a cold stare at the dog. "Which I'm not!"

Phil snickers. "You weren't kiddin'. Trouble really does find you, doesn't it? Come on, she won't be able to follow us where we're goin' anyway."

We walk about ten blocks, heading toward the same part of town I was in last night. The change from decent to shady within a city is always so subtle. You don't intend to roam into dangerous territory, but you look up and suddenly realize that's exactly where you are. And the people who run these streets, the people who survive on these streets, they see you long before you see them.

That's one of the drastic differences between the poor and the rich. The rich walk their streets oblivious to the person walking beside them because what threat could possibly be lurking in the alleyway between *Louis Vuitton* and *Versace*? The only threat they face there is looking absolutely ridiculous in something deemed *fashion* that actually looks like a garbage bag, and costs more than what most people make in three months.

Trash.

Trash litters the streets of the poor and the rich both, just in drastically different ways. Me? I'll take the streets we're currently navigating over the pompous and fake shit any day. It's not even a question.

"We're almost there, it's just down here," Phil says, interrupting my thoughts.

He approaches a half-assed, boarded-up subway entrance. Graffiti covers what's left. No doubt a gang tag marking their territory. He's about to duck underneath one of the boards when I start to question what we're doing and where exactly he's taking me.

"Hang on." Phil stops and looks back at me, pulling a flashlight from where it had been tucked into the back of his jeans. "Why are we going into an abandoned subway? What kind of answers could I possibly get in there."

He shrugs. "All of them. None of them. I ain't got a clue to what kind of answers you need, but I promise, if they exist, this is where they'll be. I'm askin' ya to trust me."

I look between him and the ominous darkness waiting for us behind those boards. The longer I stare into that darkness, the stronger the urge to enter becomes. It's the same pull I felt about coming to Chicago in the first place. I'm here for a reason, aren't I? I followed my gut this far, what's a little traipse through a dark, abandoned subway tunnel in gang territory?

"You ain't scared, are ya?" Phil's voice holds a hint of amusement. I glance at him and see his failed attempt at hiding a smirk.

"After you, old man." I gesture to the opening.

I have to practically crawl to get through the hole. Phil's

flashlight illuminates our path down wide concrete steps. Once on the platform, Phil heads to the end and jumps down onto deserted tracks.

With nothing else to do, I follow him. "You're surprisingly nimble for an old man," I say, returning a friendly jab.

I'm not surprised when he only grunts and continues along the tracks, heading farther into the tunnel. The darkness gets thicker, if that's possible, and almost...*heavy*. I've always been able to see surprisingly well in the dark, but this is different.

It feels like a warning.

A warning to turn back.

But we continue on in a strange deafening silence. It feels like we're in a soundproof, padded room; like the outside world doesn't exist. Gravel crunching beneath our shoes is the only sound we make for a long time. Up ahead, lights in the ceiling illuminate the tunnel, and Phil clicks off his flashlight as we approach, letting the lights guide us. They start off few and far between, flickering dimly, but they gain brightness as we continue forward.

That's not exactly right. The bulbs overhead isn't not what's creating the almost blinding light. It's coming from straight ahead as if we're walking directly into stadium lights, only...it doesn't hurt my eyes.

I pull to a stop next to Phil and stare into....I have no fucking idea what I'm staring into.

"Phil...."

"Yeah, kid?"

"What the fuck am I looking at here?"

"This is the portal to The Underworld."

"The what? As in...Hell?"

"No, kid. Not Hell. Although The Underworld is a type of hell all its own."

Nervousness grips my stomach and flips it. I have no idea what the hell a portal even means, what it is, or what waits on the other side. Will it hurt to walk through it? Because I'm assuming that's what we're about to do. And what am I going to discover when I do? Will I find out who I really am? Will I finally get answers I never expected to find?

"What do I do?" I ask, steeling my nerves.

"I'll walk through first then you try. If you're human, you won't be able to walk through without an invitation from me."

"And if I'm not human?" I turn to meet his gaze. He looks just as nervous as I feel.

"Then we find out what you are."

Without another word, Phil takes the last few steps toward the portal then disappears through it. His voice comes back muffled, sounding far away, but I can just make out his words.

"Your turn to try on your own, kid."

Taking a deep breath, I stride toward the portal. I don't hesitate as I reach the light. My next step has me walking through what feels like electricity. It tingles and zaps along my skin but doesn't cause any pain. I have a second to wonder if it's because I don't feel pain like a normal person or if it's the same for everyone who walks through.

It feels like a blink of an eye and several minutes all at the same time, but I'm suddenly standing on the other side, a bit disoriented. I come face to face with...*something*.

It's voice barely registers through my shock. "Well, that's interesting."

Chapter five

Peace of Mind by Villain of the Story

It sounds like Phil. It sort of looks like Phil. It's the same size and stature, and it has the same eyes, bald head, and beard, but that's about where the similarities end. Two horns, about three inches long protruding from its head, and its lower half is…the body of a goat. It's covered in dark brown fur and its feet aren't feet at all, they're hooves.

"You're taking this better than I expected." The voice still sounds like Phil's.

I'm too far past shock to react to what I'm seeing and my nervousness comes back tenfold. I immediately look down at my own body, lifting my arms in front of me to inspect them, then looking at my legs, before patting myself down, terrified that I might find my own set of horns and fur.

Nothing.

"I'm not different. Do you see anything?" I ask nervously.

"You're still you, kid. And just so you know, I'm a satyr. Essentially exactly what you see, half goat and half man, and I'm the least of the strange things you'll see here."

"This can't be real. I'm dreaming."

I've had strange dreams my whole life. Nothing more than flashes and glimpses of things I could never comprehend. Fantasies. Lore. I chalked it up to nothing more than the imagination of a kid. But this…this feels exactly like my dreams.

The sound of wings beating comes from just behind me and a huge gust of air barrels into us. I move away from the portal and turn to face the cause of the wind, not sure what in the hell I'll see next. I don't know what I expected but it's not this.

It's the dog. With wings.

Phil's laughter catches me completely off guard. "What?" I ask. "What's so funny?"

"Well, I was wrong for one. Looks like she can follow us after all. And two, she's a Pegasus," he says in awe.

She tucks her wings into her sides and waits patiently once again. I look between her and Phil, who seems utterly entranced by her. I wait for him to say more but he doesn't. I'm not nearly as patient as she seems to be, so I interrupt their little reverie.

I clear my throat. "Can you explain? As you might remember, I have no clue what the fuck is going on."

"Yes, yes, of course. Obviously, the world you know isn't the only one. Your Pegasus here, and myself, are Mageía. Long ago, we used to live alongside humans until the Titans got out of hand on their power trip and threatened the human race. Zeus created The Underworld and separated the two worlds which allowed humans to thrive. Again, I can explain more later but not here."

"Okay," I say slowly, trying to wrap my head around this new reality and failing miserably. Mageía. The Underworld. Zeus. Zeus, as in the legends and fairytale Zeus? A fucking god? I have no clue how to process any of this. The one thing I can focus on is *me*. "So, what does this mean to and for me? I passed through the portal, but I didn't…*change*."

Phil shrugs. "Like I said, interesting. If you were human, you wouldn't have been able to walk through on your own, but the portal also reveals your true self when you pass through it. This…," he gestures to my body, "is your true self. Unfortunately, it doesn't help us determine what exactly you are. All we know for certain is that you're not human."

I sigh, disappointed. "Alright, well...." I look around. The tunnel looks exactly the same as it did on the other side. Other than Phil and the dog with wings, I don't see anything *magical*. "What now?"

"Now we introduce you to your new world. That is if you're up for it?"

I look at the portal one more time and then back down at my body. This wasn't necessarily an answer but it's more than I've ever known. I need to know more. I need to know who...*what* I am.

I nod. "I'm up for it."

"Good. But before we get too far into this new world, we do need to address your Pegasus."

She's utterly still, sitting and waiting like she has all the time in the world for me to figure this shit out.

"That's the second time you've said *my* Pegasus. I already told you, she's not mine."

Phil laughs. "That's where you're wrong, kid. Pegasus' are extremely rare, only a handful of 'em even exist. They choose their master, not the other way around."

"Well, she had a master."

He shakes head. "No, she was probably captured and sold by some idiot who didn't even know what she was. And the fool who had her sure as hell didn't know what he had. If he did, he woulda never laid an unfriendly hand on her, much less given her up so easily.

"Pegasus' choose their master based on a connection to them. She's connected to you whether you believe it or not. And once you let her in, and she lets you in, you'll be connected on such a deep level that you'll be able to understand one another. It's one of the rarest pairings in our world."

"What do you mean I'll be able to understand her? Will she be able to...*talk* to me?"

"Well, not with words exactly. Alls I know is what I've been told. I ain't never been lucky enough to have a connection like that. It's a blessing, kid. Accept it."

I look back at the dog in question. The Pegasus. She's beautiful. She's unlike anything I've ever seen, even in regular dog form. I knew she was special the second I saw her and even though I tried to ignore it, I felt the pull to her too.

"What do I do?" I ask.

"You can start by giving her a name. Then, touch her. Connect with her. Get to know her."

I nod my head. "Alright," I mumble, more to myself than as a response. I slowly approach her, still sitting stoically, watching our exchange as if she understood every word. "May I?" I lift my hand, asking for permission to pet her. I don't know why but it feels important to get her approval.

She nudges my hand with her nose, and I take that as a yes. I let my hand glide over her head and along her neck. Her coat feels like silk. My fingertips gently brush over her wings. I can feel the individual feathers which are just as soft as the rest of her. They feel so delicate, but I know they must be incredibly strong. Fucking hell, I don't have the first clue what a Pegasus is, exactly, or what I'm going to do with one.

Pegasus.

"Peggy," I say softly, speaking to her as I take a step back. I look into her beautiful blue eyes. "It's not very original but how does Peggy sound?"

Something clicks into place. It settles, taking root, deep inside of me. She stands and reaches for my hand, nudging it again. This time she flicks out her tongue and licks it. A small smile tugs at my lips as I pet her again. I've never had a pet before, not even as a young kid. Though *pet* isn't the right word to use here. Companion, that's what she is.

"Peggy it is then."

"Well, ain't that sweet," Phil says, only a little sarcastically.

"Hey, I'm just doing what you told me to do, old man."

"Alright, alright," he waves dismissively. "Let's see how well you can continue to follow instructions. Whatever you do kid, stay close and leave the talking to me, understand?"

"I can do that."

"Then let's get on with it."

I once again follow in his wake with a white shadow in mine. We move down the tunnel, and I can't even imagine what a sight we make. A satyr, a Pegasus, and a...what? A man that looks human. This is insane. What the hell am I going to see next? A unicorn?

Phil approaches an enormous door in the tunnel wall. Though *door* may not be the right word. I feel like I have no right words for this world. Everything is on an entirely different scale here and I'm just trying to keep up the best I can.

He pushes the door open, and I follow him through to standing on a landing that is just as big as the subway's. Only no tracks lay below but rather giant concrete steps descending into darkness.

"You weren't kidding when you said *Underworld*, were you?"

Phil scoffs. "This is just the beginning. There's an elevator at the bottom and I'll give you one guess which direction it goes."

Words completely escape me as two bodies emerge from the Shadows as they ascend the stairs, and heading right for us. They look like women in the fact that their bodies have the curves and breasts of a woman, but I've never seen a woman quite like this. They move in sync, identical in shape and features yet they're also the exact opposite of one another.

One has skin the color of fire. She's shades of red and orange, and it appears as though flames flick over her skin. Her hair is the brightest shade of red I've ever seen. As she gets closer, her eyes land on me and I notice that her eyes match her hair.

The other woman is white. Not pale skin but white with shades of blue. If an iceberg could grow feet and walk, this would be it. Her hair is a vibrant shade of blue that no dye could ever replicate, and her eyes are a chilling match to her hair as well.

Both their eyes are on me as they approach, their gazes curious and lingering. Peggy comes to stand at my side, ears pulled back and a light snarl on her lips, showcasing very large, very sharp teeth. A warning to the newcomers not to get any closer. I sense her unease or is it mine? I can't tell, but I reach out to lay my hand on her neck anyway letting her know that I'm with her. The two...*women* address Phil without ever taking their eerie eyes off me.

"Philoctetes," they sing in unison.

"It's been too long," the one with red hair says.

"Too long indeed," the other echoes. "Who's this delicious piece of meat?"

"Delicious indeed." It's the redhead's turn to echo. "We could have a lot of fun with this one. What do you think, sister?"

"Oh yes, lots of fun, sister. But the Pegasus could be a problem."

"Problem, yes. Territorial and jealous little beast," the redhead hisses.

The way they speak is creepy, just like they are. I have no desire to get any closer than I already am to these psychos.

"Jett, meet the twins. Tianna...," he points to the redhead, "and Tillie," he gestures to the one with blue hair. "They're Titans and two of the most popular beings down here. I'm sorry to disappoint you lovely ladies, but T here ain't up for grabs. He's my newest fighter which means he's strictly off limits."

My eyes dart quickly over to Phil. What's he playing at? I'm not his fighter. I have no intention of being his fighter. The burst of laughter pulls my attention back to the Titans standing in front of us.

They both throw their heads back and laugh. Well, *cackle* might be more accurate.

"You dare bring a human to fight with us?" Tianna questions.

"Are you trying to get the sweet soul killed?" Tillie feigns concern. "Oh, you poor, poor boy." Her ice-blue eyes slide to Phil, humor sparking in their gaze. "After what happened with your last fighter, I thought you were done with this world, but Raymond is going to love you for this foolishness, Philoctetes."

Tianna turns her attention to me. "I would wish you luck but all the luck in the world won't help you down here. Come sister, let's go find our human fun elsewhere."

"What a shame. He really is a pretty one. I would have loved to eat him right up," Tillie pouts.

My tension eases slightly as I watch the sisters exit through the door which closes solidly behind them. I turn to Phil. "What in the actual fuck? I never agreed to fight."

He grunts. "What'd ya expect, kid? That you'd just waltz into The Underworld like you're on vacation? This ain't no charity fight. You want answers? Well, answers come with a price. You want access to this world then you need a reason to be in it. Trust me, being a fighter is one of the best things you can be down here. Be a great one and everyone will love you, but that's not the point. Fighters are like royalty down here. No one will mess with you outside the ring, kid. Do ya get what I'm sayin'?"

I sigh in defeat, my anger subsiding as I realize why he did what he did. "You're protecting me."

"Damn right I'm protecting ya, kid. Still, this ain't gonna be no cake walk. This place and everything in it are dangerous. It's best you remember that and start learnin' how to see behind you."

"I know how to protect myself."

"Not down here you don't. But you'll learn. Come on, we've gotta get you registered and figure out our next steps."

He descends the stairs, this time leaving his flashlight tucked into his jeans. I guess he figures there's no need for a crutch to assist a human weakness neither of us have. Phil's hooves click on the concrete steps in front of me and Peggy's claws click behind me. The sounds should echo in this massive cave-like structure but it's as if the darkness takes all the sound, along with the light, and snuffs it out.

At the bottom of the stairs another smaller platform leads up to the largest birdcage elevator I've ever seen. The door is large enough to accommodate an elephant, easily. What the fuck could be so large that The Underworld needs doors and elevators this big? I don't even want to know.

"You comin', kid?"

Phil snaps me out of my dumbfounded daze and my eyes leave the large elevator, finding Phil and Peggy already waiting for me. Inside, the three of us are dwarfed by the enormity of the cart. It feels like I'm standing in a house, not an elevator.

"Get the gate and door, will ya?"

I feel like I'm in a trance. I'm walking and talking, moving to slide the metal gate and door closed as Phil instructed, but it all feels...disconnected. *I* feel disconnected. From my surroundings. From my body. Maybe the shock is finally starting to settle in.

Once the door is latched, there's a metal grating sound and we start to descend, falling away from the platform and heading deeper underground. After the bumpy start, the ride smooths out and only a low whirring sound hums around us as we drop lower and lower. I'm not sure if I should be feeling cold dampness from the Earth surrounding us or increased warmth, but I feel nothing. It's such an odd sense of absolutely nothing.

Phil's voice is loud in the nothingness. "I don't really know how to prepare you for what you're about to see. I guess if I had to try and put The Underworld into words it would be think Time Square. For the most part, Mageía look human enough but there's usually some kind of tell. The eyes, skin, build, certain features that make them more than just humans, but sometimes it's hard to tell."

"Like me."

"Like you," he agrees. "But there are beings like me, Peggy, and the twins you just met mixed in."

I try to picture what he just said and fail miserably.

"You'll see humans too. Not many know about our world, but it does get out. You saw the twins on their way out into the human world. No doubt they'll find some poor fool and bring him back to have their way with him. And, if they don't break him, he'll probably thank them for it and ask for more."

"Do they use actual magic to control humans?"

He shakes his head. "No. The portal strips them of their magic as they pass through into the human world. Humans have to come through of their own volition, with an invitation of course. However, once here, there are no rules the Mageía have to follow. We can do whatever we want in The Underworld. And, once humans are exposed to our world, the magic and allure of the Mageía are strong. It's hard to explain, kid. Kind of like a moth being drawn to the light." He shrugs. "It just is. But if it's not careful, the moth will burn itself, possibly even killing itself, unintentionally."

I nod. "I think I understand."

All my life, people...*humans* have seemed drawn to me, but there's always been that slight hesitation. As if they could sense something else. Something different. Something dangerous. Most people feel that sixth sense and pull away but some…some people like to push boundaries. Some people like the danger. It does make sense.

Before I can drive myself crazy thinking about it, the elevator jolts to a stop. There's a moment of hesitation before I reach for the door and slide it open. Phil and Peggy lead the way down another large, dark tunnel, the only option out of the elevator. We don't walk long before we're met with the same type of door we entered through the subway. There are a lot of barriers into The Underworld giving you ample time to tuck tail and run, but here I am.

"You ready, kid?"

Am I ready? Ready for what exactly? My entire life to be turned upside down? Everything I ever thought I knew to be taken from me? Again. No, what was taken from me was my parents, my truth. Everything I've ever believed has been a lie. This is my truth so ready or not…

Peggy nudges my hand with her nose letting me know she's with me. The feel of her soft fur under my palm as I stroke her neck calms my nerves.

I nod.

Phil nods, too, then pushes the door open.

Chapter six

At The Wheel by Colorblind

The noise is overwhelming. The eerie silence and pressure of the abandoned subway is gone, replaced by clamorous, bustling energy.

Now I understand why we had to travel so far underground. I'm standing in a city. A legit city under the ground. Hell, this might as well be New York itself and we just entered the heart of it. There are buildings and skyscrapers though all I see above is a blanket of darkness. There's a sense of sunlight, but it's not coming from any actual source. There are paved roads and vehicles but no pollution. Flashing signs and billboards take up the entirety of the building walls. One, in particular, catches my eye. It's the twins, Tianna and Tillie, standing next to two men. One looks more like a mountain with human features than a man. His face looks normal enough, but his arms are literal boulders. I can't help but wonder what other body parts are made of stone. The other man is tall, *extremely tall*, considering he's towering over the others and the twins are barely shorter than me. His hair is blowing as if a gust of wind caught him as the photo was being taken but it didn't touch the others. He looks human, but considering who he's with, I'll bet everything I have that he's not. The wording above them tells me exactly who they are.

Titans.

Someone bumps into my shoulder, pulling my attention from

the billboard back down to the sidewalk.

"Watch it," the stranger snarls as he passes, flashing pointed teeth that look horrific in his human-looking face.

"Come on." Phil grabs my wrist and pulls me forward. "Just ignore him."

I let Phil drag me along, thankful for his guidance because without it I'd most definitely be frozen in place as this new world attacks my senses. As we pass through an outdoor market, so many overwhelming sights and smells fight for my attention. Booths and vendors line the sidewalk selling various foods, drinks, clothes, and trinkets. My eyes are everywhere except where they need to be as Phil weaves us through the crowd and I continue to bump bodies left and right, the sensation further jolting me.

Yeah, the shock has definitely hit me now.

Mercifully, the crowd begins to thin, and I feel like I can breathe again. I'm not sure when Phil released my wrist and I started following on my own, but he's come to a stop on a wide sidewalk with large steel buildings surrounding us on all sides. He faces me, hands on his hips.

"How ya doin', kid?"

I lean back into one of the buildings and let out a heavy breath. "That was…intense."

Peggy sits next to me, her large body leaning into my leg. My hand automatically rests against her neck. It's strange to me that it feels so normal and right to touch her. It feels like she's been mine for longer than thirty minutes. If we were anywhere else, I might question it, but how can I worry about that when I'm standing in an underground city filled with beings that have teeth like animals and skin like fire and ice. Not to mention everything else that just blurred across my vision. I'm pretty sure I saw a woman with a beak for a nose, another with actual scales on her skin, and a man that had so much body hair it was hard to make out his face.

"I'm just surprised it took you this long to react," Phil chuckles softly. "How can I help?"

I shake my head, trying to clear the daze. "I don't think you can. I just...."

When I don't finish my sentence, Phil finishes it for me. "You just need time to adjust, kid. You'll be alright."

I nod my head in agreement. I *will* be alright. I always have been, and this is no different. I fight. I adapt. I survive. Period.

"I hate to keep pushing you, but we need to get you registered and on the books as a fighter. Then we need to see what's going on in the fight world and where we can get you started."

"Alright," I concede. "And where exactly do we go to do that?"

I follow the line of sight to where Phil's pointing. Of course. We need to go to what looks like the center of the city, to the largest building I've ever seen, situated on top of a slightly raised hill, looking down on the rest of the city. The building emanates the same darkness I felt getting here. It's all shiny black metal and a sleek, powerful design.

As architecturally beautiful as it is, I don't want to go anywhere near it. Unfortunately, that's just not a choice I have. Not if I want answers.

"Alright," I repeat. "Let's go."

We walk the rest of the way in silence. As we get closer, the sidewalk starts to fill up again. It feels like this, and the market we came through, are the hubs of the city. As I become a part of the crowd, more prepared than I was in the marketplace, I inspect the people around me intensely. Some have obvious features that identify them as Mageía, but others look human, and I can't tell if they truly are or if they're Mageía that just look like me. Considering the twins thought I was human and couldn't sense any kind of magic on me, I'm assuming I won't be able to tell the difference either.

I follow Phil onto an escalator, and it quickly turns steep as it takes us up, up, up, towards the ominous black building looming over us. Once we get to the top and step off the escalator, the building is in full sight. I have to crane my neck to take it all in. It's more than large, it's massive. It's the biggest building I've ever seen and the only thing that comes to mind to compare it to is the pyramids of Egypt or the Great Wall of China. If this building was on Earth, I have no doubt it would be one of the structures you could see from space.

Incredible.

Ridiculous, but incredible.

A cold, wet nose nudges my hand, pulling my attention back down to ground level and letting me know that she's still here with me. I'm grateful to her already for keeping *me* grounded.

"Come on, kid."

I step in with the surge of the crowd and get swept up easily in the rush, but once inside I have to stop again to take it all in. It's just as sleek and impressive inside as it is on the outside. The floor is black marble with streaks of blue slicing through the large slabs. It almost looks like blue flames dancing across the floor. The large, open walkway leads out and around on both sides. Shops line the walkway with beautiful and immaculate displays of finery in their windows. Unlike the marketplace, which felt very common and practical, this is as upscale and fancy as I've ever seen.

Walking towards the railing, I look down onto an elegant and immaculate casino. As soon as I see the large machines lining the floor and lighting up, the sound seems to slam into me. The loud murmur of crowds, the clinking of tokens and coins, the ping and music of machines as people push buttons and pull levers. It's organized chaos and it makes me dizzy.

"Welcome to The Underworld, kid. The center of Raymond's money-making world. Each floor is dedicated to a certain…vice.

Gamblin' as you can see here. Up on the next level is everything revolving around sex, and down a level is where you'll find the fights. No tellin' what kind of depravity goes on behind all of this though. I know he's got his hands in the drug trafficking world too. Wouldn't surprise me one bit if he traffics people," Phil says, clear disgust in his tone and on his face. "Nothin' is off limits as long as it makes him money."

"Who the fuck is this Raymond guy and why doesn't anyone stop him?" My own disgust, mixed with my ever-present anger, rises to the surface at what Phil is suggesting.

"Trust me kid, you don't want to get on his bad side. Raymond isn't just Mageía." He leans in and beckons me to get closer. He whispers the next words as quietly as he can. "He's Zeus's brother. You've probably heard him referred to as Hades."

My eyes go wide. "Hades?" I repeat. "Son of a bitch, you mean like an actual god. The God of The...." The words die on my lips.

"The Dead. Yeah kid, one and the same. And now, here you are, in his world. I told you, you ain't even close to prepared to protectin' yourself here."

"It can't be real. They're just...they're just fairytales people tell their kids to scare them. Just like Satan and Hell."

Phil cocks his eyebrow, an unimpressed look on his face. "You're standin' in the middle of an underground world, surrounded by magical beings, walked through a portal to get here, and you still want to believe everything is a fairytale? I hate to break it to ya kid, but everything you've ever heard has come from some form of truth, even Satan and Hell, I'm sure. Though that's an entirely different world that I've never witnessed or been a part of. That I know of."

"Jesus," I mutter.

"Yeah, he's probably real too. Come on, let's go down to the fightin' level and get you squared away and get back topside where you can mull this all over."

I follow numbly as he leads me to an elevator, and we descend. We get out and walk down another fancy hallway, the black and blue marble design following us here. Phil pushes open an unmarked door and we enter into a large waiting room of sorts, only it's not stiff chairs and dull magazines that fill the room. Couches and oversized cushioned chairs and beanbags are strewn across the floor. Some of them are taken by men and women, some talking, some...*not* talking. A table running along the entire back wall is filled with food and drinks. It's more like a lounge than a waiting room.

As we approach a tall counter, Phil reaches for a step ladder that's pushed up against it, under the overhang, and slides it out. I hadn't even seen the ladder, but Phil seems to be very familiar with this place.

Climbing up the ladder to where can see over the top, he rings the bell for service. A door behind the counter opens and a beautiful woman walks through. I know immediately that she's Mageía because her hair is white as snow with eyes to match. It's a stark contrast to her flawless midnight skin. She's honestly not much taller than Phil, with excessive curves accentuated by a silky blue dress. Curves that should look ridiculous on her smaller frame but only add to her beauty. She has to climb up onto her own ladder behind the counter before she can properly see us. As soon as she sees Phil, her face lights up and a smile graces her glittery lips.

"Philoctetes! What a wonderful surprise! What on earth has brought you down here? After Achilles, I thought you were done with this place for good."

Achilles? As in the legend of Troy? No way. I can't be hearing all of this right.

Phil sighs. "I thought I was, too, but unexpected circumstances fell into my lap. I swear, Yesmín, I think I'm cursed just as much as this place is."

"You are not! I'll hear no such thing, so get those nasty thoughts out of your head." She reaches out and cups Phil's face in her graceful hands. "You're one of the good ones, Philoctetes, and I won't hear any argument about it."

My eyes practically bug out of my head at the bashful smile that breaks out on Phil's face. *Is he blushing?*

"Ah…well, I ain't gonna argue with you. I know there's no use," he chuckles giddily. "You always did know how to cheer an old, grumpy man up. It's good to see you again, Yesmín." He squeezes her hands where they're now wrapped in his.

I clear my throat loudly, interrupting their happy little reunion. Phil looks even more embarrassed now as he lets go of Yesmín's hands and stands a little straighter.

"Yesmín, meet Jett, my newest fighter."

Her eerily beautiful white eyes slowly rake down my body and back up again, a questioning look on her face, but all she says is, "Any friend of Philoctetes' is a friend of mine." She extends her hand out to me, and I take it. "It's nice to meet you, Jett."

"Just T," I say politely. "It's nice to meet you too. Anyone that can get more than a grunt out of this guy…," I motion my head in his direction, "must be special."

"Ah well, we go way back." She looks lovingly at Phil again before clearing her throat and getting down to business. "I'm assuming you're here to register?"

Phil nods. "We are."

"Come on, into the back room then," she says as she slowly climbs off her ladder, heading down a hallway on the side of the room. We pass a few doors before she opens one and steps aside, ushering us in.

I follow behind Phil and Peggy follows behind me. Our usual

little train it seems. As soon as Yesmín sees Peggy, her eyes widen and snap back to mine.

"Oh, well that makes more sense."

Phil chuckles.

I look between her and Phil, confused. "What makes more sense?"

"I thought Phil had completely lost his mind, entering a human into The Underworld fights, though I'd never say it." She winks at Phil. "But you're not human at all, are you? Quite deceiving though, I must admit." She closes the door behind us and walks further into the room. "Come," she gestures to me. "Take off the shirt, pants, and shoes, and stand over there."

Hesitating, I look to Phil. "She ain't gonna take advantage of ya, kid." He chuckles again. "She's gotta get your measurements, take your photo, and get you registered in the system."

Right.

I only feel slightly embarrassed at where my mind went. How the hell am I supposed to know what the fuck is going on? It's not like I've ever been in this type of situation before. Yesmín is definitely attractive, and I've had my fair share of flings and one-night stands, but I've never been one to have an audience. Voyeurism isn't my thing. I don't like bringing unwanted attention to myself any more than I already do. Yet here I am, getting ready to be the center of everyone's fucking attention, all so I can maybe get some answers about my life. Just fucking great.

I pull my T-shirt over my head and toss it on one of the chairs against the wall, then kick off my shoes and step out of my jeans, tossing them on the chair too. I walk over to where Yesmín is waiting, clipboard now in hand.

"Full name?"

"Jett Stephens."

"Age?"

"Twenty-two."

"Step onto the scale, please." She gestures to the large white square in front of me. I had no idea it was even a scale until she said so. I've never seen one this size before. Everything is on a bigger scale down here. She jots down the number that displays in front of us, two hundred thirty-one pounds.

"Now up against this wall, please." Following her instructions, I move to a wall with height markings all the way up to the ceiling. "Stand up straight." I pull my shoulders back and lift my head. "Good. Now arms out to your side."

She sets her clipboard down and picks up a measuring tape then, with the help of a stepstool, proceeds to take every measurement of my body possible; my arm length, the circumference of my biceps, shoulders, chest, and waist, all while standing extremely close and nonchalantly rubbing her body against mine. I can feel the hardness of her nipples through the thin silk of her dress as they brush across my bare chest.

I watch her closely as she moves down to measure my calves, but her eyes remain glued to the task at hand. Not once does she bat a flirty lash my way. I'm about to chalk it up to coincidence when she gets to my thighs and her hands graze over the front of my crotch, not once...but twice, and I catch her glancing at it. I'm surprised she hasn't asked me to pull my dick out to measure it too. I'm half tempted to take it out and see if she can tell how big it is when I shove it down her pretty little throat. If Phil wasn't here, I think this whole thing would have gone an entirely different way.

Part of me is pissed that he's here and that I won't be sliding my dick between those voluptuous breasts, titty-fucking her before I fuck her, and another part of me is extremely grateful. It saves me the pain of having to act like I care about her and her needs. It saves me from having to face the fact that I'm fucking heartless and empty, even when it comes to sex.

Once she's done measuring, she takes my photo and tells me I can get dressed. Then she walks over to a desk with a computer on it and begins typing.

"Your stats are decent but definitely not the most impressive," she says matter-of-factly. "I hope you have something special that will allow you to be a contender in the ring and not just a punching bag or worse."

If I had an ego, or any less confidence in myself and my ability, I might have been offended by her words. I don't and I'm not. She's simply stating facts about numbers on a page. Numbers on a page don't mean shit.

"Then again...," she says as she walks over with something else in her hand, "you're being trained by one of the best trainers in the world. That definitely is something special." She smiles brightly at Phil again. "Give me your hand."

Holding my hand out to her, she flips it around and places a device on the inside of my wrist. She pushes a button, and a sharp pain immediately radiates through my arm, but it's gone as quickly as it came. I'm in shock at the feel of it because I don't normally register pain.

"What the fuck was that?" I ask as I yank my arm away from her.

"I implanted a chip into your arm. It has all your stats, your photo, and your FIN."

"What the fuck is a FIN?" I rub at the spot where the chip was implanted. I can barely feel it under my skin.

"It's your Fighter Identification Number. The chip is what they'll scan when you enter a fight and it's how they'll be able to identify you if you get beaten beyond recognition or killed."

I scoff. "Killed?"

"Didn't Phil tell you? Every title fight is to the death."

I glance at Phil, and he has the decency to look a little ashamed. "You said—"

"We'll talk about it later," Phil cuts me off.

"Yesmín, my dear, it's always a pleasure," he says sweetly, as he goes in for a hug. "I guess I'll be seeing you soon."

She returns the hug and then lets him go. "Take this." She hands him a brochure. "It's all the info you need on the upcoming events. If you want to register Jett, just scan his chip in the app. You know how it works."

"Unfortunately, I do." He walks to the door, opens it, and leaves me standing in shock staring after him.

I can't believe he pulled this shit on me. I was right not to trust him but then I let my goddamn need for answers cloud my judgment. If he thinks I'm willing to die for these answers, he's wrong. I'm not going to die down here in some weird ass magical world run by fucking Hades.

I'm about to storm off after Phil when Yesmín grabs my wrist, halting my pursuit. She leans her body into me, her breasts pressing against my stomach as she tilts her head back to look up at me.

I've never had a problem getting women and it obviously won't be an issue down here either. Again, had Phil not been here, had I not just had a fucking bomb dropped on me, things might have gone differently.

"My shift ends at midnight." She gives me a seductive smile and lets her fingers dance slowly down my stomach, passing the button on my jeans, and then rubbing her palm against my dick.

It's my turn to grab her wrist, putting a stop to her groping as I step away from her. "Maybe next time," I say as nicely as I can, then head towards the door.

"You know where to find me!" she calls after me.

Peggy is waiting for me just outside the door. "Come on, Peg, let's get the fuck out of here. We've got some things to hash out with a certain scheming old man."

Chapter seven

Hollow by Execution Day

We don't say a single word as we traverse back through The Underworld. For some reason, heading back topside seems to take twice as long as it did to get here. Maybe it just feels that way because I'm ready to explode on Phil and his fucking games.

Once we're through the portal, I open my mouth to start my verbal assault, but Phil quickly cuts me off.

"Not here, kid. Still too close to The Underworld. We'll talk back at the gym."

I grit my teeth and push on, leaving Phil to follow me for once. I don't stop and wait as I climb out of the boarded-up subway entrance. As soon as I'm through, standing once again on the dirty, grimy Chicago sidewalk, I immediately feel better, lighter. Polluted or not, this air feels like new life being pulled into my body. My lungs expand on a deep inhale, and I relish the feel and comfort of this world. As I exhale, some of my earlier anger and frustration seem to go with it, dissipating into the night air.

I feel better overall, steady, and more like myself, but still not over the fact that I feel completely fucking played and manipulated. I have questions for Phil, and he better fucking provide the answers I want or else...

A warm, wet lick flicks across my clenched fist. Peggy. She's once again back in dog form, no wings to be seen, and she once again pulls me out of my nasty thoughts and calms me. It feels like a lifetime ago that I saved her and not just this morning. I didn't think I'd have time or a place in my heart for her, but I already feel like I don't know what I'd do without her.

I rub her head lovingly. "Come on girl, let's go home."

Home.

What is a home anyway?

The definition is simply where one lives permanently. Some people say home is where the heart is, whatever the fuck that means. I don't live at the gym permanently and my heart sure as hell isn't there, so I guess home to me is simply where I'm laying my head down for the night. I won't lie and say there's not a pang of longing that tugs annoyingly at my chest with the thought of actually having a home. I did have one at one point. I know what it is. I know what it feels like. And I know that I'll never have that feeling ever again. So, I push that longing away and make my way through the city with the now familiar click-clack of claws alongside me.

A few minutes later, Phil joins us at the gym. He unlocks the door, lets us inside, and then locks the door behind him again. The loud click of the lock engaging feels final. It feels like that lock has officially set me in place, set me into this new life, and these new circumstances.

Phil walks quietly to the middle of the gym, ducks under the ropes of the fighting ring and stands in the middle of it, arms crossed, staring at me expectantly. I can't help but follow him, stopping on the outside, looking up at him.

"What are you doing?" I ask indignantly. "I'm not going to fight you, old man."

"You sure 'bout that? You looked plenty eager to fight me earlier. I figure, if it's gonna happen, then might as well do it here and start your training."

"I'm not going to fight you and I don't need training. I've been fighting my whole life."

"Well, get in here and let's see then. Prove me wrong."

"I don't have time for this shit." I run my hand through my hair. "I have questions and, yeah, I'm pissed, but I'm not going to get in the ring with you. Just come out of there and answer my questions."

"I'll make you a deal, kid. You land a solid hit, just one, and we'll call it a night and I'll answer all your questions."

I blow out a heavy, frustrated breath but climb into the ring, tired of games and wasting time. "Fine, but when I knock you on your ass old man, don't break a fucking hip, ok?"

He snickers, unfolding his arms and lifting them up in front of his body, his legs wide and in a solid fighting stance. He looks at ease and comfortable, as if he's been doing this his entire life. He probably has.

I don't fuck around. I walk straight up to him and swing, though I hold back most of my strength. Despite what he says and his confidence, I do fear that if I go at him with everything I have, I *will* hurt him. Badly.

My punch gets blocked easily enough, but I knew it would. I immediately come at him with my left fist aimed at his face and a quick follow with my right to his ribs. He blocks the shot to his face and lowers his arm to stop the hit from landing on his ribs. That's exactly what I was waiting for…an opening to his face. I pull back to swing again, but in the blink of an eye he dances out of the way, and I feel a solid hit to *my* ribs as he maneuvers around me.

The hit doesn't hurt but it shocks the hell out of me. I had no idea he'd move so fast. I turn to face him again, this time going at him more quickly and from both sides. I jab, I punch, I move around him, but the damn feisty old man blocks every punch I throw. Getting more and more frustrated, I let the punches land a little heavier. I can hear the whoosh of air coming out of his mouth with every block as he continues to breathe through the onslaught of punches. Not getting anywhere, I decide to hell with this shit and these games. I take a step back and throw a kick to his side.

He catches it and holds my ankle captive against his side. "My turn," he snickers.

I don't even have time to react before his fist is in my face. Again, it doesn't hurt but surprises the shit out of me. As he punches me in the jaw, he pushes my leg away from his body, the momentum of both forces causing me to stumble. He wastes no time with his attack and delivers four fast and hard punches to my torso before sending my head flying back with the force of a vicious uppercut.

"Son of bitch!" I yell as I stumble backwards. I bring my hands up in front of me, waving off any more of his attacks. "Alright, alright, you made your point."

"Let me guess," he says as he stands in front of me, hands on his hips. "You've always just run in guns blazin', taking whoever you were fightin' off guard, or just plowing through them with that crazy strength of yours, right?"

"Yeah," I mutter.

"What was that?"

"Yes, alright! You're right, fuck!" I admit. "But it's worked for me this far." I throw my hands up in defeat.

"I ain't tryin' to be right, kid. I'm just trying to do right by you and help you the best way I can. These aren't people you've fought on the street. They're not thugs and bangers. They're trained fighters. And it ain't just that. They've got magic, too, some of 'em. You're out of your league kid, unless you let me help you."

"Oh, now you want to help me? When you've signed me up to fight for my fucking life! Literally! Now you fucking care? And if I do survive, that means I killed my opponent. I know that's what landed me here in the first place, but I already told you, I'm not a fucking killer!" I yell my anger, frustration, and fear at him.

Not fear of fighting.

Not fear of losing.

Fear of becoming the monster I already know lives inside me. Fear of unleashing all the nothingness that I feel inside of me out into the world and on to others.

Phil sighs and drops his voice lower, attempting to damper the situation and my anger. "You ain't gotta do no title fight, kid. I didn't mention it because it's not relevant. All you gotta do is make a little splash in the smaller fights, get the crowd to see you and cheer for you, make a little name for yourself, and give yourself a chance to be a part of that world and discover who you are."

His honest words deflate me. They take all the fight right out of me. Ever since the night I lost my parents, I've been disappointed, let down, and used by everyone around me. Until I figured out that even people who claimed they were helping me were selfish liars. When that realization finally broke through my naïve young mind, I refused to be anyone's pawn again. I've been the only person I can count on since *that* night. Sixteen fucking years.

"Although I wouldn't mind seeing the Titans defeated, and Hades taken down a notch...," he shrugs, "that's not something I expect you to do, kid. That's not something I think anyone can do and I'd never ask it. When I told you I'd do my best to help you, I meant it. I ain't got no ulterior motives."

My jaw clenches instinctively. Words have never been my strong suit, especially ones that are deep and heartfelt. I've certainly stopped apologizing for who I am a long time ago. I also haven't had anyone like Phil in my life that genuinely deserved one.

"I apologize." The words come out harsher than I'd like,

feeling foreign, but I mean them. "All of...," I wave my hands in the air, "*this* just has me defensive. I thought I had the world around me all figured out but turns out I don't know shit. Add that on top of the fact that I don't even know who or what the fuck I am, I'm a bit...on edge."

"That's understandable, kid. But you can't always solve all your problems with your fists."

I cock my eyebrow, amused. "Isn't that exactly what I'm doing? You did just register me as a *fighter*."

He chuckles. "I suppose you're right, but you know what I mean."

"Yeah."

"Let's go sit in the office and look at this brochure." He pulls it out of his back pocket. "Let's see what our next steps will be."

I stand behind Phil, looking over his shoulder as he unfolds the brochure on top of the desk. He looks it over and then points to one section. "This is probably our best bet. As good a place as any to get started."

I read the headline. *New Fighters! Test your mettle in our epic Battle Royale! Winner gets a spot in the upcoming Titan Tournament!*

"A Battle Royale? That's like where everyone fights at once, right?"

"That's right. I think it will actually play more to your brute strength. It's chaotic and hectic, not much skill in those battles, really."

I scoff. "Thanks for the vote of confidence."

"It's obvious you need training. You need to learn how to protect yourself, not just attack like some wild grizzly bear. The people you'll be fightin' will be fightin' back. You need to learn how to move and defend as well as how to make your hits count."

"To be clear, I wasn't using my strength on you. I could have knocked you out with one punch."

"Oh, I'm sure you could. But these fighters aren't human

either. They're Mageía. They'll be able to take your strength a lot better than a human."

"It sounds like you don't think I can do it."

"You can do it, kid. I have no doubts about that. But you're gonna have to trust me and you're gonna have to listen to me. Do what I tell ya and don't fight me on anything. We ain't got much time if we're gonna get you ready for a Titan Tournament."

"What exactly is a Titan Tournament?"

"The best of the best. Depending on how many sign up, usually between sixteen to twenty fighters all fightin' in a bracket style tournament until there's one winner. That winner then gets the chance to fight the Titans one-on-one. It would be expected but not required. You win the tournament and that's all you have to do, kid."

"Let me guess, those one-on-one fights are title fights."

He nods and sighs as if we're already defeated. "Ain't no one's beat a Titan in the ring in centuries."

I contemplate what he's saying. The gravity of what I've done starts to sink in. "You said the man I killed was a Titan."

He nods again but remains sullen. "He was topside, lost his Mageía strength and magic walkin' through the portal. Plus, you probably caught him off guard."

"Why is it that I have my strength topside if even the Titans don't have theirs?"

"That's one of the questions I just ain't got an answer for. We need to keep this information as quiet as possible. And we need to hope and pray no one saw you kill him because that would certainly lead to your death next. I imagine Raymond is fuming with the loss of one of his Titans. Any mention of him or anything else regarding the Titans, you keep your mouth shut. Not one peep that you know anything about anything. You understand?" He pierces me with a serious gaze.

I nod.

"Good. Now get some rest. You're gonna have a long day tomorrow."

Chapter eight

Fade Out by Zero 9:36

"Damn it, kid! Move your feet!"

Phil yells at me from the sidelines as I try to remember everything we've gone over in the past four days. We're working on a move called *'galloping'* which sounds ridiculous but is really just a simple four count of steps that I can use in every aspect of maneuvering forward, backward, and sideways.

I can gallop just fine. I can strike just fine. It's getting my body to work as a unit, as one, that's tripping me up. It's a lot harder than I thought it would be. I'm used to just standing in place and knocking the shit out of someone. Apparently, that's not going to be an option for these fights. So, here I am, reciting the steps like a prayer in my mind.

Gallop. Cross. Hook. Two.

Gallop. Cross. Hook. Two.

"Good! That's better!" I hear Phil confirming. "Push him a bit harder, Dwayne."

I'm sparring with Phil's current top fighter. He has an uncanny resemblance to Wesley Snipes in *Blade*, from his physique and haircut, down to his strange golden, almost orange eyes. I was a bit shocked when Phil assured me that he wasn't Mageía. He's all human and making his own splash in the fighting world topside, moving up quickly in the heavyweight division and will be challenging for the title belt soon. He's good, and at six feet tall, two hundred two pounds, he's the closest to my size.

But size doesn't mean shit against my...*power* or whatever the fuck it is. Only, I can't spar with him full-out. I have to rein in my strength and fight him on his level, which leaves me basically getting my ass kicked every damn day. I can't depend on my strength alone. I can't let it be my crutch. I have to learn the techniques of fighting or else I'm fucked. Sparing with Dwayne has shown me that.

He picks up his speed and I lose my rhythm; focused on defense and trying to keep his strikes from landing. Arms up in front of my face, I feel every vicious blow only vaguely. They'll never penetrate. They'll never bruise. They'll never break my skin. Doesn't mean that it's not incredibly frustrating though, to get my ass handed to me...for hours, every day.

I feel the ropes at my back as Dwayne corners me, moving his hits from my face to my sides. I have to curl in on myself in order to try and protect both my face and ribs.

"Get off them ropes!"

As if I don't fucking want to, Phil. I'm utterly useless in this position. Throwing all my training out the window, I dive for him, wrapping my arms around his body, taking us both to the floor.

We wrestle and fight for a dominating position. I end up on top of him, trying to move my hips up higher on his chest so I can go for the arm bar, but he's too quick and powerful. He straightens one leg and rolls, initiating a hip escape, pushing my knee back, gaining space between our bodies for him to roll and hip escape again, gaining the half guard and escaping from my mount position.

I end up with my back on the mat and him in mount position on top of me. It all happens so quickly it's hard to do anything other than react and defend. Dwayne uses my disadvantage and begins pummeling me with his fists.

"Goddamn it." I grit my teeth against the onslaught. It takes all of my control not to use my strength to get him the fuck off me, but Phil would never forgive me if I actually hurt Dwayne.

"Alright, alright. Let him up," Phil orders.

Dwayne gets to his feet and offers his hand to me. I take it and let him pull me to mine, removing my mouth guard.

"This is fucking pointless," I huff in annoyance.

"Bro, what are you talking about? You've already improved immensely since day one. You're learning and adapting quicker than anyone else I've ever seen. Cut yourself some slack. You're not going to be perfect right out the gate."

"Listen to him," Phil joins in. "I've trained a lot of fighters in my day and he's right. You're catchin' on faster than I expected."

"Not fast enough. I only have three more days until the Battle Royale and Dwayne still kicks my ass, *easily*. How in the hell am I supposed to win against...," I throw my arms in the air as words escape me, "who the fuck knows what if I can't even beat Dwayne?"

"You're not using your full strength against Dwayne," Phil says pointedly. "That's going to be a game changer for you in the ring, but you've gotta learn the basics to put under that impressive strength. You gotta trust me, kid."

Interlocking my fingers behind my neck, I look up to the ceiling with a sigh. I close my eyes, taking a few deep breaths to calm my frustration before I face Dwayne. "Alright, let's go again."

He looks to Phil for approval, who nods, and then we're at it again. I can't argue with their assessment. I am learning and adapting at an alarming rate. Every time we start again, I'm getting faster, and my movements are becoming more fluid; second nature. It's like my body is absorbing all the training. It's like this is what I've always been meant to do.

Fight.

Even with my improvement, I can't help but feel like it won't be enough. Like *I* won't be enough.

Another hour of sparring before Phil stops us. Unlike me, Dwayne can't continue to take my kicks and punches, which admittedly are landing more frequently. He tires more quickly than I do, and his human skin bruises and breaks when mine doesn't. A fact that I can't hide. Everyone here knows about the Mageía, about Phil. The older fighters don't have ambitions to venture into that world, but the younger boys seem enthralled by it.

By me.

I walk over to the mat area intent on doing some yoga. I laughed the first time Phil told me yoga would be part of my training. After ten minutes, I swallowed my ignorant statements about yoga being stupid and for chicks. That shit fucking hurts and is a lot harder than most people make it look. Yoga not only helps with mobility, but it forces you to use all kinds of stabilizing muscles that you don't use every day or in sparring. It's surprisingly been a game changer for me physically. When it comes to the whole, *quiet your mind and namaste shit,* yeah, that shit doesn't work for me. Nothing besides straight up fighting, causing pain, and seeing blood seems to quench the beast that is my mind.

"Looks like you guys beat me to yoga today," I say as I approach the occupied mat. "What's this particular move called?"

Joey looks down to where Peggy is rolled over onto her back, her long legs and big paws comically splayed in the air, clearly enjoying the belly rubs.

"Lazy dog." He chuckles.

"More like spoiled dog." I lower my big body onto the mat next to them, pulling my knees up, resting my arms on them.

Even in this position, I dwarf Joey. Hell, Peggy makes him look small too. He's average height but his body is naturally thin. Even with all the hard work he puts in daily, his body refuses to grow like the other kids. And he *does* put in the work. He outworks all the other boys yet has the least to show for it. I feel for him. I can't imagine how frustrating and disheartening it is for him to work so incredibly hard at something, do everything people tell you to do, only to remain exactly where you are. Spinning your wheels. Stuck. Struggling to understand why what you're doing isn't working for you but works for everyone else.

"Thanks for keeping her company. We both appreciate it. Though I think she's definitely reaping all the benefits."

As if she can understand that we're talking about her, Peggy snorts and stretches her legs out before returning to her relaxed position. We both chuckle and shake our heads.

"How's the face feeling?" I nod my head in his direction.

He shrugs. "It's not as bad as it looks. Doesn't really hurt anymore."

I'm not entirely sure he's telling the truth. I've never had any type of wound to heal, only ever experiencing fleeting physical pain. I can't imagine what he felt in the moment, much less the constant physical pain. It's been five days since that night. The swelling has subsided, but half of his face is covered in yellowish-green bruises. The cut on his lip is scabbed over and his left eye is still bloodshot from the veins bursting under the vicious punches he took. I don't think five days is enough for him to have healed enough not to still feel pain.

"Why'd you get involved with him anyway?" I ask, staring at him, failing to understand why such a good kid would be mixed up with the likes of Tiberius.

Another half-hearted shrug, his eyes falling to Peggy to avoid meeting mine. "You wouldn't understand."

"Try me."

"I just wanted to be a part of something bigger. Something

important. I thought it would be cool to be a part of a powerful team. I thought…," a half shrug, "I don't know, I thought if I was part of that world, *I'd* be important."

"You're here. You're a part of Phil's team, are you not?"

"Yeah, but…," he shakes his head, still refusing to meet my stare, "it's not the same. I respect Phil, I like being here, but it's just still…not enough."

He's not saying much but he may as well be screaming for help at the top of his lungs. I've seen the way the other boys pick on him and tease him when Phil's not around. Phil doesn't allow any type of bullying or favoritism in his gym but that doesn't mean it doesn't happen behind his back.

Boys will be boys.

I hate that term but it's true for those that aren't taught to believe any differently. Or the ones that don't see the benefit of being better when the world around them shows them the opposite. The world is cruel, and they learn that same cruelty whether they want to or not. And I've noticed that the boys that come here don't seem to have the best support systems outside of these four walls.

I recognize the familiar loneliness in all of them. This gym is a safe haven for them, and Phil is the one burdened with trying to keep them on the right track.

They all want to be a part of something better, some are just more susceptible to the hatred in the world than others. And on the streets, only the strong and cruel survive. And there's not one cruel bone in Joey's body. But he is strong. Maybe not physically but he's stronger willed than any of the other boys. I saw that firsthand when he didn't back down from Tiberius even though the odds were impossible.

"Joey, look at me," I say, voice stern but soft. He reluctantly lifts big, sad brown eyes to meet mine. "*You are important*. Do you hear me? You. Just the way you are. And I know the world isn't fair. I know from experience how cruel and vicious it can be. But you have this." I gesture to the gym around me. "You have Phil and I know he cares about you deeply. You have the chance to follow the right path, a *good* path. I don't want to see you end up like me."

"But I want to be like you, T!" he insists. "You're strong and confident and you're not afraid of anything!"

"You're right. But if I had a choice...." I trail off, my thoughts going back to those foggy memories of a loving mother and father, the overwhelming, unabashed affection given to me. All the hugs, kisses, encouraging words, laughs, tears, and bedtime stories before getting tucked in. A home. In this moment, I choose to be more honest with Joey than I've ever been with anyone, ever. Even myself. "I'd rather have a life I was afraid of losing than one that won't even notice if I'm gone."

To his credit, he stays silent, pondering my words. He's such a smart kid. I hate seeing him feeling so weak. I know what it's like to feel lost and helpless. That was a lifetime ago, but I remember it like it was yesterday. Just a lost little boy trying to understand Heaven and if I could visit my mom and dad there.

Finally, he nods his head, looking back down at Peggy, who is now laying her head in his lap offering comfort of her own.

"Hey," I say, making him look at me again. I don't know why on earth I care so much about this kid, but I can't seem to stop myself from wanting to help him. "As long as I'm here, I'm not going to let anything happen to you, ok?"

I don't know why I fucking say it. I want to take the words back as soon as they leave my treacherous mouth, but I can't. I mean them more than I've ever meant any other words before but how can I promise him something like that? Especially in a world I have no clue about. But the look on his face, the utter dismay and lack of confidence, wrenches my insides. He's been bullied his entire life. He's been run over his entire life. He's been ignored and dismissed his entire life. I've only known him for five short days and I'm tired of seeing his light slowly burn out. If there's anything I can do to help him get to the right path and stay there, I'm going to fucking do it. God help me, I'm a fucking idiot for thinking I could ever help this kid. I've never been able to help a single soul in my own pathetic excuse of a life but damn it if I don't want to try. For him.

His eyes light up and he gives me a smile. It's still a little weak around the edges but I'll take it over the hopelessness I saw seeping in.

"Now get off my mat," I say, gently pushing him. "I need to do yoga before Phil comes and kicks both our asses." I mimic Phil's voice, "This is a gym. Ya ain't gonna train then—"

"You know where the door is," Joey finishes.

We both laugh as we get to our feet, and I watch him walk over to the weights.

I don't know what it's like to even have a best friend much less a little brother, but I imagine this must be what it's like. It feels oddly satisfying.

And intensely fucking terrifying.

My life was a lot easier when I didn't give a shit about anyone. I can't help but think, again, that this city may just well destroy me. Because Joey looks up to me. He believes me when I say that I won't let anything happen to him. And who the fuck am I to do anything for him?

Nobody.

I'm just fucking nobody.

Chapter nine

Savages by Catch Your Breath

The noise of the crowd thunders and echoes through the tunnel, getting louder and louder with every step I take toward the exit. The beat of their clamor reverberates through the air and sinks into my chest, coaxing my heartbeat to join their excited and frantic tempo.

I haven't felt nerves this intense since I was a kid being thrown into the whirlwind of the foster system. I'm not necessarily nervous to fight, that's just engrained in my DNA at this point, but I'm nervous because I've never been in front of a crowd before. I don't know what the hell to expect about any single part of this.

I'm trying to listen to Phil, but his voice is nothing more than a murmur blending into the cacophony of a million voices. My sole focus is the end of the tunnel, waiting for the moment when the noise finally translates to people. And when I finally get to the end, I'm nowhere near ready for what I see.

My feet stop moving as everything finally comes into view. People...well, Mageía...everywhere. The stadium is much larger than I expected. Rows and rows of seats climb up three levels high, encircling the entire room. Even though the faces in the crowd are unusual and shocking, they all blend together as I spin around slowly, trying to take it all in. Two levels up, a glass box overlooks the fighting ring. I can see bodies inside, but I can't make out any faces. There's something...familiar tugging at me from inside that room though. Something that tingles down my spine and seems to crawl beneath my skin, making me itch.

A violent shove to my shoulder brings my focus back to what's happening around me. "Out of my way, *pretty boy*." A large man with the scales and eyes of a crocodile shoves past me sneering, flashing his very crocodile-like teeth.

"C'mon, kid. No time for shock and awe, we've gotta get you in the ring." Phil gives me a gentle push, getting my feet moving again.

I fall in line with the other fighters making their way toward the center of the arena. Approaching the ring, I'm shocked at how large it actually is. I was wondering how we'd all fit inside for a Battle Royale, but this ring is easily three times the size of the one in Phil's gym. This one is also completely enclosed by chain link fencing. It even covers the ring from the top in a dome-like style.

Fighters climb up the steps and enter the ring one by one, yelling at the top of their lungs, pounding their fists on their chest and acting more like animals than humans. Then again, I guess none of us are humans, are we? Though looking at me versus all the other fighters, you can't tell that I'm Mageía, not the way you can tell they are. I look human. I'm hoping this causes the other fighters to underestimate me.

I have to admit I'm not feeling my most confident self as I approach the ring. I've never contended with anyone other than a human and I'm not sure what the hell's going to happen once the fighting starts. I don't know how my body is going to react to the force of Mageía. Will my skin still be impenetrable? Will I still not feel any pain? Only one way to find out.

"Just do like we've been practicing. Stay focused and controlled. Don't let the chaos throw you off. You're not only going to have an opponent in front of you, you're gonna have 'em comin' at you from all angles. You gotta be smart and alert."

I pull my T-shirt over my head as Phil rambles on and on. He had a pair of old fighting shorts in his gym that he lent me. They're plain orange shorts, no logo or name printed on them like all the other fighters have. It's fine. They actually suit me perfectly. Who the fuck am I anyway?

Nobody.

"Hey, are you even listening to me?" Phil snaps.

"Yeah, old man. I got it. Be alert and smart," I respond half-heartedly. The truth is my focus has been everywhere else except on Phil.

Before he has time to scold me more, I'm being ushered closer to the ring. Someone grabs my arm, flipping it around aggressively, and scans my wrist. The scanner beeps, displaying my picture and stats on the screen for the enforcer to verify. He nods once and then more hands are on me, pushing me towards the stairs. I slowly climb up and then I'm walking onto the mat of the ring.

I don't yell or seek attention like all the other fighters did before me. The noise is overwhelming enough as it is without me adding to the mix. The shouts from an entire stadium, filled to the gills with bodies, are deafening. Why does it sound even louder here at its center? It's distracting and a bit disorienting. God, this is so fucking annoying and outside of anything I'd normally do. All for fucking answers I may not even get. I'm beginning to question how much I fucking care.

The loud bang and clank of metal against metal jolts my focus back to the ring. I look over my shoulder to see the door to the ring has been shut, effectively locking us inside. I guess this is it. There's only one way I'm walking back out of that door.

Either unconscious or victorious.

The announcer comes on the mic, his voice deep and booming out across the stadium, silencing the rowdy crowd with his simple, *"Ladies and Gentlemen."*

I slowly back up towards the outer portion of the ring. I'm not going to get stuck in the middle, attacked from all sides when this starts, and that's when I hear it. A low buzzing sound, almost too low to hear, but *I* hear it. I turn around to face the fencing that encircles the ring, lifting my hand tentatively towards it. Right before my hand comes in contact with it, I feel it.

Electricity.

"...The Underworld's very own, Raymond Harris, is proud to present the fifth annual Battle Royale!"

The announcer's voice comes in waves as I try to focus. Motherfucking fuck, it's an electric fucking fence. Either this is a new, fucked up and psychotic development, or Phil is going to have some explaining to do. He never once mentioned the ring I'd be fighting in, *locked in*, would be surrounded by electric fucking fencing. It may not affect me as much as some but even I'm not immune to the force of electricity.

"...let the fighting, bloodshed, and mayhem begin!"

The crowd erupts again as the announcer completes his introduction and I have no time to focus on anything else as fighting breaks out around me. Somehow the sounds of fists landing, bones breaking, and fighters screaming, grunting, and groaning, manage to compete with the noise of the crowd.

Mayhem is the perfect word to describe the inside of this fighting ring. Tangled bodies are everywhere and not just bodies with two arms and two legs; some have wings and tails, not to mention the claws and fangs on some of these...people. The back of a wing smacks me from the side, sending me stumbling into the nearest body.

The face that turns and snarls at me is the same one that

pushed past me earlier. Crocodile-man takes full advantage of my slightly shocked state and lunges for me, wrapping his body around mine and spinning, throwing my body to the ground aggressively.

He lands one solid punch to my face and that's all I need to snap me out of my daze. I use the momentum of his next punch to claim the arm bar, wrapping my legs around his upper body, trapping him there. I lift my hips in a bridge, distancing my face from his reach, and then I pull on his arm. Unlike Dwayne, I don't hold back an ounce of my strength as I bend his arm up at the elbow. It snaps like a twig in my hands. He roars in pain as I push him off me and roll to my feet. I don't get the chance to finish him off before another fighter grabs him in a chokehold from behind. Phil's voice echoes in my mind.

You gotta be smart and alert.

I leave crocodile-man to his fate as I scan my surroundings and once again put the fence at my back so no one can come up behind me. I'm happy to stand back and let the others fight amongst themselves, thinning the herd. I'll fight when it's time to fight.

Of course, it doesn't take long for that time to come. Everyone went full-out as soon as they got the green light to unleash their fury. They all went head-on, intent on proving who the better fighter is. The only problem is, when you're literally surrounded by everyone with that same mindset and it's not a fair one-on-one fight, it doesn't matter if you are the better fighter. Surrounded by chaos, luck has just as much of a chance at winning as talent.

Bodies litter the floor as Mageía are left either unconscious or cradling charred, beaten, and broken bones, unable to get up without assistance. I've managed to go unscathed, my only fight being the few seconds with crocodile-man at the start. Now I'm left facing off with the only other man standing. He's shorter than me but he has a strange advantage of reach that I don't. Wings. They're large and hairless, a burnt orange with red veins snaking through them. He's the one that bumped me earlier, only now one of his wings is bent at an awkward angle, dragging on the floor. It looks painful as fuck, but it doesn't seem to be bothering him.

My eyes are pulled away from his wings as a similar orange glow starts to form at the center of his chest. I watch in utter awe as that glowing ball moves under his skin and up his throat. I realize almost too late that it's fucking fire as a flame shoots out of his mouth, directly at me. I jump out of the way and throw myself to the ground, rolling out of its path.

I hiss as electricity sears through me as my body rolls into the fence. Definitely unpleasant. I quickly push off the fence and back to my feet; that's when I notice my chest and side have been hit. My skin is singed from the bottom of my left pec down onto my side, just above the band of my shorts.

I still don't feel any pain.

I don't know if it's because of my skin or if it's the adrenaline keeping the worst of it at bay. Before he can work up another flame, I rush him. He attempts to block with his one good wing, wrapping it around his body. I grab ahold of the wing in a death grip and then I roll, throwing the man over me and to the floor. He lands on his stomach, and I don't waste any time. I place one foot on his back and then, still clutching his wing in my fists, I pull. Even with my strength, it takes more force than I thought it would to rip his wing from his back. The sound he makes as his flesh rips would haunt me in my dreams if I was a better man.

I'm not.

For the first time tonight, the crowd disappears, and my mind goes completely silent. Nothing else matters now except the man struggling beneath me. The feeling of his skin tearing as I yank on his wing, and the blood pouring out of his back, settles me. I don't know when I became this cold, dead version of me. This monster. But I don't see a need to be any other way. Especially now, in *this* world. I have a feeling being a monster is going to be the best fucking thing I can be here.

When the wing snaps free, I toss it to the side and look down at the utter ruin of his back. There's a gaping hole from his shoulder blade down to his lower back where his wing used to be. I don't know how healing works, never having experienced it firsthand, but I don't see him healing this. No doubt I just destroyed this man's life, and I still can't be bothered by the sickening thought. He shouldn't have entered this fight if he didn't want to fucking be ruined. He's gone completely limp beneath me, resigned to simply whimpering in pain and loss.

Loss of his wing.

Loss of this fight.

The crowd and the noise come crashing back to me as someone grabs my wrist and throws my arm up in the air, the announcer's voice finally breaking through my reverie.

"...champion of the fifth annual Battle Royale, Jett Stephenssss!"

Most of the crowd is on their feet, cheering, yelling, and chanting my name. My name being shouted like a fucking prayer by thousands of strangers staggers me more than anything that happened in this ring. It's unsettling and, oddly...satisfying. I let my eyes sweep over the crowd slowly, taking it all in.

Then, I see her.

And everything changes. The world of muted greys I've lived in for the past sixteen years snaps, suddenly flooded with vibrant color.

She stands out in her normalcy. She looks like me. Human. We lock eyes as she walks past the ring. Her beautiful face is a cold, blank mask, but her eyes hold the slightest bit of curiosity as they appraise me. She holds herself like a goddess, and fuck, she may as well be for all I know. The intensity of her gaze knocks the air from my lungs and, once again, the crowd disappears. Nothing else exists besides her. Fuck. Those eyes. They could hold me captive for centuries, easily. I want to fall into them, get lost in their depths, but she breaks our stare much too quickly and continues walking past the ring, leaving my eyes to trail after her. The sway of her hips holds me in a similar trance until she's lost to the sea of bodies surrounding her.

Then Phil is by my side, slapping my cheek to get my attention. "Snap out of it, kid."

"Huh?" I look down at him, the image of her eyes still burned in my mind.

"What do you mean, huh? Boy, did you get hit upside the head and knocked silly? You won."

"I won," I echo quietly as I look up one more time in the direction of where she disappeared.

"Hey." Phil slaps me one more time, really getting my attention and rousing my anger. "Head on straight. You ain't done yet. You've gotta interview and take photos. Come on."

I let Phil lead me out of the ring, stepping over bodies that are still sprawled on the mat, injured beyond the ability to get up and walk. I pay them no mind as my eyes search one more time for her purple dress, only to be disappointed when there's no sign of her. Oh well, probably for the best anyway. The last fucking thing I need is a distraction as I'm navigating this new, dangerous world. My focus hasn't changed and *won't* change because of a pretty face.

And haunting eyes.

And a devastating body.

Fucking hell, T. Snap out of it, I echo Phil's words. And then I have no choice but to snap out of it as bright lights flash in my face and practically blind me, and a microphone is shoved in my face.

This? Yeah, I can do without this. It feels like I've stepped into a fucking circus and I'm the main attraction. I've been a lone wolf most of my life, as a choice, and this is the last thing I ever wanted or expected to happen when I came here. This isn't me. My fists clench at my sides as I attempt to rein in my annoyance and impatience. Then I feel the familiar soft coat of Peggy as she nudges my hand with her head. I open my clenched fist and lay it on her neck as she settles in next to me, and just like that, she's helped ease my rising anger.

Thanks, Peg.

"Jett?"

I shake my head, clearing my thoughts, and finally focus on the blonde woman with the neck of a giraffe and large animal-like eyes standing in front of me, holding the microphone. God, this place is fucking weird.

"What was the question?" I ask.

"What was your gameplan going into the fight tonight?"

Twenty minutes and twenty-one fucking questions later, I'm finally set free and slip away to the locker room. I stand under the hot water of the showerhead and let it wash away the blood I hadn't even noticed splattered on me. As the winner of the Battle Royale, I've secured a spot in the Titan Tournament, and I need to decide what the fuck I'm going to do.

Do I want to stay and fight? To potentially learn who, or what, I am? Do I want to deal with this…attention? All these fucking eyes on me, watching my every damn move?

Or do I want to just say fuck it and leave? Like I've left so many other places in my life without a second fucking thought.

Then I remember that one set of haunting eyes standing out amongst the thousands. An encounter that lasted no more than ten seconds but seems to have left an imprint on my mind. Maybe I'll stay just a little longer after all.

Chapter ten

I shouldn't be surprised to see him here. Especially not after what I saw in that alley. I shouldn't be surprised that he's Mageía. The way he utterly destroyed Tiberius should have been all the proof I needed that he wasn't human, but damn, looks sure can be deceiving.

Just like he looks like a gods-damned living breathing angel. I knew by his size and the way he carried himself that he would be in peak condition but seeing him without a shirt on nearly gives me a damn heart attack. Hell, palpitations at least.

His golden skin shines like the sun, pulled tight across a sculpted chest, broad shoulders, and insanely cut abs. His obliques are so prominent that the deep V-cut low in his abdomen is criminal. It should be illegal for anyone to walk around with a body like that. His legs in those orange shorts…gods. He could probably crush the world between those muscular thighs like it was nothing more than a watermelon. I think I'd die happy if I got crushed between them. There are definitely worse ways to go.

But what catches my attention the most are the matching snakes that wrap deliciously up his jacked arms. Starting at his wrists, they wind up his arms in an unnervingly lifelike way. The heads of each snake mirror the other, mouths open and menacing on each of his solid pecs. Gods, arms are my weakness, and his arms are devastating.

Then there's the lion head that takes up his entire back. Again, the artwork is so incredibly detailed and beautiful you expect the lion to blink and roar to life, jumping off his skin to devour you. I wouldn't mind letting *him* devour me. Sigh...*get a grip Meg.* He's just another conceited and self-centered asshole. The fighters always are.

Only he didn't act like the other fighters in the ring tonight. I'm annoyed to admit that I watched him closely. This was the first fight I've ever watched where I felt utterly riveted and didn't once want to look away. Not even at the brutal ending. Because watching him fascinated me.

He walked into the ring like he didn't belong there, like he was annoyed at even having to be here. And once the fighting broke out, he stood back to watch it all unfold with a look of boredom and...I wanna say a look of disgust on his face. Maybe even a little bit of hesitance.

But as soon as he was pulled into the fighting, he changed. He came alive. There was not one second of hesitancy as he easily broke the first man's arm. And when it was down to him and the drakon fighter, when he had him pressed to the mat and ripped off his wing with his bare hands, he looked almost...peaceful. What does that say about him?

Even worse, what does it say about me?

That I couldn't drag my eyes away from him. That I wanted to watch him move that impressive body with such elegant and lethal grace all night. That I had the most devious and heated images of that body tangled up with mine. That the mere sight of watching him fight has my panties wet.

The realization has me shook. I've been surrounded by nothing but violence my entire life and I hate it. I absolutely fucking hate it. So why am I reacting this way to him? To this stranger? He's hardly the first attractive man I've seen. Though I have to admit he's definitely in a league of his own. Or maybe that's just my lonely and neglected vagina talking. Either way, that mischievous curiosity of mine is piqued. That small dying fire inside of me that' I'm desperate to stoke stirred to life at the mere sight of him.

Then our eyes lock. I barely manage to school my features in time. The action comes easy after a lifetime of learning how to lock down my thoughts and emotions. To show no fear. But it's not fear I have to try and keep off my face now. Especially with the way his eyes bore into mine, never once lowering to trail down my body. I can't tell if he's also schooling his features or if he really has nothing more to show than slight curiosity.

Except this type of eye contact is more than simple curiosity, isn't it? It's heavy and deep. It's raw and real. It's…more than I want to try and understand, so I break our intense stare and continue on my way.

The last fucking thing I need in my life is an arrogant, selfish fighter, no matter what my traitorous lady parts say.

Chapter eleven

Animals by Call Me Karizma

As I'm walking down the hall leading out of the fighters' locker rooms, I see her. She's pushed up against the wall by a disgustingly fat centaur. Fucking hell, *a centaur*. I'm not sure when I'll get used to seeing all of this but today isn't the day. Peggy lets out a small growl as we approach them, obviously not thrilled about the situation either. Or maybe she's sensing my anger.

The centaur's chunky hand is wrapped around her jaw, holding her in place. "And what do I get in exchange if I say yes?"

"You get to be a part of his empire. You should be so lucky. How dare you ask for more. Now, if you know what's in your best interest, you'll get your fucking hands off me," she says, with absolute confidence and defiance that doesn't support the situation she's in.

He pushes his naked, sweaty torso harder against her, his free hand running down her bare arm, and he leans his head in closer, inhaling deeply. "I don't think he'd care if I took a little taste of what he so willingly puts in my path. Besides, what are you to him besides a burden? I can make him money. What value do you serve? No, I think I like my chances. So, I'm going to take you—"

He's so focused on her that he never even hears me coming. "She clearly said no, motherfucker." I grab his wrist from where his hand had started to travel up her stomach and twist his arm behind his back until I hear the bone snap.

He roars in pain as he lets her go, stepping away from her to face me. He swings his good arm at me, aiming that fat fist at my face. I duck under it easily and give three quick jabs to his gut. I hear the air whoosh out of him as he staggers back on his horse legs.

The next thing I know he's rearing up, those dangerous hooves kicking in my direction. Peggy's wings snap out, blocking his view of me and giving me a chance to drop to the ground and aim a kick to his back leg, right at the knee joint. The loud pop tells me it's dislocated, if not broken. Another roar of pain and he staggers to the ground. He uses his front legs to climb to his hooves again, not putting any weight on the back leg I injured, leaving him off balance and he knows it. His right arm hangs limp at his side, broken at the shoulder.

"Who the fuck are you?" he asks, eyes darting between me and Peggy as he tries to decide if he should keep fighting or walk away.

"No one. But the lady said no, so I suggest you fuck off before I become someone you need to worry about."

He snorts. "Mr. Harrison isn't going to be pleased you injured one of his potential investments. You'll pay for this. He'll see to that."

"Like I give a fuck." His eyes go wide as he continues to stare at me like I just grew another head or some shit. "Well, go on. Tuck your tail and run off to tattle like a little bitch. Unless you want me to break another limb?"

He turns his hateful glare to where she still stands against the wall, throwing him her own glare of dangerous twin daggers. "You're not even worth it," he sneers, then his attention is back on me. "We'll see how much you talk when you don't catch me off guard like a pussy. I'll find you," he threatens before he turns and limps off.

"There's a good boy," I prod. "Run to daddy." I watch him until I'm sure he's not turning back, then I finally give my full attention to...*her*.

Fuck. She's even more beautiful up close. Her long, dark hair is pulled into a high ponytail and looks as smooth as melted chocolate. Her sand-colored skin sparkles lightly like the sun glinting off the distant waves at a beach, and her curves....

Jesus.

Her body is capable of a TKO without even throwing a punch. Her deep purple dress hugs her thick hips, accentuating her small waist, and leaves very little to the imagination when it comes to her breasts. I can only imagine how beautiful she'd look with those thighs spread open underneath me and those breasts set free to bounce as I slam into her. My cock twitches as the image plays in my mind. My gaze continues to travel up her neck, over plump lips, rosy cheeks, and a straight, dainty nose. But then...those eyes.

Dazzling, if not a bit angry, amethyst eyes capture mine and hold them hostage. I've never seen eyes like hers before, and I'm instantly entranced by their depths. She's downright seductive and she knows it. I realize her lips are moving but I haven't heard a word she's said. Her fingers snap in front of my face, pulling me out of my daze.

"Did you hear what I said?"

I shake my head, clearing the fog. I ignore her question, asking one of my own. "How'd a girl like you get mixed up with a jackoff like that?"

"That *jackoff* is one in a million down here. It comes with the territory. I could have handled it myself, but instead you jump in with some kind of fucking hero complex that's only going to attract the wrong kind of attention and get people hurt, *for real*." She crosses her arms over her stomach and pushes out a hip. "Next time, why don't you mind your own damn business. I swear, you fighters are all the same."

I snort. "I'm nothing like them."

She rolls those beautiful eyes. "Oh please. You're a

casebook, grade-A douchebag. I can see it written all over you."

Peggy lets out a growl from where she stands next to me. I reach out and pat her head, sending calm, reassuring thoughts her way.

"Is that right?" I can't help the hint of amusement in my tone. She's so confident in her appraisal of me. "By all means, enlighten me to my grade-A douchebags ways."

"You saw a female in a rough situation, and you immediately thought she was weak and needed you to rescue her. Chauvinist much? I may be a damsel, but I'm not in distress, that was your first mistake. I bet you've been told your entire life how *special* you are, which has caused you to think way too highly of yourself and made you feel entitled to whatever you want. And the lack of discipline and consequences in your life makes you more willing to hurt others to get it. How am I doing so far?"

"Wow. You nailed it," I say sarcastically, slowly clapping my hands for emphasis. "You've really got me pegged." I stare at her, studying her, trying to see who *she* truly is behind her tough act. Her assessment of me says more about her than it does about me. She's way off the mark but it says exactly how she's been treated and what she's come to expect from fighters. Hell, from guys in general. We're dicks and I'm no exception, just not in the ways she mentioned. And, unlike her, I'm not one to judge a book by its cover. Her mask is good, I'll give her that, but not quite good enough. "But I've got you pegged too. And you don't belong here."

She pulls her head back slightly as if my words physically hit her. "And you don't know shit about me."

I step into her space and slam my fist into the wall next to her head. She flinches and gasps, pushing her back into the wall in a failed attempt to get distance between us. I'm flooded with the scent of some kind of flower blossom I can't even begin to describe. It's subtle and yet…intoxicating. It's something exotic and beautiful. A scent that I feel seeping into my senses, burrowing in to torment me as a memory once it fades.

A confident smirk tugs at my lips and I huff out a laugh. "You might fool all those other *jackoffs* who don't care to actually see you, but I see you." I trail a finger softly across her jaw, the simple touch causing her heart to race. I know it's racing because her chest is heaving like she just ran a mile. As she loses control of the mask, her eyes drop to my lips for a fraction of a second before I watch as she physically steels herself to my presence. "I see the uncertain girl behind the bravado," I whisper.

"Don't touch me."

I catch her wrist before her fist can connect with my jaw, my arrogant smirk deepening. "Trust me, Little Firecracker…," I keep her wrist held in one hand while I trace the thumb of my other along her bottom lip, "you'll know when I touch you, and you won't be telling me to stop." Her other hand comes up to my chest, trying to push me away from her.

When that doesn't work, she tries to turn her head away from me, but I grab her chin and force her to look at me. I force her to give me those big, beautiful eyes. She's trying so hard to be cold and angry, but there's no denying the heated desire I know is running through her veins, making her eyes shine the way they are.

"When I touch you, you're going to beg me not to stop. Do you wanna know how I know?"

She tries to lift her chin in defiance as she looks up at me, clamping her jaw tightly, refusing to answer. But she never breaks eye contact, allowing me to see so much more than she realizes. Eyes very rarely hide what a person is feeling inside.

"Because I see the truth in your eyes; you like that I see you. I'm the flame that just lit your fuse, Little Firecracker, and it's only a matter of time until you detonate *all over me*."

If looks could manifest physically, her glare would scorch my skin even more than it already is. And I would gladly welcome her flame because maybe, for the first time, I feel pain.

I let go of her wrist and step away from her. Whatever moment of weakness and vulnerability I saw seconds ago is gone. Her mask is firmly back in place, and she finally finds her voice.

"You'll *never* touch me."

I can't help but smirk again, knowing she's lying to herself. The only question is, does she acknowledge her own lie? Or does she believe it?

As the distance slowly grows between us, the rest of the world starts to come back into focus. The hall is busier now, filling up with fighters and…fans. I was so caught up in her that I hadn't even noticed the bodies moving around us. As my eyes scan the now crowded hall, a woman locks eyes with me. She twirls her blonde hair around her finger as she walks towards me, an exaggerated sway in her hips. All the sway in the world wouldn't give this girl hips. She's tall and thin with tits that are way too big for her body. They don't move a muscle as she saunters toward me. God, I hate fake tits.

"Hey," her voice comes out all syrupy and sweet. "You're Jett, right?"

Peggy steps between us, ears back, snarling.

"It's alright, Peg," I say as I step around her. "Yeah."

The woman eyes Peggy warily but still smiles flirtatiously. "I'm Jennifer. Wanna go somewhere?"

Hell, it's been a while since I slept with a woman, and I do have needs. I also just won the fucking Battle Royale; I deserve to celebrate. Deserve. I guess I am feeling a bit entitled after all. Besides, my encounter with little-miss-know-it-all has my body wound up and needing a release. And since she said I'll *never* get to touch her, fuck it.

"Yeah." I sling my arm over the blonde's shoulder, tucking her rail-thin body into my side.

Before I lead us away, I look over my shoulder to where she still stands against the wall, arms crossed. The fire in her eyes would definitely burn me if they could. She's angry. Angrier than our little chat warrants. I know I didn't mistake the way she responded to my touch, and I can't help but wonder if she's jealous. It dawns on me that I don't even know her name.

"See you around, Firecracker." I wink at her, which causes her to simmer with even more rage as she clamps down on her jaw.

I lead my little barbie down the hall, but I can still feel her eyes on me. I feel the heat of twin amethyst daggers in my back, promising me the most delicious type of pain.

And I can't fucking wait.

Chapter twelve

Shackles by Steven Rodriguez

My dick is rock solid as I play back our little encounter in the hallway. Her voluptuous hip pushed out, begging for my hand to grip it and sink my fingertips into her supple skin. Her full, natural breasts, straining to be let out of that skintight dress. Her long hair, waiting for my fingers to slide through it before wrapping it around my wrist. Her venomous, smartass mouth, tempting me to taste it. Her flowery-fresh scent, enveloping me.

Those eyes.

Fuck. Those eyes, calling to me, desperate to be seen.

A groan escapes my lips as her mouth greedily slips up and down my cock. Her hair lightly tickles my thighs as her head bobs up and down.

"Do you like that?"

An annoyingly sweet, high-pitched voice pulls me out of my fantasy. I look down to meet two blue eyes staring up at me, a sly smile on her lips. Blue eyes. Probably beautiful to most men. Hell, most men wouldn't even notice the eyes with her large, round tits on full display.

Neither of which does anything to keep me aroused. I'm suddenly irritated as fuck. This isn't who I want kneeling between my legs. These aren't the eyes I want staring up at me. Her smile falters as my dick starts to soften under her touch. I push to my feet, sending her sprawling on her ass, her fake tits still not budging.

"Hey!" she exclaims. "What the fuck?"

I tuck myself into my jeans as I button them back up. "Listen...." *Shit, what the fuck is her name,* "Jess—"

"Jennifer," she snaps, angrily.

"Listen, Jennifer," I start again, "I'm not in the mood." I grab her dress and toss it to her where she's still sitting on the floor. She's so shocked she doesn't even move to catch it as it falls in her lap. Yet again I have an angry set of eyes looking up at me. The only difference is, I don't give a fuck about these ones.

"What do you mean you're not in the mood? I was literally just giving you head."

I look down at my now limp dick, safely secured behind my zipper. "Not very well, obviously," I point out and she scoffs. "Get dressed and go."

She's frozen on the floor, mouth hanging open in an 'o' of surprise, an embarrassed flush on her cheeks. "You're not seriou—"

"I said get the fuck out," I growl as I lean down, grabbing her arm and yanking her to her feet. Reaching back down, I grab her dress and press it into her chest. Still holding her arm, I lead her to the door, and shove her out while she's still only wearing a thong and heels.

"You're such a fucking assh—"

I slam the door in her face, cutting off her annoying voice. God, if I would have had to hear her high-pitched voice as I pushed into her, I may have just gone in-fucking-sane. Dodged that bullet. The assault on my ears has stopped but the irritation running through my veins is still alive and well.

Irritation at the sheer confidence in which she said, *"You'll never touch me."*

Irritation at the fact that the mere minutes I spent with her have already affected me.

Irritation at being turned on by the simple thought of her and not getting my release.

A knock on the door has me growling as I yank it open and yell, "I told you to get the fu—"

"Dayum, T! I know I said I wanted to be like you, but I *really* want to be like you. That girl was so fine. Man, all the fighters get the sexiest—"

"What do you need, Joey?" I managed to rein in my irritation, only a slight rumble in my voice as I question him.

"Phil sent me to get you. He wants to see you in his office, and he *did not* sound happy," he grimaces.

"Great," I sigh, and rake my hand through my hair.

"Getting called into the principal's office already, huh?"

"Last thing I need right now is another fucking lecture," I seethe as I join Joey in the hall, shutting the door behind me, irritation and unspent desire still raging hot in my veins. I need to get it under control. The last person I need to yell at right now is the only person helping me.

"Kind of wound up for a guy that just got laid, aren't you?" Joey shoots a nervous glance my way. I don't bother correcting him as I turn to descend the stairs. His footsteps fall quickly behind mine. "You killed it in the ring tonight!" I can hear the smile practically splitting his face in half. "The way you ripped that guy's wing ri—"

I stop and turn so abruptly Joey slams into my chest. I grab his shoulders, pushing him away from me so I can glare at him. "You watched the fights?

"Duh! I wouldn't miss it for the world!"

"How the hell did you get into The Underworld?"

He shrugs. "I just walk through the portal like you guys do."

"What do you mean you just walk through? No one invited you across?" He shakes his head and I narrow my eyes at him. "Are you Mageía?"

He scoffs. "I wish. You know I'm not," he says defeatedly.

"I don't want you going down there," I practically yell in his face.

"What? Why? I always go down there."

"Because it's dangerous."

"It's no more dangerous than up here! Do you know how many times I've been approached by a gang? Do you know how many times I've been jumped just because they could? Because I don't have any protection!" He angrily pulls out of my hold. "You don't get it, T! And you never will." He storms off before I can even attempt to say anything else. I know how cruel the streets are better than anyone else but he's right, I'll never know what it's like to be the weak one on the streets. He needs help and guidance, but I have no idea what to do, or hell, even what to say obviously.

"Fuck," I grumble, letting him go and heading to Phil's office. I knock on the open door. "You wanted to see me?"

"Come in. Shut the door."

It takes everything I have not to sigh and roll my eyes. I'm not fucking twelve. Hell, even when I *was* twelve, I wasn't fucking twelve. This is why I'm a lone wolf. This is why I don't get close to anyone. I hate anyone telling me shit. But I just step inside his office and close the door, leaning against it with my arms crossed, waiting for the lecture I know is coming.

The only sound in the office is the clicking of the keyboard as Phil finishes whatever he's working on. Once he's done, he pushes the laptop to the side and leans on the desk, finally looking up at me. Here the fuck we go.

"I ain't tellin' ya what you can and can't do with your life, but you won't do it here. Ya wanna get your rocks off then by all means, but don't bring 'em here. The boys don't need that kind of distraction, ya hear me?"

I grit my teeth but nod in agreement. "Loud and clear."

"Now let's talk about the fight and what comes next. You won the Battle Royale which guarantees you a spot in the upcoming Titan Tournament. The fighters that join this tournament are the best of the best, on a mission to prove themselves against the Titans. What you fought against tonight were the bottom of the barrel. It'll only get harder from here on out. You ain't gotta' join the tournament, but it'll be expected and it's the only way to keep ya safe in The Underworld, so you can continue looking for whatever it is you're looking for. So, what do ya wanna do, kid?"

This decision has been weighing on me since I agreed to all this shit. I'm here for a reason. This is the closest I've ever been to understanding why I'm so different. Do I think I'll find all the answers I seek? Probably not. But this is my best chance. I tell myself the flash of purple across my mind has nothing to do with my decision.

"I'll do it."

He nods. "Good, because I already registered you an—"

I scoff. "Of course, you did."

"And this came for you."

Pushing off the door, I walk toward the desk and take the item out of Phil's hand. It's a business card. All it says on one side is *Raymond Harris* and on the other is a date and a time.

"Am I supposed to know what this is?"

"It's a calling card from *him*."

"Hades," I say, the name sounding ridiculous on my lips. I can't believe the God of the Dead is not only real but runs an underground world, and goes by the name of Raymond Harris.

Phil nods. "He obviously wants to meet with you since you won the Battle Royale. It's not something ya have a choice in, kid. You'll go to see him or end up in The Pit of Souls."

"The Pit of Souls?" I deadpan, waiting for Phil to elaborate. When he doesn't, I can't help but ask. "What in hell is The Pit of Souls?"

"Exactly what it sounds like. You get tossed into The Pit, there's no gettin' you out. It's a death trap. A place your soul will remain, locked in torment, forever."

"Jesus Christ," I run my hands down my face. "And what does he want with me?"

A shrug. "Probably what he wants from every potential champion. To own you."

"Well, I'm not fucking interested."

"Regardless, kid," Phil says in defeat, sounding tired, "you'll go and see what he wants. And after you meet with him, we'll attend the pre-tournament announcement party. Here." He opens a drawer and pulls out a cellphone and card, holding them in my direction. "I got you a phone so you can get all the updates and track the fight progress. I've already downloaded the app for you. I also opened a checking account in your name."

I take the items from him. I've never had a cellphone before. I don't know the first thing about using it. I'll ask Joey to teach me. That is, if he's still talking to me. I slide the phone into my back pocket and inspect the card. Sure enough, it's a Bank of America debit card with my name on it.

"What did you open this up with?"

"What, ya think the most lucrative sport in The Underworld doesn't pay? There's a reason people want to be fighters, kid."

"How much?"

"I only took ten percent for training ya and puttin' ya up here. I'll increase that to fifteen for the tournament winnings. I ain't a greedy man but I got bills to pay."

"I understand. How much?" I repeat.

"There's two thousand on that card and twenty-five hundred

on the chip in your arm. You can pay for anything in The Underworld by scanning your chip."

I quickly do the math. "So, the Battle Royale paid five grand." Phil nods. "How much do the tournament fights pay?"

He shrugs. "Depends on how big it is, how many fighters join, but typically the first-round fights pay about ten and increase as you move forward. The highest I've seen the champion receive is one hundred."

"One hundred...*thousand*?" I ask, not sure I'm hearing him correctly.

"Yeah, kid. One hundred thousand dollars. It's nothing compared to what the fights bring in for Raymond. Talk about a greedy bastard. He'll also be holdin' bets on the fights and The House very rarely loses. If they do, the winners typically turn up missing not too long afterward. Money and death are his two favorite things."

Well, fuck. One hundred grand. I don't even know how to wrap my head around that much money. I've never had more than a couple hundred dollars on me at a time. Even forty-five hundred is unimaginable. I can't believe that this is all real. And it didn't even cost me much to earn it. Hell, I've fought harder on the streets for less.

"Take that card and buy yourself something to wear for the party. Something other than jeans and a T-shirt. We'll train first thing tomorrow mornin' unless you need a day off after the fight tonight?" He cocks an expectant eyebrow at me.

"I don't need a break. I'll be ready to train."

"Good." He returns his attention to the computer, pulling it back in front of him, and I guess I'm dismissed.

Before I walk out of the office, I turn back around. "Hey, did you know Joey goes to The Underworld?"

He grunts. "I told that boy if he keeps lookin' for trouble, he's gonna end up findin' some he can't get out of."

"He just told me that he crosses the portal without an invitation."

That gets Phil's attention. "Impossible."

I shrug. "That's what he said. I don't know why he'd lie?"

"Unless he's protectin' the one who keeps inviting him across because he doesn't want you goin' after 'em."

Considering what he saw me do to Tiberius, I guess I don't blame him. I nod.

"Get some rest."

Rest. A four-letter word that should be easy for me to comprehend, and yet, the last time I actually felt rested was too long ago to even remember. Rest. I think the only time I'll ever rest is when I have no choice. When my eyes close for the last time. Until then, there will be no rest for the wicked.

Chapter Thirteen

Kill Beautiful Things by DED

He's got his face practically buried in a naked ass that's bent over his desk. There's a loud snort before he lifts his head, wiping at the remnants of white powder. His eyes lock with mine and darken with the familiar anger I'm used to having aimed my way. A loud smack has the girl jumping with a surprised yip as he lands a heavy hand on her ass cheek.

"Give me a minute. I've got a meeting."

Shit. I sigh internally. He only dismisses his whores when he wants to discuss something serious.

"Yes, sir," she complies, though she pouts and runs her fingertips down his tie as she turns and walks my way.

A tie that no doubt cost a few hundred dollars. Because his appearance is everything, even if all he's doing is snorting coke off a skanky ass. Gods forbid he looks anything less than the king he is.

The girl sways on her six-inch platform heels but somehow manages to stay on her feet. He always likes humans because they can't process drugs as quickly as we can. No doubt she's high as a fucking kite right now with no care in the world. One of those cares being the fact that she's entirely naked. There's not one shred of modesty to be found in her as she walks by me with her head held high. Literally on cloud nine, I'm sure.

He comes to stand in front of his desk, leaning against it, crossing his arms and ankles. There's not one wrinkle or crease in his tailored black slacks and his black shoes are buffed to an impossible shine. He's tall and lean compared to the enormous bodies I'm usually surrounded by, yet no one makes me feel smaller than he does. He looks relaxed but I learned from a young age that there's nothing safe about him at any time, no matter how disarming he's pretending to be.

When I was younger, I was so taken by him. He was the most beautiful thing I'd ever seen. The thick sweep of dark hair styled to perfection. A strong jaw, always slightly covered in a ten o'clock shadow, only adding to that rough, yet sexy look. The intense black eyes that match the rest of him, all beautifully dark and brooding. I wanted nothing more than to please him. To do whatever he asked of me. To have all that devastatingly handsome darkness directed my way. Then again, he always claimed to be my savior and I was too young to know any better.

But one can only remain young and naïve for so long. Sometimes I wish I still was. Sometimes I wish I didn't understand or have to be witness to the cruelty of this world. The cruelty of him.

"You sent for me?" I'm careful to keep my chin tipped down, voice soft and low, with my arms loose at my sides. I can't give him any type of reaction. I can't show emotion. I can't appear to be scared, defiant or weak. I have to be the perfect blank canvas which is harder to accomplish than you'd think. Even with my twenty-one years of practice.

"What the fuck went wrong with Nessus? I sent you to convince him to be on my fight card, and he ends up with a broken shoulder and fractured knee?"

"He wanted more than I was willing to give him and I—"

He's standing in front of me in the blink of an eye, his hand gripping my jaw painfully. Spittle hits my face as he yells, "I say what you're willing to give, not you! Don't forget that I fucking own you, Meghana! You know what's at stake."

Of course, I fucking know what's at stake. I think about it every gods-damned day I'm in this hellhole. As if I could forget when he's happy to remind me every time I fail. As much as I try to be numb to his threats, to his anger, my body constantly betrays me. My heart hammers in my chest and I know he hears it. I pretend I'm strong anyway.

"Look, it wasn't my fault. Some guy saw Nessus getting a little handsy and thought I needed help. I told him to mind his own business, but you know how these young, new fighters are. Cocky and arrogant and out to prove they're better than everyone else."

His grip never loosens as he asks, "What new fighter?"

"The one who won the Battle Royale. He thinks he's some gods-given *wonder boy* or something and—"

"What did he want?" His black, soulless eyes narrow on me.

"What?" I ask, confused. The pain of his grip starts to throb and steal my focus.

"The new fighter, genius. What did he want? Did he ask you about me? Was he trying to get information? Tell me!" He jerks my face, bringing me closer to him, his body taught with anger. I can feel the heat radiating off his body and his fingertips start to heat up against my skin. He's seconds away from unleashing his hellfire that will burn my skin as easily as if it was soaked in gasoline.

His questions are throwing me off. Why would this fighter be asking questions about him? What information? It takes me a few seconds to stutter out, "Nuh…nothing. He didn't ask anything."

"You know what will happen if I find out you're lying to me." His shrewd gaze holds me just as tightly as his fingers digging into my skin. It's so painful, tears start to well in my eyes despite how much I'm trying to fend them off. It's not uncommon for him to leave bruises on my skin, but he's never left them on my face before. My face is too important to him for that. So, even though he's one to never give anything away, this blatant lack of control speaks volumes. I just don't know which part of this scenario is causing him to react this way.

"I swear," I barely manage to say through the pain of his hold on my face.

He finally snarls and pushes me away, releasing my face as I stagger under his strength. It takes everything in me not to caress my jaw. Instead, I stand up straight, gaining composure once more.

Raymond walks behind his desk and takes a seat, running a hand down his tie, regarding me with a cool calm that is the exact opposite of his demeanor just seconds ago. I'd get whiplash if I wasn't used to his extreme mood swings.

"You're going to get close to this new fighter. I want to know everything there is to know about him. His strengths, his weaknesses, all of those closest to him."

My brows furrow and stomach dips with what he's suggesting. He's never hesitated to use me as bait, to lure in whoever he wants, but he's never ordered me to get close to anyone before. This is different.

Just remembering how *his* hand felt wrapped around my wrist brings the encounter flooding back. His grip was firm but never painful. The gentle caress along my jaw. How those deep cerulean eyes devoured me. And the way he smelled like fresh air on a summer breeze. I wanted to close my eyes and breathe him in deeply. I wanted his scent to smother me right along with his large body. The memory is overwhelming, causing my heart to race for entirely different reasons than it was mere minutes ago. This task is

dangerous in ways I don't even want to acknowledge, but all I can do is nod obediently.

"You disappointed me with Nessus, pet." He laces his fingers together, placing them in his lap as he sits back in a relaxed position. "Do it again and I won't hesitate to add her soul to my collection in The Pit."

Dread grips my chest, making it hard to breathe. It takes a few attempts to speak through the rising panic gripping my throat like a fist. "I understand."

"Then get fucking to it."

Chapter Fourteen

Closer by VRSTY

I'm ushered into the most lavish space I've ever seen. Hell, his office's waiting area was so disgustingly foul, this makes me want to use words like *opulent*. I don't know what most of this shit is; the art, sculptures, and what I'm sure are one-of-a-kind collection pieces, but I know enough to know none of it is cheap. It's all the same to me.

Trash.

The blatant show of wealth is nauseating, and I've never been more uncomfortable in a space in my entire life. Give me the raw, real honesty of the streets any day over this pretentious shit.

The man casually sitting behind the desk reeks of entitlement. I try to hide my revulsion, but I feel the hint of a sneer pull at my lips. I've never been one to fake shit, but I've also never stood in front of a fucking god before either. I'm trying my best to be polite.

"Ah, Jett Stephens," he announces, in a sing-song voice. "Come in, come in. Please, have a seat." He gestures to one of the large black leather chairs in front of his desk.

I walk stiffly, uncomfortable not only in this situation but also in this suit. It's a damn fine suit as far as I can tell, nothing wrong with it other than it's on me. It required a bit of tailoring but now fits like a second skin. I shouldn't feel so stuffy, but I do. Taking a seat, I watch the man across from me just as shrewdly as he's watching me.

There's something about him that feels…familiar. I haven't a clue what the fuck it could be, but it's a feeling in my gut and my gut is never wrong. I know I need to be wary of him, but I also recognize something in him. It's nothing more than a feeling of likeness but it's a strong sensation, nonetheless.

"Brittney, bring us two drinks," he orders the naked girl standing by a drink cart.

I don't bother to tell him I don't drink. Let him waste whatever high-end alcohol he has on me. It's the least he can do for having demanded this meeting. A few minutes later, a crystal glass is handed to me, its clear liquid cooled by one large, perfectly round ice cube. I internally roll my eyes and scoff. Even this fucker's ice is rich. The strong scent of alcohol wafts up to me, burning my nose at the barest scent. Whatever it is, it's potent.

As the girl walks around to his side, he grabs her around the waist and sits her in his lap. She immediately leans into him, snuggling closer. His hand moves to rest high on her ribcage, his thumb caressing the underside of her bare breast.

"I can also get you one of these if you want."

My eyes leave his hand to meet his black gaze and he winks with a smirk as if he caught me staring when I shouldn't be. Hell, maybe I shouldn't but I wasn't staring at her. Weak and submissive women have never been my thing. Not to mention one that's clearly high on something much stronger than whatever is in this glass.

"I can get you one that's eager to please," he says proudly. "Be a good girl and suck daddy's dick." The girl doesn't even glance my way or hesitate as she drops down under the desk. I hear the slide of the zipper and I know she's doing exactly what he ordered her to do.

"Why am I here, Mr. Harris?" I ask as politely as I can, still holding his gaze. I watch as the interest and amusement turn to cold and calculating in an instant.

His relaxed posture never wavers though. "You're the winner of the Battle Royale. I wanted a chance to meet the man who not only took my five thousand dollars but who won in such an...*understated* fashion."

"I didn't *take* anything," I say defensively. "I earned it."

"Yes, yes." He waves his hand dismissively. "Of course, you did. I saw that you also entered the Titan Tournament. It's my job to not only know every fighter but every person in my city." His tone has the slightest edge of accusation. "Why are you in my city...Jett?"

"Fighting. What does it look like?"

The muscle in his jaw ticks and I can see the tension pulling at his body, even though he's trying to hide it. I have no doubt that this man is used to everyone submitting to him and groveling at his feet, just like the girl currently kneeling before him. I'm sure they all cower in fear simply because he is who he is. Phil told me enough about his cruelty and temper, but I don't give a flying fuck who he is or what he can do to me. I'll never submit or cower ever again, before anyone, a god or not.

"So that's it then? You're just here to fight? Not for women?" He grabs the girl's hair and yanks her up. He sits her down on his lap, spreading her legs wide, and proceeds to finger her right in front of me. She doesn't seem to mind as she closes her eyes, tilts her head against his chest and moans, writhing in his lap. "Or pleasure? Or alcohol, obviously." He gestures to the untouched glass in my hand.

I'm sure he's expecting his shrewd display to rattle me, but it doesn't. "I'm here for money. I heard the best way to get it is by fighting, and I've always been good at fighting. I can assure you I have no other interest in *anything* in your city."

"Ah, yes. Money. Some say it's the fruit of all evil." He shrugs. "Maybe that's true, maybe it's not. But if it's money you're after, I can definitely help you." He gestures around the office while still also fingering the girl in his lap who's started to jack him off. "As you can see, money is what I do. I can make you a very rich, popular, and well-pleasured man. You'll want for nothing."

"I don't need your help getting money. I already told you, I'm good at fighting and I work best alone."

His eyes narrow as he continues to appraise me. "Do you know who I am? Do you know what I'm responsible for?" His eyes bore into mine and I swear he can see the very essence of my soul. If I had even the barest survival instinct I might be scared, or at least cautious.

I don't and I'm not.

"Look," I set the glass down on his desk and stand, buttoning my suit jacket as I do, "I don't give two fucks about anything you do here or what you're responsible for. I'm here to fight and that's what I'm going to do. So, if you'll excuse me, I'm going to head over to this ridiculous pre-tournament party and scope out my competition. Thanks for...the opportunity," I say, with only the slightest sneer as I turn to walk out of the office.

"I'll be watching you closely, Jett. If you do anything I don't like, our next meeting won't be so civil."

I don't bother looking back or responding. He can threaten me all he wants but I'm really not here for anything that has to do with him. I'm here for answers about who *I* am but that's information he doesn't need to know. I'm not going to admit shit to this man or give him any insight into my life, no matter how little I actually have.

Phil is waiting for me in the hallway. The relief on his face is immediate and I'm not sure how to process his concern. I know he genuinely cares about me, but in a world where I've mostly been treated cruelly, I'm not exactly sure how to handle it. And I sure as hell don't understand it. The man barely even knows me.

"How'd it go, kid?"

I shrug. "I'm not dead or being dragged to The Pit of Souls, so

I guess fine."

"And?"

"And what?" I ask as I hit the button to call the elevator and get us off this damn floor.

"What'd he want?"

Stepping into the elevator, I let Phil dictate our next destination. After all, I have no clue where the fuck we're going. "He tried to play nice, bribe me with alcohol and women, but he asked why I was here in The Underworld."

"And?"

"And I told him the truth, mostly. That I'm just here to fight and win money."

"And he didn't try to recruit you?" Phil's looking at me with the intensity of a detective, trying to read all the clues a suspect would try to hide.

I shake my head. "He said he'd be watching me closely." I scoff. "Whatever the fuck that means."

Phil sighs. "Oh, he'll be watchin' you and the other fighters closely. Mark my words kid, he will try to recruit you at some point. He'll offer you a deal you can't refuse, and he never makes deals he can't win. He always ends up on top, no matter what."

"So, what am I supposed to do then?"

His lips purse and he shakes his head in defeat. "I wish I knew, kid."

The elevator doors swish open, and I follow Phil down another hallway. It's already littered with Mageía and from what I can gather a few humans here and there, all dressed to impress. Even Phil is wearing a suit, tailored to his half-goat body and everything. It's oddly perfect for him. Hell, he looks more comfortable in his suit than I do.

We slow to a stop as we reach the entrance to the ballroom. There's a line forming and what looks like security at the door, scanning chips before allowing entry.

"Let me guess…," I lean down and whisper, "only the best of the best are invited to his parties."

Phil nods. "Only the richest or most beautiful. It's all about looks and superficiality with him."

"Well, there must be an exception if he's letting you in, old man."

A grunt is all I get in response, and I smother my smile as we reach the man at the door. Phil goes first, scanning his chip, beeping with approval. As I step up, the man's eyes take me in, and his eyebrow cocks in curiosity. He probably thinks I'm human like everyone else assumes but he refrains from saying anything or reacting further. My chip beeps with approval and I follow Phil into the massive room.

I don't understand how the rooms in this building are so enormous. Don't get me wrong, the building itself is massive, but I still struggle to understand the structure. Then again, I'm literally in an underground magical world. I'm sure magic plays into everything down here. There's really no other answer because everything about this place defies logic. It's a place that plays by its own set of rules and I've got to learn these rules as quickly as possible.

As we weave our way around bodies, I hear whispers as we pass by. Most people seem to know who Phil is and their eyes quickly scan over me as I follow in his wake like a large shadow.

"I can't believe he's trying again."

"How many fighters does he have to lose before he gives up?"

"Is he really bringing a human to fight here?"

"The old man has truly gone insane."

"Did you see him in the Battle Royale?"

"I didn't know he was Phil's fighter."

And on and on the gossip spreads as we pass. Phil seems

oblivious or maybe he doesn't care. I knew Phil had fighters before me but what do they mean *he's lost fighters*? Does that mean they've all died going up against the Titans?

We end up in front of a table laid out with food. Phil grabs a plate and begins heaving portions onto it.

"Hungry?" I tease.

"The food is the only good thing about these parties, kid. Might as well take advantage."

We stand at a small high table, Phil standing on a platform, pointing people out to me as he eats and I simply people-watch. He shows me who the richest, and foulest, people are. The ones that bet the most on the fights and the ones that sink their nasty claws into Raymond's drug and sex world. I'm surprised to see a few females in the mix, but I guess females can be just as nasty and cruel as men. I know this from foster homes, so I don't know why I'm still surprised.

Excited whispers ripple through the crowd moments before everyone falls into complete silence. I follow their stares to the entrance and watch as he walks in with confident strides. The crowd parts for him like he's a knife slicing through them. Following closely in his wake are the Titans. The manic whispers erupt again as they pass, making their way to the stage at the front of the room.

Hades, or Raymond Harris as he goes by, moves to stand behind a podium, turning the microphone on as the Titans line up behind him.

"Ladies and gentlemen...," his voice booms through the speakers, "thank you all for coming to the first of many tournament parties! I am happy to announce that this year's Titan Tournament is the biggest one yet. We have a total of thirty-two fighters who will compete in several rounds of fighting. Each winner will move forward in a bracket-style format until we get down to the two fighters that will compete for not only the title of Champion but the chance to challenge my Titans!"

The Titans all smirk and chuckle at this announcement, as if it's comical that anyone would attempt to challenge them. According to the murmuring crowd, it seems they agree. There's a small voice somewhere deep inside me warning me to get out before it's too late, but the fighter spirit in me is screaming at a chance to wipe the smirks right off their arrogant faces. I've never tolerated bullies, and there's no doubt in my mind that I'm looking at four of the biggest bullies I've ever seen. Someone needs to take them down a notch. Why not me?

"I'm also happy to announce that since this is the biggest tournament we've ever had, it's only fair that the prize should also be the biggest, should it not?" The crowd heartily agrees. "Each beginning round will start at ten thousand dollars to the winner and will increase by twenty thousand each round thereafter. The championship fight will be a grand prize of two hundred and fifty thousand dollars. Which means, if you've done the math, the Titan Tournament champion will have earned a total of five hundred thousand dollars."

The crowd erupts in shouts and excitement, and my own excitement joins in. I've never been one to care about money, mainly because I've never had it, but I can't deny the thought of winning half a million dollars doesn't excite me. I want to win. I'm going to fucking win. What the fuck I'll do with half a million dollars? No damn clue, but I'll cross that bridge when I get there.

"Well, shit," Phil says next to me, pulling my attention back to him.

"Half a million dollars is a lot of money."

"Yes, it is."

"We're gonna win," I say confidently.

"I wouldn't have entered you in if I didn't think you could win, kid. But it won't be easy. Pay attention." He nods back to where Hades is still addressing the crowd. "He's about to announce the fighters."

"Our fighters are here tonight, scattered around the room with you. When I call your name, raise your hand so the people will know who you are, and then we can start the festivities. First up, we have the winner of our Battle Royale, Jett Stephens."

I raise my hand and clench my teeth against the sudden onslaught of a hundred pair of eyes staring at me. I'm suddenly missing Peggy and the grounding and calmness she provides me when I touch her. Maybe leaving her at the gym for this party was a bad idea. I've grown more and more connected to her every day, and I feel her absence deeply now.

It was different in the ring. I knew the audience was there, watching me, but they felt a million miles away. Nothing mattered except my opponent. This…this is too intimate, too close, all these people literally staring at me like I'm the newest exotic animal at the zoo. I'm thankful when Raymond continues announcing the other fighters and the attention is taken off me.

"Laszlo "The Lion," Shea "The Slaying Hydra," Manawyden "The Boar," Nessus "The Crushing Centaur," Mordecai "The Menacing Minotaur.…"

I can't help but notice mine is the only human name. It's clear I'll be going up against some fierce competition.

His voice fades when I see her. She enters the room stealthily, slithering in while everyone's attention is on Raymond and the fighters he's announcing. But I see her. I felt her presence the second she entered the room. My eyes follow her as she inconspicuously slips through the crowd and heads to the bar.

"I'll be back," I whisper to Phil. I'm gone before he can object or try to stop me.

I slip through the crowd just as easily as she did while everyone's attention is still glued to the front. I vaguely hear the drone of voices as I approach her. There are a few others at the bar but it's mostly empty. She stands off to the side, waiting for the bartender to make her drink. Her back faces me and I take the time to thoroughly check her out. She's wearing another skintight dress, this one a vibrant fuchsia with simple purple flowers stitched into it. It almost brushes the floor as it cascades over her body. It wraps tightly across her chest, leaving her shoulders and arms bare. Her long, luxurious hair is pulled into another high ponytail, taunting me. As I approach her, I see the faint sparkle on her creamy skin, as

if she's dusted herself with a layer of crushed diamonds.

I hover behind her, placing my hands on the bar to each side of her, caging her in. She inhales a sharp, surprised breath, her body stiffening immediately at the intrusion. I lean down to whisper in her ear, but it takes a second to find my words as her intoxicating scent takes hold of me. It's familiar and yet still so new and exhilarating. She smells smooth and sweet like vanilla mixed with something tangy like…cherries. I have to restrain myself from pressing my body against her. My mouth waters, and my voice comes out huskier than I intend it to.

"Hello, Little Firecracker."

Her body relaxes ever so slightly. "Well, if it isn't the one and only, Wonderboy himself." Her voice is catty and filled with sarcasm. I fucking love the it.

She turns in my hold, leaning back against the bar, and looks up at me. The second her eyes land on mine it's as if she's sucker punched me in the gut. Her beauty is even more stunning in these bright lights than in the dim hallway I saw her in last. I thought her eyes were merely purple before, but I'm suddenly lost in their kaleidoscope of colors, an intricate mix of lilac, plum, and amethyst with a hint of indigo. Hell, probably more colors I don't know the names of. Different shades are highlighted as her eyes dart back and forth between mine, catching the light at different angles.

Neither one of us says anything as we stare into each other's eyes from inches away. The tension between us is so thick I can feel it like humidity in the air. I finally manage to tear my gaze away from her hypnotic eyes only to travel a few inches south to her beautiful light pink lips. They shine with a layer of gloss and the illusion that they're wet makes me lick mine, desperate to sate my suddenly parched mouth by drinking her.

"Ahem." A throat clearing breaks our trance. "Your drink Ms. Williams," the bartender says, placing her drink on the bar next to her.

"Thank you." She twists to pick the glass up then faces me again. "Did you come to save me from making a bad drink choice? Because I'm afraid you're too late."

I watch as her lips part, gently resting on the edge of the glass as she takes a sip of something red that smells fruity. I watch her throat swallow it down and notice the rapid rise and fall of her cleavage. She's acting nonchalant but once again her body betrays her. Her tongue darts out to lick her lips and I suppress a growl. I want to lean down and run my tongue along her bottom lip. I want to slide my tongue inside her mouth and taste the drink on her tongue. But her words from before keep me rooted in place.

You'll never touch me.

"Any drink is a bad choice because they lead to more bad choices. You may be in need of saving yet. Better to be safe than sorry."

"Oh?" She takes another drink. "Bad decisions like taking someone home from the bar?"

"Depends on who that someone is."

"Hmm." She chews on her bottom lip, eyebrows furrowing as if she's truly contemplating this. My dick twitches at the sight. "So, if I had too much to drink and made the choice to bring you home with me...," she trails a finger down my tie and looks up at me seductively through her lashes, "would you be saving me then?"

"Yes. Because I'd never let you take anyone home if you're too drunk to realize what you're doing. Not even me."

"Well, you're shit out of luck then, Wonderboy, because piss drunk is the only way I'd ever bring you home with me."

I smirk and lean down to whisper in her ear, my lips gently grazing against her skin. "You're such a bad liar."

I'm about to pull away when something large and heavy slams into me. I brace myself against the bar but not before being pushed into her slightly.

"My bad, man. Are you alright?" A deep, grumbly voice says from behind me.

I turn around and come face-to-face with one of them. A Titan. The one that has boulders for arms. His suit is sleeveless, leaving those massive rock-like arms on full display. I would say it looks ridiculous, but I can't imagine what a suit with sleeves would look like trying to cover those massive arms. I quickly glance around us, but the bar is still empty. There's no reason why he would have bumped into me unless it was on purpose.

"Why don't you watch where you're fucking going?" I growl.

"Why don't you walk away if you know what's good for you?" he counters and reaches around me to grab her by her arm and pull her out from behind me.

"Damn it, Tison!" She yanks her arm out of his hold. "What the fuck is your problem?"

"This...," his eyes scan me up and down and he sneers, "this nobody is my problem, Meg. He doesn't deserve to touch you."

I step into his space; we're eye to eye. "I wasn't touching her. But if you grab her like that again, I swear to God, she will be the last thing you ever fucking touch."

"Do you have any idea who I am, punk?"

He shoves me in the chest, but I was ready for it, and he barely budges me. Typical fucking bully move, resorting to name-calling and pushing. He'll sucker punch me if I give him the chance. I've seen a million guys just like him in foster homes and on the streets.

"Tison, leave him alone! He wasn't doing anything." Her voice sounds pissed. She's still standing next to us, trying to be heard.

"I know exactly who you are, nothing but a fucking bully who needs to be taken down a notch."

He throws his head back and laughs. "You've got some huge balls I'll give you that. You're lucky I don't fight unless it's in the ring and I'm getting paid. Although I may just make an exception to ruin your pretty face."

"I'd like to see you fucking try," I say through clenched teeth, my fists balled at my sides, itching to be set free. Itching to destroy him like I did his Titan brother. He doesn't know it was me and the thought of ending another one of these shitheads makes me smirk.

"What's so funny, pretty boy?"

"I heard there were five of you. If you're so indestructible…," I glance around the room, noticing that we have an audience now, "where's the other Titan? Or did something happen to him?"

He reaches out, balling my suit in his fists as he yanks me closer. "What do you know about what happened to Tiberius?"

"Nothing, but you just confirmed it you dumb piece of shit. You *can* be killed. And I'm coming for you."

"Tison, that's enough!" Meg yells as she struggles to get his hands off me. "You better talk to Ray before you start acting on shit you can't take back."

His attention slides to her, something finally registering behind his crazed eyes. He shoves me and I stumble slightly. He points a threatening finger at me. "I'll see you in the ring. And you…," he turns to face Meg and scoffs, "his little fucking whore. You're not worth it."

I lunge, wanting to make him regret those words ever left his mouth, but her hands are on me. They're so small and so weak yet their touch stops me in my tracks. She sounds exhausted. "Let him go. He's the one who's not worth it."

I watch and make sure he's leaving and not coming back before I give her my attention. She looks sad and defeated and nothing seems more important right now than to cheer her up. I want to see that defiant spark in her eyes, not this lost puppy look.

"Did I imagine it or did the Little Firecracker spark and come to my aid?"

She rolls her eyes and fights a smile. "The only thing that needs aid is your suit. I'm so sorry, I must have spilled my drink on you when he bumped into you."

I look down and, sure enough, there's a bright red stain running down the front of my white shirt. The suit and tie are black, hiding whatever mess is on them as well, but no doubt, it's there.

"Fuck," I grumble. "This is why I don't buy expensive shit. It gets ruined just as easily as cheap shit, so what's the goddamn point?"

"It's not ruined, just needs some love. Come on, I'll take care of it. It's the least I can do."

I gently pull on her wrist as she turns to walk away. "Hang on a minute. Let me get this straight. You're going to take me home so you can clean my clothes for me?"

She crosses her arms over her stomach, that defiant attitude back full force. "That's exactly what I'm going to do and not one damn other thing. So, get any ideas you have out of your head right this instant."

I smirk and lift my hands in surrender. "After you, Firecracker."

She shakes her head as if she's annoyed, but I don't miss the smile on her lips as she turns away or the exaggerated sway of her hips as I follow happily behind her. The tension between us both times we've met in public has been hard to ignore. With no eyes on us, I don't doubt for a second that it will lead to more if we're both not extremely careful. And I'm not about to be on my best behavior.

I'm burning up at the thought of touching her. Tasting her. And whether she wants to admit it or not, her fuse has already been lit. It's only a matter of time until the flame meets the explosive at the other end.

Chapter Fifteen

Give Me A Reason by Versus Me

Fuck me. Oh gods, I'm going to let him fuck me, aren't I? And why wouldn't I? The man is stunning. I've seen him shirtless which should be one of the Wonders of the World. I've seen him in a T-shirt and jeans. Now I've seen him in a fitted black suit. And damn, he's the snack, the entrée, and the dessert. Though the polished look doesn't suit him, not that I know him personally, I just get the feeling that he's more at home in his T-shirt and jeans. But I don't care what he's wearing, I just want to *look* at him.

As soon as he leaned over me at the bar and whispered in my ear, my heart started to race, and it hasn't stopped. It doesn't seem to care that my mind is screaming at it to calm the fuck down. To put up a brick wall. To not let him in. I have a job to do but that doesn't mean I need to let him in.

I won't let him in.

I won't let him in.

I won't let him in.

If I repeat it like a mantra in my head, it will become true. Besides, it's not like I need the constant reminder. He's a fighter through and through. I'll never forget that about him and that's enough to stop me in my tracks. I won't let another fighter break my heart, no matter how good-looking he is.

We get in the elevator and as soon as the doors shut, locking us in, I'm overwhelmed by his presence. He was literally just in my space moments ago, but he feels much more suffocating in the elevator. His sheer size is overwhelming. His scent is overwhelming. But even though I feel like I might suffocate, I want nothing more than to pull his scent into my lungs and hold it there. It's the opposite of this stuffy elevator and this underground world. He's everything light and airy and free.

And dangerous.

So very dangerous.

He chuckles and the sound tingles along my skin, causing goosebumps to dance down my arms and spine. "Are we actually going somewhere, or did you just want to get me alone in here?"

His words filter through my daze slowly. I blink, realizing I've been gawking at him like a lunatic. He's leaning against the elevator wall, ankles crossed, hands in his pockets, looking completely at ease. His eyes dance with amusement as he watches me, and I feel the heat rush into my face. There's no way to hide that I'm officially embarrassed and feel like a fool. I clear my throat and reach out to the enormous number panel, hit ninety, then lean against the opposite wall, crossing my arms and trying to act as relaxed as he is when I'm anything but.

"A hundred floors." He shakes his head. "This building defies all logic and sense. I don't understand how there's this much space inside this building."

I scoff. "You act like you're not familiar with magic."

"I'm not."

That admission finally manages to break through my muddled brain, and I look at him, really look at him. Gods, he looks so human. But he can't be. Right? The fire from the drakon in the ring would have destroyed a human but he barely seemed to feel it. And the strength it would take to rip a wing from its back....no human has that kind of strength.

"I don't understand. How can you not? You look human but you're not. What kind of Mageía are you?"

"I was raised in the human world. This is all...," he hesitates, "new to me." Before I can question him further, he turns the questioning on me. "You also look human, for the most part. What kind of Mageía are you?" His blue eyes bore into mine and I feel so vulnerable under his gaze. It's such a simple, normal question, but I feel like it's deeper than that. That he sees me deeper than just what kind of Mageía I am.

"I'm a nymph. I don't know who my father is, but he's human, and my mother is a Muse. The Muse of music, lyrics, and poetry," I explain with a small smile. "It's been said that my mother is known for her beauty and voice, which can hypnotize both men and women."

"She passed that ability along to you then." His voice is low and deep as if he's spilling a secret he shouldn't.

When I meet his gaze again, there's no denying the hunger I see in them. Even though he hasn't moved a muscle, and he still looks relaxed and at ease, it feels like I'm trapped inside a cage with a wild beast. A beast that looks at me like he wants nothing more than to ravish me thoroughly with his hands and teeth. Gods, the way he looks at me sets my heart galloping and stomach flipping. It's unlike any other look I've ever been given by a man and, honestly, I don't know what to do with it. I know how to handle a man that looks at me like I'm a prize to be had, a thing to conquer and brag about, but I don't know how to handle *this*. I don't know how to handle *him*.

Luckily, the doors slide open, and I let out a shaky breath. "This is us." I rush out of the elevator into my receiving room. I don't wait for him to follow as I hurry across the large lobby to the main entryway doors. I lean down slightly, looking into the retinal scanner to unlock my suite doors. It beeps with approval and the sound of the locks releasing is loud in the charged silence. I open one of the large doors and step inside, gesturing for him to follow.

"Well, this is me. Come on in."

He strolls through the lobby and into my home, eyes raking over every inch of space he can see. I'm suddenly nervous about having him here. You can learn a lot about someone by going into their personal space. I glance around the living room, trying to see it through his eyes, seeing it for the first time.

The space is huge and wide-open, with a formal lounge and bar to the left, and a cozier seating area to the right, complete with a velvet cream-colored sectional sofa situated next to a large gas fireplace. The sofa is adorned with a few too many colorful pillows and two different throws. It's my favorite place to be so it's a bit messy. A seventy-five-inch screen TV hangs on the wall above the fireplace. The far wall is made up of nothing but floor-to-ceiling windows overlooking The Underworld.

The dining room and kitchen are visible from where we stand, the stainless-steel appliances gleaming against the white cabinets and black countertops.

The rooms are a mix of elegant and lived-in with pops of color everywhere, from the art and paintings on the walls to the pillows, candles, and décor. I think it's homey but what does he think of it? What does he see? What does it say about me? Why do I care?

Before he can retort or comment, I clear my throat and shut the door behind me. "You can go ahead and take your jacket and shirt off here, and I can get started cleaning them." I hate that my voice shakes slightly, showcasing my damn nerves like they're one of the décor pieces to be scrutinized.

"Alright." Unlike mine, his voice is calm, giving nothing away.

He walks toward the bar and then turns to face me where I stand like a damn statue by the front doors. He shrugs out of the jacket, discarding it on the back of a barstool. Next, he unknots the tie and slowly slips it off his neck. The swish as it slides through the stiff collar of the shirt makes my stomach flutter. I watch, transfixed as he starts to unbutton it. He starts at the top, slowly revealing that golden skin inch by inch. I'm certain he can hear my heart pounding viciously against my ribcage.

Then the shirt is untucked, the last buttons undone, and he pulls it open, sliding it off his arms until it's nothing more than an insignificant piece of material hanging from his hand. Once again, I'm aware that I'm gawking but I can't help it. Seeing him with his shirt off in the ring was one thing, seeing that incredible body this close...*in my home*...is something entirely different.

The light works hand in hand with the shadows to highlight every dip and curve, every muscle, every beautiful inch of his glorious skin. And the way his muscle ripples underneath his skin as he walks toward me. *Oh gods, he's walking toward me.* His body is so much bigger than I let myself realize. He towers over me as he reaches me, his body laughably dwarfing mine. I want to run my fingers up his arms, tracing the lines of ink that make the snakes come to life. I want to trace every dip, valley, and mountain of muscle. I want to feel what it's like to be at the mercy of his power.

"Meg."

My name on his lips utterly shocks me. I finally register that the door is pressed against my back and his hands placed against it on both sides of me, once again caging me in with his massive body. I hadn't even realized I had backed away from him.

I meet his eyes again, another flood of embarrassment coursing through me. "Meghana," I elaborate. "My name is Meghana. I can't believe you're standing half naked in my home and we haven't even been properly introduced."

He shrugs his shoulder. "I don't know, Wonderboy pretty much sums me up."

I scowl, trying desperately to quell the heat racing through my veins. "The nickname *isn't* a compliment."

Another shrug. "It's whatever I make it."

I duck under his arm and take a few steps away from him, the space allowing me to clear my thoughts. I cross my arms over my stomach and channel my inner *deal with Hades Meg*. "I'm Meghana Williams," I hold my hand out to him, "and you are?"

He bites his lip, attempting to smother a laugh. I hate the fact that he's been laughing at me since we stepped in the elevator, but I don't hate how good he looks when his beautiful lips curve in a smirk. Gods forbid the man actually smile at me. I may combust on the spot.

His hand engulfs mine. "Jett Stephens, but you can call me T." He jerks my hand and I stumble forward, colliding with his body as he holds me against his chest. His voice is a whisper against my skin. "Remember it, because when I'm making you pant and beg, you'll pray to me like I'm your god," he says in a low seductive voice.

Heat pools low in my stomach and my thighs clench together at the thought of him making me cum. I can't even fathom what that would be like. No man has ever brought me to a release. I don't care how attractive he is, he's no different than any other man.

And he's definitely *not* a god.

I pull out of his hold, and he releases me. "I think you've had your head hit one too many times because you're delusional. Shirt." I extend my arm, palm up, demanding. He hands it over. "Wait here," I order, and race off around the corner, down the hall, and into my bedroom before he can pull any more moves to get close to me.

I storm into my bathroom and lean against the counter for support. My damn knees feel like they belong to a newborn foal. I stare at myself in the mirror and barely recognize the flushed face staring back at me. My pupils have dilated slightly, the colors of my irises brighter than I've ever seen them, and my skin is sparkling like I'm a damn strobe light.

"Get it together, Meg." I splash cold water on my face, close my eyes, and take a few seconds to breathe. The only problem is all I can smell is him. I feel his large hand at the base of my spine, holding me against him. I shake my head and walk to my storage closet, rummaging through it until I find the baking soda. It's not the first stain I've had to clean out of clothes.

I stand at the sink and start to scrub at the stain, taking all my pent-up frustration and sexual tension out on his damn shirt. I'm so damn focused on the shirt that I don't even hear him approach.

"What did that poor shirt ever do to you?"

I jump, my hand slamming over my heart at the sound of his voice behind me. I scowl at him in the mirror. "It had the nerve to be on *you*, who bumped into *me*, spilling *my* wine." I break eye contact, leaving his shirt in the sink and walking over to the one next to it. I focus way too hard on washing and drying my hands, all the while careful not to look at him through the mirror again. The only problem is, I can't hide from him. I take a deep breath and turn around, leaning against the counter. "The shirt needs about twenty minutes to soak, then you can be on your way."

"Hmm." He grabs his chin and rubs his finger over his lips, eyebrows knitting together in deep concentration. "Since I have some time to kill, maybe you wouldn't mind if I rinsed off." I'm about to adamantly object when he stalks toward me with lethal grace. I snap my mouth shut, tilting my head back to maintain eye contact with him as he stops in front of me. He reaches out and grabs my wrist, then plants my hand firmly on his abs. "Because you got me all...*sticky*." My hand does slightly stick to his skin as he pulls it off.

"It was from the fr-fruit," I stutter, "I was drinking Sangria."

"Well, if you don't mind...." He unbuttons his pants and my

heart leaps into my throat. I start to object, but if he's in the shower, that means he's out of sight and out of reach. Once that dawns on me, I'm all too eager to allow him to use my shower. Hell, I'll let him use a bath bomb if he wants to take the entire twenty minutes and soak in the tub.

"No!" I blurt out aggressively. "I mean, no, I don't mind. Not at all. Help yourself." I squeeze by him and practically run out of the bathroom, securely shutting the door behind me.

I power walk to my bed and sit down on the edge. My heart is beating so fiercely I can feel it in my entire body. I feel like one big, sensitive, turned-on pulse. Gods, was he just going to undress right there in front of me? The absolute nerve of this man. I want to scream at him and push him away while simultaneously letting him undress and have his way with me.

The sound of water echoing off the shower walls makes me hyperaware that he's in there. In my shower. Naked. My mouth waters at the thought of that glorious body dripping wet, the suds flowing over every muscle making his skin slick and smooth, water droplets hanging onto his lips as if they're dying to kiss him too.

I hesitate for only a second before opening my nightstand drawer and pulling out my bright pink, penis-shaped vibrator. I have time while he's in the shower to give my body the release it's been screaming for since he walked up to me at the bar. Then, maybe, I'll be able to face him without being driven by my damn weak body. A release to clear my head and satiate my desire. Yes, that's exactly what I need.

Hiking my dress up and laying back on the bed, I turn on the vibrator and move it between my legs. Holy shit my clit is sensitive, and I gasp at the first vibration. My entire body feels like I've been skinned alive and left to feel every slight sensation on my skin. I close my eyes and all I see is him. Those incredible blue eyes staring into mine. Those full lips pulled into a sexy, arrogant smirk. His smooth skin and muscles rippling like waves beneath it. When he placed my hand on his stomach, all I wanted to do was touch more of him. Feel more of him. That stupid V has been taunting me since the first time I saw it and I want to see it in its entirety. I want to see where those lines lead.

"What's going on in here?"

I yell and practically fall off my bed in an attempt to right myself and my dress. My bright pink vibrator goes flying, rolling on the floor in his direction, stopping almost at his feet. I swear the sound of the vibrator against the carpet is way louder than it should be.

He takes a step and picks it up before I even have the chance to move. I think I'm frozen in shock. In utter embarrassment. My face is so hot I'm sure I'm as red as a damn stop sign. I can't believe he just walked in on me using a fucking vibrator. What the hell was I even thinking?

"I was going to ask you where the towels are, but I think this is a much more exciting conversation," he says as he holds my vibrator up and inspects it. "This is quite the impressive toy. Although I don't vibrate, I am bigger and know how to move better than this thing."

"That's unlikely," I say, finally finding my voice.

"That's beside the point," he says as he walks over to where I'm leaning against my bed, my dress askew, barely covering me. "The point is what were you doing with this in the first place with me literally in the room next door? Did you want me to catch you?"

I snatch the vibrator out of his hand and hit the power button. I pull my shoulders back and lift my chin. I don't have any reason to be embarrassed. Ok fine, he caught me using a vibrator. And? "For your information, since you seem unfamiliar with women, we have needs just as much as a man does. I needed a release. So what?"

He moves closer, pants still unbuttoned, hanging low on his hips, the band of his underwear showing, and gods-damn my treacherous body loves what it sees. I tilt my head back to hold his heated gaze. The way he looks at me...I clench my thighs together and, of course, he doesn't miss it. He drops his hand onto my leg, just above my knee, and slowly starts to slide up my thigh.

"You need a release because your body wants mine." Not a question. A statement. He places his knee between my legs and nudges them apart. I don't know why I don't fight it. I can't think past the depth of his eyes watching me and how incredible his fingers feel touching me. His fingertips roam higher, tickling the sensitive skin of my inner thigh as he reaches my core. "I'm the reason you're on edge." I gasp at the barest brush of his fingers caressing my clit over my panties. "Therefore, I'm the one who should give you your release."

"You can't."

He tilts his head, still holding my gaze. "Why not? You clearly need it. Let me give it to you."

"No one ever has."

His hand stills but he doesn't remove it from between my legs. "Are you saying you're a virgin?"

"What? No. Of course, I'm not a virgin. But no man has ever given me an orgasm. I don't care how much I may be attracted to you; you'll be no different."

The smirk is back. "So, you *are* attracted to me." I roll my eyes and his other hand reaches out and clamps down on my jaw. He leans down, getting right in my face, and his fingertips start to caress my clit again. I'm torn between focusing on the feel of him between my legs and the attention he's demanding with his eyes. "Those eyes," he whispers, more like he's speaking to himself than to me.

"What about them?" I barely manage to speak through my heavy breathing.

"You like to roll them. Well, I'll give you a reason to roll them. Stand up," he orders, pulling me to stand by his grip on my face. I have little choice but to follow or cause myself pain. He maintains his hold on my face while the other hand bunches in my dress and pulls it over my hips. "Take them off."

Again, I don't know why I comply. Maybe it's the way he demands, leaving no room for argument. Maybe it's the intense hold he has not only on my face but on *me*. He holds me captive like I'm nothing more than a helpless little doe caught in his massive claws. The only difference is I'm a willing captive.

"This is pointless," I protest, but my fingers hook under my panties, sliding them down my hips. His hold keeps me from bending down so I wiggle my legs until the panties fall the rest of the way down my legs.

He releases his hold on my face, and the next thing I know, I'm slightly airborne as he lifts me up by the backs of my thighs and tosses me onto the bed. No sooner is my back on the mattress before he pulls me forward, my ass hanging almost all the way off the edge of the bed. He kneels down and wastes no time looking at me or going slow and teasing. Just like he fought with no hesitation in the ring, there's no hesitation now as his mouth descends on my pussy. I can't help the loud gasp for air as the first feel of his tongue stuns me.

His strokes are confident. He goes straight for my sensitive clit as if it's another fight to be won and he won't be satisfied with anything less than a TKO. A reluctant moan escapes my lips as his lips tighten on my clit and he sucks on it while his tongue moves against it side to side. My fists grip the comforter tightly and I throw my head back, eyes closed, reveling in the sensation. Holy shit, it's never felt this good.

I push up onto my elbows to watch in astonishment as he utterly devours me. He snakes his hands under my thighs and grips them tightly, pulling me harder against him. His eyes look up at me and he lifts his face, making a show of his tongue flicking back and forth against my clit. He never stops. He never comes up for air. He holds me captive with his determined gaze, his blue eyes looking like wild flames, threatening to burn me alive.

Pleasure builds inside of me, and I throw myself back on the bed, closing my eyes and focusing on every single lick and flick and suck. The room fills with moans of pleasure, and it takes me a few seconds to realize it's my voice filling the space. I don't have time to think about it or be embarrassed at how vocal I'm being, because he slides a finger inside of me and I cry out.

"Yes! Just like that. Don't stop." My voice is foreign to my ears. It's raspy and sensuous, breathy, and lost to the pleasure that's coiling deep in the pit of my stomach.

His finger continues to slide in and out, in and out, as his tongue continues to massage my clit in a steady rhythm. His mouth is locked onto me and gods, he's relentless. I've never felt this kind of pressure before. It's building up inside of me and I feel like I'm going to explode. All I can do is hold on and ride it out. My hands somehow end up in his hair and my hips are rocking, moving to the rhythm of his tongue, chasing that pleasure that I've only ever known by my own hand.

"Oh gods, whatever you're doing, don't stop. Please don't stop."

He growls with his mouth still pressed against me and that's all I need to throw me over the edge. I pinch my eyes shut tight as my body physically breaks. It feels like a dam inside of me has collapsed and pleasure floods my entire body. I feel the sensation of my release from the tingle in my scalp all the way to the curl of my toes as I scream my pleasure to the ceiling. I've cum a million times but it's always been surface-level. I've never felt an orgasm penetrate so deep. I can feel the intense pulse of my pussy as it spasms around his finger, my clit so sensitive the feeling of his tongue is almost painful. I try to shove away from him but his one hand on my thigh holds me with an insane amount of strength as the pleasure bows my spine and I writhe and fight against him.

I think I hear him whisper, "Beautiful," but I could have imagined it as I struggle to stay conscious.

Ever so damn slowly the pleasure fades, as if leaving my body almost reluctantly. I jerk and spasm until finally, I'm lying on the bed spent and panting. My consciousness also resurfaces, slowly at first, and then all at once as I realize what's just happened. My eyes snap open and I look down my body at him.

Jett has rocked back on his heels, a very arrogant smirk on his lips. "You were saying?" he teases, holding my gaze as he wipes the glistening remnants of my orgasm off his lips and chin. I feel the flush of my cheeks even though my body is already overheated.

"I didn't think…I've never…." I struggle to find my words and understanding of what's just happened. "That's never happened before."

He stands up and my eyes travel down his massive body. He looks so large standing over me where I'm still sprawled out on the bed. My eyes drop lower, and I see the impressive outline of his rock-hard dick where it's straining against his pants. He reaches a hand inside, my eyes glued to his crotch, waiting anxiously to see what he's working with, and if his body is equally proportioned.

Only, all he does is adjust himself, and then he buttons his pants back up. I'm so thrown off, I open my mouth to ask him what the hell he's doing, but no words come out. He leaves me lying, confused as all hell, on the bed as he walks back into the bathroom. I manage to sit up, pulling my dress down to cover me, when I hear the shower turn off. He walks out a few seconds later with the wet, white shirt clinging to his chest like a second skin. He runs his hand through his hair, straightening out the mess I made of it.

"Thank you for cleaning the shirt," is all he says before he starts walking out of my bedroom.

"Hey!" I jump off the bed, chasing after him. "What the fuck? You're just gonna leave?"

He stops and turns around to face me. "I don't see the problem. Did I not satisfy you?" He makes a show of sticking his finger in his mouth and sucking on it, pulling it out slowly. "Mm, because it tastes like I satisfied you."

I can't help but blush again. Gods, this man is so infuriatingly arrogant. "Yes, but...," I hesitate, "what about you?" I point to his dick, still hard and pressed against the pants.

"I'm not going to take anything from you. Not yet."

I scrunch my eyebrows, confused. "You're not taking anything if I'm willing. You clearly need a release too."

He closes the distance between us, his hand falling on my face again, gently this time. "It's not about keeping score. Besides, I'm not going anywhere, Little Firecracker. There's plenty of time for me to fuck you, and make no mistake about it, I will fuck you." His thumb trails along my bottom lip before he pulls away and heads back out the way he came.

I stand in silence, staring at the door long after he's disappeared behind it. What in the actual fuck just happened? Did he really just give me the best orgasm of my life? Yes. Did he just leave instead of claiming his own release? Yes. But why? What the fuck did he mean by not taking anything from me? Did he not believe me when I said I'm not a virgin? That must be it. It's the only thing that makes sense.

I finally shake myself free of my trance, walking back to my bedroom. The sight of him kneeling between my legs is fresh in my mind. I can still feel the slick wetness of his tongue between my legs and the tight grip of his fingers on my thighs. I remove my dress and walk into the bathroom, looking at my reflection. The evidence of his hold is red and already bruising on my thighs, and the sight of it causes my body to clench in pleasure all over again.

My body heats up and I'm grateful the water was running the entire time because I need a cold shower like I need a miracle.

"Gods, save me. This man is going to destroy me."

Chapter sixteen

Getting her out of my head has been harder than I'd like to admit. I haven't been stuck on a girl like this since I was twelve and thought I was in love with Stacey. She was another foster kid in the last home I was sent to. She was a few years older than me and tried as much as she could to help take care of me. With my unnatural strength, I didn't necessarily need protection, but I did need food and water. She did what she could to make sure I didn't starve, but honestly, she wasn't much better off. None of us were.

At the time, I was still too young and naïve to fully understand everything that was happening in the world around me. Ever since the attack, I haven't been a good sleeper. When all the other kids were fast asleep, I was awake. That's when I heard him come in and take her. Every night, he would come in after everyone was asleep and take Stacey out of bed. She would come back thirty or forty minutes later and slip into bed.

The sounds of her quiet sobs tormented me for days. Until I couldn't take it anymore and started climbing into her bed, trying to comfort her. Trying to show her the same kindness she was so quick to show me. I would lay behind her and put my hand on her shoulder, just letting her know she wasn't alone. I didn't know what else to do. And she always let me. We never addressed it, not verbally, but I think it helped her too. Though nothing would ever make what happened in that home ok.

We were bonded, her and I.

Bonded in our loneliness.

Bonded in our anger.

Bonded in our trauma.

And I held on to the kindness she gave me like a lifeline. She didn't smile much but she always managed to smile for me. And when she did, when they were real and true, I thought she must be an angel sent just for me.

Until she was taken one night and didn't return. I climbed into her empty bed, waiting for her. I waited and waited until the sun rose. I stayed in her bed through breakfast, lunch, and dinner. No one came looking for me. No one cared. And when the sun fell again, and she still hadn't returned, I knew she never would. Just like my parents, she had been taken from me too. And just like that night, I had done nothing. All the strength I had in my body and what good had it done? What good was I?

I left that night and never went back. I never went back to any foster home and have been on my own since. Stacey's smile haunted me for a long time. Especially at night, when I would find a dark corner to curl up in. Alone. Truly alone for the first time in my life. All I had were haunting memories of those I had lost. There's no doubt in my mind that I loved Stacey. But I was only twelve. What did I know of love?

And this, now, with Meg? It's not love by any means, but it *is* something. She's all I see when I close my eyes. She slithers into my chaotic thoughts, unbidden, stealing my focus. I feel the same type of bond with her that I did with Stacey. There's a familiarity between our souls. Something that we both recognize in each other, regardless of whether or not we know what it is. We don't need to know what it is to feel it. I feel it. And it terrifies me because everyone I have ever gotten close to has been taken from me.

There's not a lot in this world that I know, or that I'm confident in, but I do know one thing for sure. I'm cursed.

"Where you at, kid?"

Phil's voice pulls me out of my depressing thoughts. I haven't thought of Stacey in years. I need to get my shit together. Now is not the time to reminisce on a life lost. Not when half a million dollars is on the line.

"I'm here."

He grunts and I watch as he finishes wrapping my hand with expert efficiency. "I know ya ain't one to talk about what's in that head of yours, but you need to focus. Now ain't the time to be daydreamin'."

"I'm here," I say with more conviction. "So, you trust this guy?"

Phil drops my hand when he's done with it and looks up at me, contemplating how to answer. "As much as I can trust anyone, I s'pose. I've known him since he was a kid, and his father was a friend. He was raised right, but at the end of the day, he is your competition kid, and you better not forget that."

"I don't understand why we're even doing this. Like you said, he's my competition. If we're training together, that will just give him the opportunity to learn my style and my weaknesses."

"Well, you're just gonna have to hold back some of your tricks and not let him see your full potential. It's still better than training with Dwayne. At least with Mordecai you can use your strength and not worry about killing him with a single punch."

"Whatever you say, old man. You're the coach. I'm just here to fight."

"Well, let's get to it then." He throws his leg over the bench we're sitting on, and I follow him out of the large locker room. We're back at the hotel in The Underworld, using Hades' training gym and amenities to get me ready for the tournament. I'm not keen on the idea of spending any more time here than necessary but their equipment and setup are made for Mageía, therefore made for me.

Mordecai is already on the training mat when we arrive. I vaguely remember seeing him at the pre-tournament party being introduced by Hades. I was a bit distracted at the party, and now that I'm taking a good look at him, I'm grateful to Phil for setting this up. I definitely need experience fighting other Mageía. I've never had to fight anyone other than human until the Battle Royal and that was a clusterfuck. There wasn't much fighting involved. More like brawling.

As I approach the mat, Mordecai assesses me as much as I'm assessing him. The only part of his body that resembles a man is his torso. The rest is that of a bull, from the hooves to the tail, to the snout and the horns. I have to admit, the horns have me slightly concerned. I don't know the extent of my impenetrable skin, but those horns have the promise of slicing me up if I'm not careful.

"Jett...," he walks to the end of the mat, arm outstretched, "I'm Mordecai, it's nice to meet you."

To say that a voice coming out of a bull's face is odd would be an understatement. His voice is a deep, smooth bass with no inflections or accent. I can understand him perfectly. But what's even stranger, and something I didn't expect, are the rich, chocolate-brown eyes looking at me. They're human. Or whatever human is in the Mageía world.

"Nice to meet you. Thank you for being up to this."

"Ahh, it's all good. I could use the training, too, but when I beat you in the tournament don't take it personally, alright." He smiles, at least I think he smiles, and winks. "Come on, let's get warmed up."

I look back at Phil, who shrugs and nods, taking his post up by the mat to guide me. Looking around, I notice other fighters and trainers scattered throughout the gym but no one else is near our mat.

"Where's your trainer?" I ask as Mordecai positions himself in a fighting stance at the center of the mat.

"It's just me. My dad taught me how to fight at a young age. I just need to hone my skill at this point. Phil refused to train me when I asked, and I don't want anyone else, so...."

I look over to where Phil is standing, legs wide, arms crossed, waiting for us to start.

"Phil's good people," Mordecai comments. "I was surprised he took on another fighter after he said he was done with the fights here in The Underworld. Losing his last fighter really got to him."

"You know what happened?"

"Of course."

"Hey, I didn't bring ya here to bond and sing kumbaya. Get to trainin', boys!" Phil instructs from the sidelines.

"You heard him." Mordecai grins wide, and then he's on me.

He's deceptively fast for his large frame, charging with the speed of a raging bull. I manage to block the fist headed in my direction but when I try to throw a punch of my own—"

"Watch for his tail!" Phil shouts too late.

Mordecai's tail lashes out at me and knocks me off my feet. I fall hard onto the mat and barely manage to roll out of the way of an enormous hoof coming down on my stomach. I get back on my feet, mind focused on every aspect of my opponent now. He wastes no time coming for me again. We go toe to hoof, trading punches. I feel his fist land on my jaw like a distant hit. He's powerful but it doesn't faze me.

I return the blow and it lands with a loud smack on his face. He stumbles backward, losing focus and almost dropping to the ground. He goes down to one knee, arm steadying his body as he takes a few seconds to gather his bearings. Since this is the training mat, and not a fight, I give him a chance to recover.

Bad choice because he roars and charges. He pushes off the mat and launches himself toward me head-first. I have half a second to panic before his horn connects with my sternum, knocking the air out of my lungs. I somehow manage to remain on my feet, planting them in the mat and fighting to gain back some ground. My arms wrap around his head still buried in my stomach and I feel the pinch of pain where his horn pierces my skin.

I throw my body to the side and swing his body in the opposite direction, twisting him in the air and throwing him to the mat. I land on top of him, pinning him with my body. I manage to get a few hard punches into his ribs and then Phil stops us.

"Alright boys, alright. Back on your feet."

I stand, offering my hand to Mordecai. He takes it with another grin, his eyes dancing with amusement. "Damn man, you got one hell of a punch." He rubs at his jaw, then wipes his mouth, his hand coming away with a little blood.

"And you tried to fucking gut me." I look down to see blood on my shirt too. I don't remember ever seeing my own blood before. I lift my shirt and find a small nick in my skin, no bigger than a dime, but it's significant. It's the first time my skin has ever broken which means it *can* break. Perhaps only by another Mageía. Fuck, I really wish I knew what the fuck I am. I wish I knew what I am, and am not, capable of.

"I did try to gut you," he laughs as if it's fucking funny. "You're one strong motherfucker. These would have done some serious damage to anyone else," he says as he touches one of his horns. "That skin of yours is interesting."

Shit. There goes my intent on hiding that little nugget of information. I ignore the comment and steer the conversation off me and my body. "We're supposed to be training not trying to fucking kill each other before the tournament even starts," I growl out.

"Calm down, bro. I wouldn't have hurt you. I would have felt my horn slip into you and pulled away. I know I look like an animal, but I assure you, I'm not. And I'm not a dirty fighter either. Though I'm one of the few who can say that. You're gonna have to watch your back when it comes to the others."

"He's right, kid," Phil chimes in. "It ain't his fault, I told him not to hold back, you need Mordecai to push you and test your limits. Now, stop bitchin' and moanin' and get back at it. The first fight is in four days, and you've got a long way to go."

I may have a long way to go when it comes to technical ability, but I'll be damned if I let any of these fighters beat me. Technique is only part of the equation. Determination and the flat-out refusal to quit is another. I don't know the other fighters, but I know they haven't lived the life I have. They haven't fought for every breath, every day, every second, to be on this Earth.

No one is going to outfight me.

Chapter Seventeen

In The Dark by Solence

I stand with my nose practically pressed against the glass overlooking the ring. It's the night of the first round of the tournament and my stomach has been tied up in knots all day. It's not like these are the first fights I've ever seen, far from it, but I'm more anxious than I've ever been. The only reason for that is...*him*. I haven't seen him since the night of the pre-tournament party, five days ago. Five days to sit with the fact that he gave me a mind-blowing orgasm and then disappeared. I don't even have his phone number to try and reach out to him. Not that I want to, but according to Hades, I have to.

"You're looking suspiciously nervous, pet. Someone got you feeling...unsteady?"

Think of the devil.

I close my eyes and release a calm, steadying breath. Fuck. I need to do better. I was so focused on seeing him again that I forgot whose presence I'm standing in.

"Just doing what you asked me to do. Watch him, get to know him and his weaknesses."

"Mm-hmm, I see. And how's that going so far?"

"I haven't had a chance to...." I haven't had a chance to what? Get close to him? His face was literally tongue deep in my vagina. If that's not close, then I don't know what is. I just wasn't thinking about him as a mark as he was successfully seducing me. "I haven't had a chance to learn anything yet. But I will."

"Good," is all he says in response. He doesn't need to threaten me, he's already done that, but I can feel his gaze on the back of my head like a damn laser is burning a hole in it.

I hug myself tighter and keep my eyes locked forward, resisting the urge to shudder under his watchful gaze. Luckily, the announcer's voice booms through the speakers and two images light up the big screens hanging beyond the ring. My heart sinks into my stomach.

"Ladies and Gentlemen, the Raymond Harris Arena thanks you once again for coming out to support our fighters and our infamous Titan Tournament! We've come to our final match of the evening, so without further ado, let's meet our final contenders."

The lights dim and a spotlight drops to the entrance of the tunnel that leads back into the locker rooms. Everyone's eyes fall to the entrance and a hushed silence rushes over the crowd as they eagerly wait for the first glimpse of the next fighter.

"Fighting for The House, a fighter you're all familiar with. He has nineteen fights under his belt, all nineteen wins, with eleven knockouts. He's the crowd favorite. Give it up for our current undefeated lightweight champion, Laszloooo, The Lionnnn!"

Replacing the announcer's voice is Laszlo's fight song, Lion by Hollywood Undead. A little too on the nose if you ask me but the crowd goes wild when they hear it. A few seconds later, Laszlo emerges from the tunnel with a roar that sends a shiver up my spine. Laszlo is merciless. He's no Titan but he's one of the best in the tournament, along with a handful of others that make me nervous.

I watch as he makes his way into the ring, roaring and throwing his clawed fists in the air. His team surrounds him, echoing his energy, egging the crowd on even more. They live for this shit.

"And his opponent, fighting out of Philoctetes' Gym, new to The Underworld but the winner of our fifth annual Battle Royale, Jett Stephenssss!"

Once again, the lights dim, and the spotlight floods the entrance to the tunnel. My heart is pounding so hard in my chest I'm slightly concerned I'm going to pass out before the fight even starts. He walks out cool as a cucumber. No roaring or shouting. No music to hype the crowd up. Just a look of pure determination on his face as he makes his way silently up to the ring.

Unlike Laszlo, everything about him is understated. The sheer confidence it takes to walk out alone and not miss a step when the crowd goes utterly silent speaks volumes. I can't decide if he's just confident or extremely fucking arrogant.

I vaguely hear Raymond and Tison discussing numbers behind me. There are always bets on the fights and even more so during the tournament. The numbers will continue to increase as the rounds progress and Ray will be winning big no doubt. The House always does.

"You bet against your own?" I hear Tison's shocked question and glance over my shoulder.

Raymond catches my gaze and holds it as he says, "I have a feeling about this one."

I don't know why that makes me uncomfortable. I quickly return my attention to the ring. There's no referee in the ring with the fighters. There are no rules to these fights except for no killing. Fighting to the death is reserved for title fights against the Titans but that doesn't stop many of these fighters from trying to kill off their competition anyways. Some even succeed. The only slight sense of relief I feel is knowing that Laszlo has never attempted to kill anyone. That can't be said for others in this tournament but one fight at a time.

"...let the fighting and bloodshed begin!" The announcer's voice gives the final command, initiating the start of the fight. The crowd goes wild, shouting and screaming at the top of their lungs. I don't know how the fighters manage to tune them out.

They launch at each other. Laszlo comes in hot, swiping at Jett with his massive claws. Jett ducks under the swing, comes up, and throws his entire body weight into a punch. He swings and his fist connects with Laszlo's cheek, sending him flying a few feet and crumpling to the ground.

The crowd goes silent. We all stare at his body, the seconds ticking by as he remains on the mat.

Five seconds...

Ten seconds...

Fifteen seconds...

He doesn't get up.

Jett turns and walks to the gate. He glares at the security guard, his mouth moves, and the gate unlocks. He storms out of the ring, down the lane that leads back to the tunnel, and disappears. The lion tattoo on his back feels like a taunt as he walks away. He didn't even wait to be announced as the winner. He didn't stay to conduct the interview.

My chest starts to burn, and I realize I've been holding my breath. I release the air from my lungs at the same time the rest of the crowd comes back to life. It starts off low, whispers and hushed conversations rippling through the crowd, until finally, someone yells out, "Jett!" And the crowd begins chanting his name like a prayer.

He won. Holy shit, he won. Not only did he just win but he knocked out Laszlo in literally five seconds. One punch. The first fucking punch. It wasn't even a fight. He dominated the ring. He demolished his opponent before he ever had a chance at fighting back. The night was filled with amazing, nail-biting fights, but this Is the only thing anyone is going to remember. This is going to be the talk of the tournament. He'll be ambushed at the afterparty. Not to mention all the trophy bunnies that will be clambering to get their greedy little manicured hands on him like that blonde, *Jennifer*, after the Battle Royale.

Why do I fucking care? And why do I even remember that bitch's name? I wanted nothing to do with him until I was ordered to get close to him. I need to remember that he's no different than any other fighter. Though, after what I saw tonight, I'm not so sure.

"I'll see you at the party," I address Raymond as I move to leave the suite that overlooks the ring.

"Don't forget about your task. I expect an update soon."

I nod and leave him and Tison to handle the bets. I've never liked the business side of things. I hate the way he makes his money and do my best to stay out of the middle of it. He's allowed me that much at least, only calling on me to be his sweet little messenger and pretty bait to hook who he wants, when he wants.

I'm one of the first people in the ballroom and I make my way straight to the bar. Alcohol always helps get me through these things and I feel like my nerves need its soothing properties now more than ever. Gods, he has me so riled up! And for what?

"Good evening, Ms. Williams."

"Good evening, Nick."

"Your usual?"

"Yes, please," I say with a smile as I take a seat at the bar, eager to relax and get him off my mind but also eager to see him again. The two desires fight against each other but, just like tonight, there's one apparent winner. Him.

I'm almost done with my first glass of Sangria when a man slides onto the stool next to me. "Mind if I sit here?"

I quickly glance over at him before returning my attention to my drink. "You can sit wherever you like."

"What can I get for you?" Nick asks my new unwanted guest.

"IPA. Whatever you have on tap. And another round for the lady."

I roll my eyes. Gods, he's one of those men. Assuming and pushy. I feel his eyes on me.

"So, what brings you to the afterparty?" he asks.

"Work."

"Oh yeah? You a reporter or something?"

"Or something," I say, taking the last drink of my Sangria as the new full glass is set in front of me.

"I'm Ricky." I see his hand come up, offering to shake my hand.

I sigh and turn to face him, finally getting a proper look. He's got bright yellow hair that matches his yellow-slitted eyes. His face is practically covered in freckles, and I can see them on the backs of his hands as well. I have to physically restrain a grimace when his split, lizard-like tongue darts out of his mouth.

"Look...." I begin to offer my tired excuse about how I'm sure he's a nice guy and all, that but I'm just not interested when I see *him* out of the corner of my eye.

He just walked in and already a girl has practically glued herself to his side. She's wearing a see-through dress with nude underwear, giving the illusion that she's naked, but no actual details are visible. Her dark hair is cut in a sharp bob, framing her soft face. Unlike me, she's got the perfect amount of curves, not overstated, and no thunder thighs. I hate to admit it, but she's beautiful, and they actually look good together.

He's wearing a pair of dark blue jeans and a simple white V-neck T-shirt with white sneakers. The suit looked good on him but this.... gods, that golden skin on display, the ink winding up his arms, and the material of the T-shirt pulled tight across his chest is downright sinful. I don't blame the girl one bit for being handsy, even though I'd like to slice those fingers right off her hand...*calm the fuck down, Meg*...but I'm surprised to see that he keeps his hands to himself as he talks to her.

The jealousy that slaps me in the face is shocking. It's the same jealousy I felt watching him walk away with the blonde barbie. I clear my throat and return my attention to the man sitting next to me.

"I'm Meg," I say, placing my hand on his knee. "What was your name again?"

He looks at where my hand is on his leg and grins, leaning toward me slightly. "Ricky."

"Right. Ricky. Thank you for the drink."

"My pleasure."

"So, what brings you out tonight, Ricky?"

He shrugs. "Why not? I've got no one keeping me at home." A hint that he's single, not that I needed one.

I sense Jett approach and can make out his large form out of the corner of my eye. I may have been talking to Ricky, but my attention has been stuck on Jett the entire time. My heart picks up its pace, sending adrenaline racing through my veins. I pretend not to see him as he comes to a stop next to my stool.

"There you are," he says as he slides his arm around my back, gripping my side and pulling me into him. My body leans in without a single ounce of resistance. His other hand grips my chin, pulling my face toward him when I refuse to acknowledge him.

His stormy blue eyes land on mine and my heart skips a beat. There's no need for words. It's clear as day he's not happy with the current situation. I can feel the tightness in his body, as if his muscles are clenched, ready to fucking snap.

Ricky clears his throat, breaking our charged stare. "Are you guys together."

"Yes," Jett says at the same time I say, "No."

"Hey man, if she doesn't want you here—"

"You should be careful," Jett says, still holding me hostage and staring into my eyes like his life depends on it. "She's a real firecracker, this one. She's bound to hurt that little ego of yours. Consider this interruption a favor. You can leave." He addresses the guy sitting next to me but never once glances his way.

"I think it's up to her to decide if she wan—"

One look from Jett has Ricky practically swallowing his serpent tongue. "Firecracker," he addresses me, "do you want him to leave?"

"Yes." I barely manage a whisper through the damn thud of my heart. My pussy clenches at the low rumble of his voice and the sheer threat in his eyes as he stares down a now sweating Ricky.

"You have two seconds to fucking leave before I snatch that disgusting tongue and rip it out of your mouth with my bare hands."

Ricky is so scared he rushes off without taking his full glass of beer. Then, his eyes are mine again, still storming. I manage to find my voice though it doesn't come out as steady as I'd like. "Wonderboy strikes once again. Saving my fragile, feminine sensibilities. How will I ever repay you?"

"I can think of a few things." His eyes heat as they finally leave my eyes and trail down, stopping on my lips before lowering to where my cleavage is heaving with my heavy breaths.

"What? No Jennifer tonight? Or perhaps the new trophy bunny? I'm sure *sheer dress* over there would be happy to give you whatever you want."

"I'm sure she would, but I'm not talking to *sheer dress*, am I?

I'm not sure why I'm playing hard to get when my body is practically throwing itself at him. The memory of him kneeling between my legs is still fresh in my mind, as if it was just hours ago and not five days ago. I clench my thighs together, my pussy practically screaming at me to stop being a cockblock. Then I remember Raymond's words from earlier tonight.

I expect an update soon.

"Well then, I suppose you should probably take me to your place," I say seductively.

He shakes his head curtly. "No"

Gods, he probably has a loyal, oblivious girlfriend waiting for him at his place and that's why he refuses to take me there. He never even hesitated or thought about the possibility of taking me to his place. I sigh internally, frustrated that I'm even in this position in the first place, and even more frustrated that I'm glad I get to use the order from Ray as an excuse to still go home with him. Because even though my mind is screaming against the wrongness of it all, my body is all too happy to oblige.

He gently pulls me off the barstool, his large hand warm and powerful against the base of my spine as he pulls me into his solid body. He whispers in my ear, "Either take me home or I'll find a dark corner to fuck you in. Doesn't matter to me but choose quickly."

Arrogant. He's definitely arrogant. But gods, he has every right to be. His words make me feel like putty in his hands, but I refuse to let him know how much he affects me.

"Just because you gave me one orgasm, doesn't mean it will happen again. One orgasm is hardly bragging rights or gives you the right to demand my body."

"A dark corner it is then," he growls out as he grabs my hand and pulls me behind him.

I have little choice but to follow him or cause a scene. At least that's what I tell myself as I hurry to keep up with his large stride. Of course, every pair of eyes is on us as we make our way through the throng of people and out the doors into the crowded hallway. He doesn't slow down as we weed our way through the crowd until the hallway becomes empty.

Doors with nameplates next to them line the hall. Conference Room A. Conference Room B. Great, we just so happened to walk down the hall filled with large, currently empty conference rooms.

I jerk on his hand as he reaches for one of the doors. "Wait, just wait a damn minute."

"Wait?" He turns on me so fast I gasp. The hunger in his eyes is unmistakable. Definitely a wild beast. "I've waited five days to see you again. Five days of remembering how fucking good you smell. How fucking good you taste." He forces my hand onto his hard cock, and I gasp again. "Five days of fucking my hand, fantasizing about what it would feel like to slide inside you. If you don't want this...," he rubs my hand up and down his dick, "tell me right fucking now and I'll go find someone who does."

I swallow, hard. He's been thinking of me for five days just as much as I've been thinking of him. That knowledge satisfies me way more than it should, and my body wants him way more than it should. The thought of him leaving me standing here, all hot and bothered, while he goes and finds some whore to fuck, makes me angrier than I have any right to be.

"Not here," I say finally. "My place."

"Let's fucking go."

Chapter Eighteen

Like You Mean It by Steve Rodriguez

As soon as we get into the elevator, I let go of her hand and move to the opposite side.

"What's wrong?" she asks, looking slightly worried as I shove my hands in my pockets.

"If I touch you now, I'm not stopping. So, unless you want me to push you up against the wall, lift up that dress, pull your panties aside, and fuck you right here...," my voice drops to a dangerous growl, "don't tempt me."

She swallows hard and leans against the opposite wall, nodding her head too quickly. I can tell she's nervous and anxious, but I know she wants this as badly as I do. Even if she can't say the words, her body speaks plenty.

The elevator dings and the doors slide open, revealing her suite lobby. I let her walk out first, keeping a healthy distance as she opens the door and steps aside to allow me entry. Then the door is closed and locked, and she leans against it, hands tucked behind her back. Definitely nervous.

I take my time appreciating her beauty. Her curves are slightly hidden in the teal dress she's wearing. It's tight on top, her breasts straining against the material, but it flows and pleats down her thighs, stopping right above the knees. Even though the dress isn't skintight, there's no way she could ever hide those luscious hips and thighs. I can't wait to spread them apart again, only this time lower myself between them and feel them wrap around my waist.

As beautiful as she is with clothes on, I can't fucking wait to see her naked. Neither one of us moves a muscle as we stand in the entryway of her suite, staring at each other with a mix of anticipation and nerves. I know the second I put my hands on her, it's done.

"Take off the dress."

"Excuse me?"

"You heard me, Firecracker. I want to watch you undress. So, take it off. Slowly."

She takes a step away from the door, then turns around. She pulls her long ponytail over her shoulder, then her hands move behind her back, and she slowly starts to unzip the dress. My eyes follow the movement like a laser, drinking in every inch of pearl skin that's revealed. She slides the straps off her shoulders and lets the dress slowly slide down her body.

Her round ass is almost on full display, the light pink and white lace underwear doing little to cover her cheeks. I can't fucking wait to see that ass in the air, with my handprint on it as I pound into her from behind, gripping those damn hips. She steps out of the dress and turns around. Her high heels make her legs look long and flawless. Her thighs come together, then her hips swell, falling into a toned waist, and up to her big, beautiful breasts. I can't wait to feel their delicious weight in my hands and watch them bounce as I fuck her.

My dick is impossibly hard and throbbing in my jeans as I take in all her glorious skin and curves. I'm having a hard time staying rooted in place and not attacking her like I attacked my opponent in the ring tonight, but fuck, she's making it difficult. I pull the T-shirt over my head and toss it, then kick off my shoes, and the jeans follow, leaving me standing in my dark blue briefs. She returns the favor and thoroughly checks me out. I grip my hard dick and she swallows again, her thighs clenching in response.

I smirk, then remove the briefs, finally allowing her to see me. I stroke my cock. "Is this what you want?"

Her voice is barely a whisper. "Yes."

"Take off the rest."

She reaches behind her again, unlatching the bra, slowly letting it fall to the ground. Then she hooks her panties, bending over to step out of them. She reaches for the buckle on her high heel.

"Leave them on." Fuck, is that my voice? I'm a barely contained body of wild desire. I've never felt this intense need and attraction with anyone before, and when she stands back up, revealing her entire naked body....

Jesus Christ. She's fucking perfect.

I don't need this type of distraction right now when I need to be focusing on the tournament, but how the fuck am I supposed to focus on the tournament when she's all I've been thinking about for too many fucking days?

I need this to clear my mind. I lie to myself.

I want her even though I shouldn't.

Before I lose any other good sense, I reach down to my jeans and pull a condom out of my pocket. I rip it open, about to roll it on, when she finally speaks.

"What are you doing?"

I look up at her. "I always wear a condom."

"But you're Mageía."

"And?"

"You can't get any type of human...sickness. We don't have STIs in our world."

That shocks me. I guess that would explain why I've never been sick. I've lived on the streets and I've never even so much as had a runny nose.

"What about pregnancy?"

She shrugs. "I'm taken care of it when it comes to that."

I stand utterly still and look straight at her as I ask, "Are you saying you want me to fuck you raw?"

She looks a little uncertain, but she nods her head. "I want to feel you."

I fucking lose it. I stalk to her in three strides. Her eyes widen, and her chest is heaving, but she holds her ground. I grip her jaw and lift her face up to me.

"Are you sure this is what you want?" I search her eyes.

A nod. "This doesn't mean I like you," she says, managing to sound adamant despite the fact that we're both naked and she knows I'm about to fuck her.

"Ditto."

The only movement is the rise and fall of her chest as we stare at each other, the air between us so fucking charged I can feel it prickling against my skin. I think we both know we're about to unpack something neither one of us will be able to put back. And I'll only be another asshole in her life when I leave. It's what I always do. I leave. And she doesn't deserve it but I'm going to do it anyway.

"I don't do soft. I don't do sweet words," I warn, giving her one last chance to change her mind.

"Then stop talking and fuck me like you hate me."

Her words unleash me. My mouth crashes onto hers. She eagerly lets me in, opening her mouth so my tongue can slide inside, colliding with hers. She kisses me back with equal force. Her tongue sweeps into my mouth, teeth grazing and biting at my lip. My hands slip down her body until I'm gripping her ass in my hands, pulling her against me. I have seconds to relish the feel of her breasts pressed against my chest, and then her hand wraps around my dick and I groan. She pumps me a few times and that's all I can take.

"No more teasing." I spin her around and push her up against the door. I reach down and slide my fingers between her legs, a growl rumbling in my chest. "So fucking wet." I slide two fingers inside, not to tease her, but so I can taste her again. I stick my fingers in my mouth. "Mm." I pull them out and lick my lips. "So fucking good."

I grip my cock and line it up to her opening. She gasps as the tip slides in, and I continue pushing, feeling her body opening to receive me. I groan again. I have to pull out and push again to get all the way inside her. Fuck, she's so soft and so tight.

"Holy shit," she breathes out as I start to pump inside her.

I hold on to her hips, her hands planted on the door above her head, and she pushes her hips back toward me. I'm driving into her long and deep, utterly focused on the feel of her pussy around my dick. Her voice pulls me out of my trance.

"I thought I told you to fuck me like you hate me."

"Just remember, you asked for it." I grin and wrap her hair around my fist, pulling her head back. She cries out as I pound into her, her moans and cries being restricted because of the angle of her neck. I spit onto the fingers of my free hand and lower it to rub her clit. The guttural moan that escapes her throat as I do drives me fucking wild. "And you're going to cum for me again, Little Firecracker."

I keep my relentless pace, driving into her hard as I hold her hair hostage, and my fingers rub back and forth against her clit. I can feel her pussy getting wetter and I know she's close to cumming.

"Come on, give it to me," I whisper in her ear.

She's breathless as she says, "Yes. Close. Don't stop."

Fuck, the sound of her voice laced with heat and passion, the desperate plea begging me not to stop, I'd die happy if this was the last thing I ever heard.

"Oh gods!" she tries to scream as the orgasm finally hits. I feel her pussy pulse and squeeze my dick, feel her orgasm spill around me, and her skin shines like a fucking diamond. I continue pumping into her until her shaky legs start to give out. I let go of her hair and her head slumps in defeat.

I slide out of her just long enough to turn her around and hoist her up. She wraps her legs around my waist, and I slide back inside her. I grab her ass and lift her up and down the entire length of my cock. Her hands are in my hair and she's kissing me again. She's kissing me like she's the fighter and I'm the opponent she needs to beat. It's fierce and demanding and wild. Just how she makes me feel inside.

I slam her back into the door. She breaks the kiss to scream her pleasure to the ceiling as I continue to fuck her like I hate her. Her breasts are bouncing beautifully, and I watch them for a few seconds before leaning down to wrap my mouth around a nipple. I flick it and tease it, feeling it harden under my touch. I suck it into my mouth and bite down, causing her to cry out again. Her hands are clinging to me like her life depends on it, pulling me closer, and I feel her nails trying to dig into my shoulders.

"Fuck, Jett...." My name on her lips is a drug. It sinks into me, settling in my chest, and I'm already desperate to hear her say it again.

I claim her beautiful mouth, swallowing down her cries as I drive into her harder than I've ever fucked anyone. I can't get deep enough. I can't get enough of her.

"Fuck, I'm gonna cum. Where do you want it?" I don't know how I manage to still think clearly, giving her the option to decide.

"I want you to cum inside me," she says, breathless.

"Fuuuck," I growl as I pound into her a few more times. She squeezes my dick with her pussy, and I groan as I sheath myself inside of her, my orgasm ripping through me. The pleasure shoots up my spine and I shudder as goosebumps erupt across my skin. "Jesus

Christ." I'm out of breath as I lower my forehead to her shoulder, her legs still wrapped tight around me as I hold her up against the door.

The only sound is our heavy breathing and my heart pounding much too loudly in my ears. It's telling me that I'm fucked. It's never felt like this. Not physically. Not emotionally.

I finally slip out of her and even with my release, I'm still not completely soft. I'm too fucking worked up, too attracted to her. I already feel the need to slide back inside of her, but I manage to slowly lower her to the ground. She winces as I do.

"I hurt you."

"I'm ok," she says, but the grimace on her face says otherwise.

I take her in my arms, and she immediately protests. "I said I'm fine, Wonderboy. You didn't fuck me so hard that I can't walk."

"You sure about that?" I tease as I head to her bedroom.

"Yes," she scowls up at me.

"But I did make you cum. Again." I can't help the satisfied smirk on my lips. I hold her gaze and watch her cheeks tint pink. I chuckle. "I'm well on my way to earning the title of Wonderboy."

"It's not a compliment," she reiterates.

"It will be," I assure her as I set her down gently on her bed. "Shower or bath?"

"With you?" she asks, taken aback.

"Not if you don't want to."

She swallows. "Bath."

I nod and head into the bathroom, going straight for the jacuzzi tub. This thing could easily fit four people in it. Then again, maybe not with me inside, but there will be plenty of room for the two of us. The two of us. Fuck me. Why am I even doing this? Why am I staying? Nothing fucking good comes from staying. But the grimace and small little hiss of pain she made as I set her on her feet sent a pang of something I don't even want to acknowledge through my chest. Not to mention I'm hungry to be deep inside her again. Not one part of me physically wants to leave her. This is not a good fucking sign.

I'm about to go grab her when she announces herself in the bathroom. "I knew it. Of course, you don't know how to properly prepare a bath."

"You plug the tub and add hot water. There's not much more to it than that."

She heaves a heavy sigh. "Typical male. But can he learn? That is the question." She walks over to where I'm sitting on the edge of the tub and drops a large purple ball into the water. It immediately starts to melt, turning the water purple and filling the air with the scent of lavender.

She leans over the tub and starts to light the candles that surround it. I grab her wrist and pull her toward me. Her palm lands on my chest, holding herself up. That one small touch sears through me. Her face is inches away from mine and all I want to do is kiss her again as I pull her down on my dick. The thought of it has me stirring back to life but all I do is trail a finger softly across her cheek.

"I think you know there's nothing typical about me."

She scoffs. "That's yet to be decided. I don't know anything about you."

"I'm not hard to figure out. What you see is what you get. And not only do I think you like what you see, I think you also like what you get."

She rolls her eyes and pulls out of my hold to continue lighting the candles. "You're so fucking arrogant."

"Confident."

"What?"

"The word you're looking for is confident," I correct her as I climb into the tub. "We both know my actions…deliver."

She finishes lighting all the damn candles, then turns off the lights, wraps her long ponytail up on her head, and finally slides into the tub with me. She closes her eyes as she sinks under the hot water, her legs brushing against mine as she settles. A sexy moan escapes her throat and has my cock twitching at the sound. We sit in companionable silence. She seems content to just enjoy the bath as if I'm not even here. Meanwhile, I can't take my damn eyes off her.

Her pouty lips are slightly swollen from our aggressive kissing and are the perfect shade of pink. They look like a rose petal, and I know now they're just as soft. Her long lashes lay beautifully against her flushed cheeks. Her skin shimmers lightly, a result of the steam clinging to her skin and the sparkle that just seems to be a part of her.

"You're staring," she scowls but doesn't open her eyes.

"Do you blame me?"

She slowly opens her eyes. Fuck, those eyes. Even in the dim candlelight, they gleam like gems. Everything about her is flawless and radiant. I've never seen anything more beautiful. Her eyes lower to the water, where her entire body remains hidden in its depths, before leveling them back at me.

"Why?"

My brows scrunch together, and I cock my head to the side, studying her. "What do you mean, why?"

"Why are you staring at me? You can't even see me."

I find her ankles and wrap my hands around them, gently pulling her toward me. She narrows her eyes but otherwise stays silent and allows me to pull her. I lift her legs over mine, wrap my arm around her back, and bring her the rest of the way onto my lap. She gasps when I drag her across my hard dick and her hips rock against me instinctively. Our bodies respond to each other without us even having to think, or seemingly having control. Even though her beautiful breasts are above the water, I make sure to keep my eyes on her face.

I bring my hand out of the water and gently rub her cheek with my thumb and then look down at it, but it comes away clean. "When I first saw you, I thought you were wearing glitter or some shit."

She scoffs. "Or some shit?"

I shrug. "Yeah, girly shit. But this...this sparkle you have, it's just *you* isn't it?"

She nods.

"And when you cum, you light up like a star in the night sky."

She laughs softly, a little embarrassed. "Not just when I cum, but when I'm happy, yeah, my body reflects it."

I hold her chin gently in my hand, looking into her eyes. They look deep purple in this light, and if I'm not fucking careful, I may just fall into their depths with no hope of ever climbing out. "How could I *not* see you?"

She drops her gaze. The compliment obviously makes her uncomfortable and I hate that it does. She can go toe-to-toe with the best of them, holding her ground and using that sharp tongue, but when it comes to someone being nice to her, *seeing her*, she doesn't know how to handle it.

She clears her throat. "What about you? What do these stand for?" she asks as she traces one of the snake heads on my chest. Her featherlight touch feels more like a scalpel, slicing me open, trying to reveal my secrets. I don't know why she has this effect on me, but it's both exhilarating and terrifying.

I drop my hand to rest on her thigh. Both hands gently grip her lush skin, and I'm still extremely aware of her slick opening pressed against my dick, but I hold her gaze and give her an answer.

"I've had nightmares for as long as I can remember of two snakes...hunting me. When I was a kid, it terrified me, but I always woke up right when they were poised to strike. As I got older, I became less frightened of what I saw when I closed my eyes because the real world was much worse. So, when they came to me again, I didn't wake up. I let them strike and then I killed them with my bare hands. I took my fear and confronted it. Controlled it instead of letting it control me. When I woke up, they were etched into my skin, and now I have a daily reminder that I have nothing to fear."

She looks up at me curiously. "They're not tattoos?"

I shake my head. There's no more of an explanation I can give her. I don't exactly understand what happened myself. Her eyes follow the trail of her roaming finger as it traces the snake up and over my shoulder and down my arm. "Did it work?"

"Did what work?"

"Confronting your fear."

"Yes. There's nothing that I fear anymore."

She looks at me, her eyes searching mine. "That can't possibly be true. We're all scared of something. Even if it's not directly related to us. There's always something that...*drives* us to do what we do. To be cautious."

"Maybe for most but not for me."

"Not even death?" she asks curiously.

"I'm not afraid to die."

"That must be why you fight the way you do."

I shrug. "It's why I live the way I do. It's why I go after what I want." I move my hand across her thigh until I feel the warmth of her core. I slide my fingers against her slit. Her breath hitches and a heavy breath escapes her lips when I sink a finger inside. "And what I want is to be inside you again."

"Yes." Her voice is a raw whisper.

"Are you sure? You're not hurt from earlier?" She shakes her head, eyes never leaving mine. "I need to hear you say it. Give me that sharp tongue of yours," I demand as I remove my hand and replace it with my dick. I stroke my tip up and down her opening, teasing her, and waiting for her to tell me she's ok.

"I'm not fragile. You're not going to break me."

"Maybe not your body but make no mistake about this, Firecracker, make no mistake about *me*. If you do, I will break you. Do you understand what I'm saying?"

"You're not going to break me," she says defiantly as she takes control and lowers herself onto me. "I don't even like you."

I grip her hips tightly and shove into her, ripping a scream from her throat. "Then fuck me like you hate me," I echo her earlier words, then claim her mouth as she starts to ride me. I know she's poison, but fuck, she tastes so sweet.

Despite what she says, I know she doesn't hate me.

But she will.

Chapter Nineteen

THE BREACH by STARSET

Another night, another fight. This is round two of the five-round tournament. You never know who your opponent is going to be until your pictures are displayed right before your fight. Or you're in my position and left for the last fight. They're saving the best for last. Not that I'd say I'm the best. Every other fight has been entertaining but I've definitely been the most talked about. So, I guess they're playing to the crowd's anticipation, making them wait to see what I'll do next.

The way I handled my last fight has definitely earned me notoriety, though that was not my intent with the way I handled it. I actually hoped for the opposite. I hoped that if I refused to play into their sick game, refusing to give them bloodshed and brutality, that they'd ignore me. Boy, was I fucking wrong.

Eyes follow me everywhere I go. Whispers follow in my wake. Most people stay a good distance away from me, but some are brave, asking to shake my hand or take a selfie. It's so strange, being seen. Being popular. It's everything I wanted when I was a kid but it's nothing I want now. Leave it to life to play its own games and truly fuck with you. To hell with what we want, life just likes to toy with us. Perhaps it's the god I grew up believing in, or maybe it's the gods the Mageía believe in, controlling all our fates. I can picture them looking down at us, laughing at our pain, enjoying the shit show. Cue the fucking popcorn.

"It's time." One of the fight coordinators walks into the locker room, pulling me out of my thoughts.

I stand and follow him down the tunnels, turning a few times until we reach the main one that will lead me to the arena. He nods and leaves me to my fate. I continue walking toward the exit, the soft thud of my steps against the concrete already drowned out by the loud murmur of the crowd. Once I appear at the exit, just like last time, the crowd goes completely silent, watching me.

I keep my eyes focused on the ring in front of me, ignoring everything else around me. The crowd isn't here. The lights aren't blinding. Nothing else matters except my opponent waiting for me in the ring. I stop in front of the enforcer and hold out my wrist for him to scan. The scanner beeps its approval, but before I can make my way to the steps that lead up to the ring, the enforcer stops me with a hand on my shoulder and points to a wall of weapons I hadn't noticed.

"Choose your weapon," he says curtly.

My eyes shoot to Phil where he's standing with Peggy next to the ring. He looks apologetic but all he does is shrug and nod, confirming that I need to choose one. I look at my opponent in the ring and notice that she's grabbed a sword. Fucking hell.

I go for the daggers. They've got a shorter reach than the sword but I'm hoping I'll be able to move more comfortably while still being able to use both hands separately. I don't have any experience wielding weapons much less a fucking sword, so the logical choice seems the best for me.

The daggers are a nice, solid weight in my hands but they're foreign to me. I have no idea how to properly wield them. As I approach the steps, I lock eyes with Phil and seethe, "You didn't tell me I'd have to fight with weapons!"

"I didn't know, kid. Just trust your instincts, and if you have to get rid of the daggers, then get rid of them and fight how you need to fight."

I nod, and then I'm in the ring, the gate slamming shut behind me. My opponent stands on the opposite end of the ring. She's quite a bit shorter than me, her buzzed head no higher than my shoulders. Her eyes are completely black, no whites whatsoever. Just black pits staring at me like I'm in their way and they're eager to rip right through me.

She stares at me as she unties the cape draped over her shoulders then tosses it to the side. I'm not sure what expression I make as I watch two dragon-like heads appear from behind her back, rising about a foot above her head. They're weaving and bobbing, serpent tongues darting out and vicious fangs snapping, promising to pierce skin and break bones if they get their jaws locked onto me. I don't want to test the theory of my skin being impenetrable with these two…things.

She grins as she unsheathes her sword. The announcer's voice barely registers as he announces the start of the fight, and she lunges for me. Her sword comes down straight at my head and I barely manage to get my daggers up in an X to block her strike in time. The two dragons on either side of her head strike at the same time and I stumble backward to stay out of their reach.

She takes advantage and spins, bringing her sword in for a cut to my side. I throw myself on the ground and roll beneath her swing. I swipe my leg out, connecting with her knees, and she goes sprawling to the mat as I spring back up to my feet. I don't waste any time going for one of the dragon heads as she's down. I swipe a dagger across its neck and its heads tumbles to the floor, rolling a few feet away from us.

She climbs to her feet and hisses at me. I'm preparing to attack again when I stop dead in my tracks. Rising above her shoulder where the dragon head used to be, are two more.

"What the fuck?"

She laughs maniacally, and I'm almost too stunned to move as she charges me again. I spin out of her path, bringing my dagger up to slice through another long neck as it reaches for me. Again, two more heads grow out of the place one had been.

"Damn it, kid!" Phil's voice finally registers as he yells at me from outside the ring. "Stop with the head slicing!"

"What the fuck am I supposed to do then?" I yell back, but whatever his response is, I don't hear it as she comes for me again.

I use my longer reach and the daggers to keep her somewhat at bay. We're basically just circling each other, her trying to get her sword to connect and me blocking it while dodging not two, but now four, serpent-like dragon heads snapping their teeth at me.

I have no clue what the fuck to do or how to fight her. There's no way for me to get close to her without getting bitten, and there's no way for me to restrain her *and* all her little demons.

A loud bark grabs my attention. I glance over to where Peggy is standing next to Phil. She approaches the ring and jumps up, placing her front legs on the side of the ring, careful not to touch the electric fence. I only lock eyes with her for a second before I'm forced to move again. My opponent seems unfazed by our standoff, her attacks never once slowing or weakening, but the connection to Peggy is enough.

Once I focus on that link, it's suddenly overwhelming. I can feel her in my mind almost as if she was whispering in my ear.

The main head. You've got to shut off the central brain.

I toss my daggers to the floor and yell as I charge. I duck my head and go for her legs, trying to get low and stay out of reach of the heads. I pick her up and slam her back into the electric fence. I hold her there for a few seconds and I can feel her body convulsing as the shocks zap through her body. Her sword clatters to the mat, and then

I release her. Her body slumps to the floor and I rush to get behind her.

I wrap my legs around her torso, locking her arms to her body, and then I wrap one arm around her neck, my other arm pulling it tight as I start to choke her out. She comes to as the shocks leave her system and she starts flailing her body, trying to get me off her. The dragon-like heads also gain consciousness and start attacking. I'm within striking distance now and my hands are occupied as I try to knock her out so I can't fight them off. I vaguely feel teeth puncturing my skin up and down my arms, but I refuse to let go.

I grit my teeth and pull tighter. "Come on, pass out already," I plead.

It feels like I've been holding on for hours when I'm sure it's only been minutes, but she finally goes limp in my arms. The dragon-like heads follow suit. I let out a heavy breath as I release her, rolling her body off me and standing. I look up to the glass box where I know Raymond is watching me. I have the urge to flip him off, but I turn around and head toward the gate instead.

Once again, I have to ask to be let out. I don't need to stand here and let some guy hold up my arm like an idiot. Everyone just watched me win, I don't need to have my arm raised above my head to be deemed the champion. I also don't need to be fucking interviewed.

Once the gate is open, I hurry down the stairs, where Phil and Peggy are waiting for me.

"Well, that's one way to do it, kid." His eyes take in the blood dripping down my arms. "You alright?"

"Fine," I grumble as I continue walking back to the locker room. My name is being chanted again but I don't acknowledge the crowd. I don't want to wave and give the impression that I care or, for fuck's sake, that I'm approachable. Let them chant because they want to chant, not because I'm encouraging them to do so.

Peggy trots up beside me, her nose nuzzling my hand. I rub her neck as we walk. "Thanks for the insight, Peg. I owe you one."

I wait until we're in the locker room before asking any questions. Phil is helping me take the wraps off my hands. "I don't know why I even wear these; they don't actually make a difference."

"Appearances."

We're quiet for a bit, but when it's clear he's not going to provide any information, I ask. "Why did they want us fighting with weapons?"

"Why do you think, kid? For the excitement. For the blood. For the pure chaos. Pick a reason but don't expect anything to make sense. Raymond does things solely for his own entertainment or benefit. Plus, how else were you going to cut a head off the hydra? He put a blade in your hand because he knew how'd you'd use it and what would happen."

"Did you know their heads did that?"

He sighs. "Yeah, kid. Everyone knows that about them."

"Everyone except me because I'm not from this godforsaken world. What else is going to trip me up because I don't know any better?"

"We're down to eight fighters now. We can study the other seven, well six, we know Mordecai, and we can focus on any that might cause a problem. There were too many before and we didn't know who you'd be paired against. We'll prepare better for the next one."

I sigh and run my hand through my hair. "It's only fight number two and I'm already tired of the fucking games."

"I know, but we're in it together. Not to mention if you win, this will change your life even if you don't find the answers you're looking for. Half a million dollars will set you on a good path."

All I can do is nod in agreement. I know he's right, but it doesn't mean I have to like it.

"You want me to have the doctor look at those?" He gestures to the punctures in my arms.

"I'm fine," I say again as I get up and head into the showers. "I'll see you at the party."

These stupid parties are the only thing I actually look forward to now because it means I get to see her. And if I have my way, which I'd bet money on that I will, I'll be deep inside her again within the hour.

Chapter twenty

The Deep End by Colorblind

Tonight's fight didn't go quite as easily as his first fight did, but he still took Shea out in under five minutes. That's impressive considering she's one of the ones I was worried about. That bitch is a tough cookie, not to mention those extra heads. I sure as hell wouldn't want to fight her. And when he started to choke her out, all I could stare at was the blood running down his arms as they attacked.

As soon as he knocked her out, he was out of the ring and gone again. He seems to have no desire whatsoever for the fame that comes with being a fighter down here. Everyone else relishes in the limelight, eager to be seen and known, but he can't get away fast enough. It makes me wonder why he's doing this at all. Then again, half a million dollars is incentive enough.

I hurry over to the ballroom where the afterparties are held, but this time, I don't go inside. Instead, I stay in the hallway, away from the crowd, but with a clear line of sight to the elevator and the entrance to the party. I want to be able to see him when he gets here and I'm hoping he'll want to avoid the party altogether. I know I do.

I don't have to wait long before he shows up, but when the elevator doors slide open, revealing another gorgeous girl on his arm, my heart sinks to my stomach. The jab of jealousy I feel, right in my damn bleeding heart, is intense and almost unbearable. Not to mention

I feel...betrayed. I don't know why. It's not logical. We've slept together, sure, but it's not like we're dating. I never asked him to be exclusive and he never gave me any reason to believe it meant anything. Actually, he warned me that he'd break my heart and all I did to acknowledge that was tell him I don't even like him.

So why does seeing him with another girl on his arm hurt so much?

I don't want to watch but I can't look away either. The way she's holding on to his muscular arm, her body brushing against his as they walk, the clear desire written all over her face. And him? He's completely unreadable. I have no idea what he's thinking but he's clearly not opposed to this girl's desires if he's parading her around on his arm.

When they reach the entrance, the security guard scans her in, but Jett doesn't follow her inside. They exchange some words; she looks frustrated but tries to hide it behind a fake smile. Then he turns away from her and starts walking down the hall. Toward me.

I stand up straighter where I'm leaning up against the wall, arms crossed over my stomach. My heart seems to have risen back into my chest and pounds to the beat of his steps as he approaches. Once he's standing in front of me, he braces himself against the wall and leans into me, gently grabbing my chin, tilting my head back and forcing me to look up at him.

"Did you think I didn't see you standing here, Firecracker?"

He smells so good. I want to wrap my arms around his waist and pull him closer, but I manage to restrain myself and only lift a shoulder in a half-shrug. "You looked a little preoccupied." I'm grateful my voice comes out cold and distant, not betraying the hurt I feel.

"She asked me to escort her to the party. I didn't see the harm in being nice."

"I'm sure you didn't."

He runs his thumb over my bottom lip, and I have to resist the urge to open my mouth and wrap my lips around it. Gods, he brings out the little she-devil in me.

"Is that jealousy I hear?"

"You wish."

"I don't actually." I open my mouth to ask him what the hell that even means when he pins me with his piercing blue eyes and slowly lowers his mouth onto mine. His tongue slips inside and he kisses me thoroughly without ever closing his eyes. Mine flutter for a second but I force them open, meeting his heated gaze. "So, what exactly are you doing out here...Meg."

He says my name like I'm in trouble, or about to be in trouble, and it makes me clench my thighs together. The heat that's already spreading from my core is embarrassing. Such a simple question. Such a simple thing, my name on his lips, but his tone and the look in his eyes ignite me.

"Waiting for you," I admit, almost breathless already and all he did was kiss me once.

He quirks an eyebrow and smirks. Damn him and that fucking smirk. "Did you want to walk in together or did you have something else in mind?"

"Something else." Another admission.

"Good." He reaches down and grabs my hand, lacing his fingers with mine as he leads us down the hall, back to the elevator, and away from the party. I don't know why the feeling of his hand holding mine feels so good, but it does. I have to smother a smile as I eagerly let him guide me.

Once in the elevator, he hits the button that will take us to my suite. I don't even care that he's acting like it's his suite, and he has every right to it. I just want to get there and get naked with him as soon as possible.

"Stand over there." He gestures to the other side of the elevator.

"Why?"

"Because I want to look at you. I want to appreciate the way that dress stretches over your curves before I rip it off you and set your body free."

Gods, his blatant words always make me blush. He may as well be the sun in my underground world the way he makes my body heat. I do as he asks and stand on the other end of the elevator as his sky-blue eyes slowly make their way down my body.

"Turn around." His husky voice adds chills to my skin.

I start to spin in a slow circle, allowing him ample time to drink me in. A gasp escapes my lips when I feel his large body press into mine. His hands slide around my waist and up my stomach to palm my breast as his hips push into me from behind, pressing his hard dick against my ass.

"Look at what you do to me, Firecracker." His voice is raspy with barely restrained desire, and I shudder against him. "You make me feel like I'm going crazy."

"You make me feel—"

The elevator dings and the doors slide open. I'm lifted off the ground as he carries me through the receiving room and to my suite doors. I'm grateful for the interruption because I'm not sure what awful truth was about to be whispered. He sets me down in front of the door and I unlock it, allowing us both access.

Once the door is locked behind us, he turns to me. "You have about ten seconds to get rid of that dress if you want to save it."

I look down at the beautiful peach-colored silk dress before lifting my gaze back up to his. "Actually, I'd rather you rip it off me."

His nostrils flare and his fists clench. There's a beat of absolute silence before he growls and stalks toward me. His hands are on the dress, gripping the plunging neckline, and then his incredible strength is unleashed as he literally pulls the dress apart. The force of the initial tug jerks my body into him, and I use it as an excuse to run my hands over the hard planes of his abs.

He pulls on the dress until it's ripped wide open. I shrug out of the tiny straps still holding onto my shoulders and I'm once again standing before him in my lingerie, a delicate nude lace set that gives the appearance that I'm naked.

His hands are on me instantly, as if he's been dying to touch me all day. I feel the heat of his hand through the thin material of the bra as he gently massages my breast.

"God, you're beautiful."

My nipple peaks under his touch and he takes it between his fingers and squeezes firmly, drawing a deep moan from my throat as I lean into his touch.

My hands slip under his shirt, and I slowly drag them up his stomach and over his sculpted chest. The softness of his skin over hard unforgiving muscle is a delicious juxtaposition that I just can't get enough of. But when the shirt comes off, it's an entirely different sensory overload as my eyes roam over his body.

I trace the deep V and slide my fingertips across his skin, tracing the band of his jeans before making their way to the button. He doesn't stop or assist as I lower the zipper and begin pulling his jeans and briefs down his hips. I move slowly, eagerly watching as inch by inch of his hard dick is revealed until finally, it springs free.

His jeans are forgotten as I run my palm up his large dick, completely in awe at how perfect it is. It's a little darker than the rest of him, not quite as golden, but the perfect symmetry, a beautiful round head, and a thick vein running underneath it. I grip it in my hand, not quite able to touch my fingers together, and start sliding my fist up and down. His skin is just as soft here, if not softer...and harder.

I'm so in awe of him, so lost to his perfection, that his voice startles me. "Are you going to do something with that or just look at it all night?"

I laugh, only a little embarrassed, and look up at him. Gods, he's so incredibly tall. I feel like I'm looking up a damn mountain of muscle as I finally make my way up to his eyes. They've darkened and I've never seen this look before. There's heat and desire, yes, but also something deeper than that. I don't even want to think about what it is because I know I'll only hurt myself if I start assuming. If I start thinking there's something more to this than just sex.

He finishes stepping out of the clothes as I settle onto my knees, getting comfortable. Then I lean in, still holding his gaze as I glide my tongue from his balls all the way up to his tip, licking the pre-cum off the slit, causing him to suck in a breath and his dick to jump in my hand. Then I slide my mouth down on him and swirl my tongue around the tip. The muscles in his jaw twitch as he continues to watch me.

I use my hand in sync with my mouth as I stroke him from base to tip, getting lost in the feeling of him sliding in and out of my mouth, and his sexy moans of pleasure that keep me going. Then, his voice breaks my concentration.

"Give me those eyes," he demands as his hand wraps around the base of my ponytail. I look up at him and he moves his hips back, pulling his dick out of my mouth. "Hold your hands behind your back." I do as he asks. "Stick out your tongue." I automatically comply.

"God, look at you. So fucking beautiful." He leans down and drops a thick layer of his spit on my tongue and then slides his hard dick back inside my mouth. He uses his hold on my ponytail to move my head up and down the length of him at his will. When he starts to hit the back of my throat with force, I move to steady myself with my hands on his thighs.

His voice is a deep growl as he repeats, "Hands behind your back, Firecracker. And give me those eyes."

I roll my eyes up to him and watch as he watches me swallow his dick. He forces his way down my throat, and I gag at the intrusion. He pulls out, giving me a second to take a breath, and then he's on me again. He pushes all the way in and holds my head hostage on his dick.

"Mm, that's a good girl," he praises. I gasp for air as he loosens his hold on me, then he starts thrusting his hips, his other hand on my head now, too, as he fucks my mouth. "Fuuuck," he growls, then pushes down my throat again. "You're doing so good." He grips his cock and pushes it against my cheek as he pulls it out, making a popping sound. Then he does it again, before lifting it up, stroking himself as he pushes my head down.

I lick and suck on his balls as he jacks himself off. He groans, then wraps his hand around my throat, pulling me up. His mouth clashes with mine and he kisses me long and deep. I moan into his mouth, feeding his desire with my own. I've never been so fucking turned on and wet in my life. I love how rough he is, and I love knowing he likes what I'm doing.

I'm suddenly off the ground and in his arms as he carries me into the kitchen. He sits me down on the island and kisses me again, slower this time but just as deep.

"God, I love this smartass little mouth of yours," he says when he pulls away. He reaches a hand behind my back and unhooks my bra with expert swiftness, unleashing my heavy, aching breasts. They want his touch. They want his mouth.

And he delivers.

His mouth is hot as he wraps it around my nipple, sucking on it and flicking it with his tongue, causing me to arch into him, a moan on my lips. But then he's gone. He grips the side of my underwear and pulls, tearing them on one side, then the other. They're no more than a scrap of material, falling away, leaving me bare in front of him.

He slowly rubs his fingers down my center, gathering my wetness on his fingertips and then caressing my clit with them. "Mm." I bite my lip at the sensation, the pleasure already building. I'm so fucking horny I feel like I'm about to cum with just a few more strokes. "Oh gods." I moan. "It's never felt this good."

"It's about to get better. When we first met, I told you it was only a matter of time until you detonated all over me. Do you remember?"

"Yes," I barely manage to speak over the rising pleasure building up inside of me at his relentless fingers. But then the feeling is gone as he sinks those two fingers inside of me.

"Well, it's time," he says as he curls his fingers up and practically jackhammers them inside of me.

"Oh gods." The feeling is unlike anything else I've ever experienced. Even the last couple of orgasms he's given me haven't felt like this. This is coming from a different place entirely. Like he's drilling into the very heart of me, into my soul, and coaxing it out of my body.

The sounds my body is making, not only between my legs but out of my mouth, would be embarrassing if I wasn't on the verge of fucking breaking. I'm whimpering in a voice I've never heard and then all of a sudden, I'm screaming.

"Fuck, Jett! Jett! Jett!" I cling to him with all my strength. He's the only thing grounding me as my orgasm literally shoots out of my body.

He removes his fingers to rapidly rub my clit, causing my orgasm to last forever. My cum is all over his chest and stomach and running down my thighs. I start to feel embarrassed, but then his fingers are gone, replaced with his mouth. His tongue licks me up and then falls to my sensitive clit. He barely uses any pressure, just rubbing it gently in slow circles. The second orgasm floods through me without any notice whatsoever. It's so close to the first that it feels like I've been cumming non-stop for five gods-damned minutes.

"Damn, you taste so fucking delicious." He wipes at his stomach, gathering my cum, and then sucks on his fingers. I've never seen a man enjoy the taste of me like this. If I was thinking clearly, I'd definitely be embarrassed. But he doesn't give me any time to recover before he pulls me to the end of the island.

He lifts my legs up onto his shoulders and then he's pushing inside of me. I can feel his cock stretching me open and I fall back onto the counter and moan. He slides all the way inside me and then starts to thrust in a slow and steady rhythm.

"Give me those eyes, Meg."

I blink my eyes up to him, still trying to focus on reality. He's so fucking gorgeous. His eyes are crystal-clear blue shining down on me like the heavens, his body is glistening with a light sheen of sweat, and his abs are rippling as he moves his hips back and forth.

"Harder," I manage to whisper.

He pulls my body closer, arms wrapping around my thighs as he pounds into me. I grip the end of the counter to help hold myself in place as he drives deep inside of me, making me cry out in pleasure every time he thrusts in.

"Let me feel you squeeze my dick with that tight pussy." I clench around him, squeezing and then releasing, squeezing and then releasing. "Fucking hell, you feel so good."

All I can think is, *same, you feel so fucking good*. But I can't form the words as he continues to utterly punish me in the best possible way.

Finally, when I feel his rhythm falter, I manage to find my voice. "I want to finish you with my mouth."

A deep rumble reverberates through his chest. He pulls out of me. "Come here."

He helps me off the counter. My legs are still weak from the orgasms, and I quickly get to my knees. He pumps himself in front of my face and I open my mouth wide, sticking out my tongue, ready to accept his release.

"I'm gonna cum," he says, and shoves his dick in my mouth. He thrusts a couple of times and then his fist clenches my ponytail as he holds me still, releasing his orgasm in my mouth.

He's salty and thick but not unpleasant, and I drink down every last drop. I lick and suck him clean until he slowly pulls out of my mouth. He grips my jaw and tilts my head up.

"Let me see," he orders. I open my mouth and stick out my tongue. "Good girl." He drops to his knees in front of me and kisses me again. It's slow and lingering. His tongue slides against mine almost lovingly, caressing me as he gently pulls me into his lap.

I've never had a man kiss me after cumming in my mouth and him doing it is one of the sexiest things I think I've ever seen a man do. He breaks the kiss when he turns to sit against the counter, holding me across his lap and against his chest. I lay my head on his shoulder, thankful that he's holding me because I feel fucking weightless. I feel like I could float up into outer space if he lets me go.

We sit in silence for a long time. He continues to hold me tight against him, his cheek resting against my head and his fingers drawing lazy designs on my thigh. I've never felt this comfortable after having sex with anyone before. I don't feel insecure about my naked body. I'm not stressed about how I look; if my makeup is smeared or my hair is a mess. I feel at peace. And so fucking satisfied. I don't even want to think about using my vibrator which is usually my first thought after sex.

The loud groan of my stomach breaks the silence. He

chuckles, his chest jolting me slightly as it shakes. "I think I've worked up an appetite," I laugh.

He looks down at me and I lift my head off his shoulder to look up at him. My heart skips a beat with the way he's looking at me. This is too intimate. This is too dangerous. I need to say something. What? I don't know. But I know that he needs to leave.

"I think—"

But he interrupts me. "How do you feel about breakfast for dinner?"

"Oh, I uh…I actually love breakfast for dinner."

He smiles. A genuine smile that shows his perfect white teeth, his canines a little bit sharp. This smile is real, and it changes his entire face. His eyes crinkle slightly at the corners and his blue eyes shine with a happiness I haven't seen in them before.

He takes my chin in his hand and kisses me. Just a chaste kiss. A simple press of his lips to mine. But it overwhelms me. My chest feels tight and my stupid heart stutters again. When he pulls back, the smile still pulling at his lips, all thoughts of why he needs to leave are gone. Washed away by that beautiful smile.

"Then let's make breakfast," he declares, climbing to his feet with me still in his arms.

I cling to him tightly. Desperately. Not wanting to let him go even though I know I should. All I manage to do is nod as a smile of my own finds my lips and I say, "Ok."

Chapter Twenty-one

"I have to admit I don't actually know the first thing about cooking," he says as he pulls on his briefs.

"Why? Did your mom never teach you or was it just not *manly* enough for you?" I tease, pulling his T-shirt over my head.

My smile immediately falters when I see his face. That lightness that was there just seconds ago is gone, replaced by something darker. Something deeper.

"I...I'm sorry," I stumble over my words, apologizing, but not sure what I'm apologizing for. I didn't say anything bad. I have no clue what I said to cause this drastic change, but obviously I said something wrong. "I didn't mean to—"

He clears his throat. "No, it's ok. To answer your question, I never had anyone to teach me, so it looks like the task falls to you." He approaches and his hand goes to my chin, tilting my head back in a move that's becoming achingly familiar. "You think you're up for the challenge?" He smirks, pushing past whatever demons made an appearance and falling back into his comfortable pattern.

Flirting.

I love his smirk. I love his hands on me, his attention on me, but I'd give anything to rewind the clock one minute and have that smile grace his face again. It's gone too soon and I'm mentally kicking myself for being the reason why, yet not knowing exactly what I did in the first place. All I can do is move forward with him and hope that whatever dark cloud seems to follow him around will clear out and allow the happiness to shine through again.

"He doesn't know how to prepare a bath and he doesn't know how to cook. Hmm." I make a scene out of contemplating my options, tapping my lips, and scrunching my eyebrows in concentration. "But can he learn? Let's find out, shall we?"

I slip out of his grasp and turn on the lights under the cabinets, illuminating the countertops and stove, then start rummaging through the kitchen, looking for ingredients.

"We've got eggs," I say as I place the carton on the counter. "Ooo and we have bacon! That's pretty much all you need for breakfast as far as I'm concerned. Bacon is a whole meal."

"You're a whole meal," he says matter-of-factly, from where he's leaning against the counter, watching me with an amused look on his face.

I blush slightly and choose to ignore him as I place butter on top of the carton. If I let him distract me, we'll never eat, and I'm starving. "We have some fresh fruit." I add that to the counter and then move to the pantry. It takes a minute to spot what I'm looking for. "There." I point to the highest shelf. "Can you get that down?"

Jett walks up behind me, placing a hand on my hip as he reaches above me, pressing his entire body into mine, causing my heart rate to spike even though I'm doing my best to remain cool, calm, and collected. "This one?"

"Yep. And the bottle of syrup next to it."

Once everything is spread out on the counter, I pull out the cooking pans, mixing bowls, utensils, and plates. "Right." I turn to face him. "I'm assuming you at least know how to cook bacon?"

He hesitates, looking a bit uncomfortable. "In theory."

I smother a smile. Never in a million years would I have guessed this arrogant man, who exudes nothing but confidence and strength, would be uncomfortable with the idea of cooking.

"Well, here." I hand him the package of bacon. "Open this up and place the bacon in a single layer in that pan. Then turn the burner to about medium heat. Cover the pan with the lid or else we'll get grease everywhere."

He takes the bacon and proceeds to do as instructed. I pretend to busy myself with other things, not wanting to make him any more uncomfortable by watching him. Once he's done, I explain what I'm doing next.

"Now we make the pancake batter. It's really easy. The box will tell you to measure out x amount of mix with x amount of water, but you don't really need to measure. Just dump some of the pancake mix into a bowl and add water slowly until you get the desired consistency."

"But if you don't measure, how will you know what the right consistency is?"

Gods, he's fucking adorable, and I'm fighting the urge to grin like a damn idiot right now as he watches me intently, hanging on every word, actually interested in learning. "Here." I hand him the bowl with the mix in it. "Pour some water in and start stirring. You want to make sure all the dry powder is gone and make it as smooth as possible. You want it to be pourable but not runny."

"Pourable but not runny," he repeats. "Alright." I stand next to the sink and watch as he slowly adds water to the mix, a look of absolute concentration on his face. I only get a little distracted watching his muscles move as he stirs. "How's this? He breaks my little moment of staring and I look at the batter.

"It's perfect! See, you're a natural." I take the bowl from his arms and move back to the stove. "Now we're gonna turn on this back burner and let that back pan heat up. While we wait, let's check on the bacon."

I lift the lid and my stomach growls again. "Mm, I swear the smell of bacon is one of the best things in the world. Here." I hand him the tongs. "We need to flip each piece over so that it cooks on the other side."

"Alright." He takes the tongs and proceeds to flip the bacon, grease popping a few times as he does, but if grease lands on his arm, he doesn't show it. His arms. Shit, I forgot that he had been injured in his fight tonight. I glance down, remembering the blood running down them just hours ago, but all I can see now are red marks.

"Your arms," I say in awe as I grab his free arm and lift it up, inspecting it. "I saw blood running down your arms after the fight. Those hydra heads bit you. I saw it happen. But...." I trail off, tracing the red marks with my fingertips. "Your arms are healed." I look up at him, his focus still on turning the bacon. "How?"

He shrugs. "It's just how I am. Their fangs barely punctured me, and I heal fast."

"You never told me what kind of Mageía you are."

"Because I don't have an answer."

"What do you mean you don't have an answer? How can you not know who you are?"

"Look." his voice is deep and stern, his eyes cold and angry as they flash to mine. "Not everyone has the luxury of knowing their history."

"Of course. You're right. I'm sorry." It's my turn to clear my throat. I move around him to the other side of the stove, focusing on cooking and letting the tension slip away. "So, once the pan is heated, you want to spray some oil on it, so the batter doesn't stick to it." I show him the can and then spray the pan. "Then, just pour in the batter. You can pour in a lot and make big pancakes, or you can make a couple of smaller ones at the same time. Then, once you see some air bubbles and the batter is cooked up the sides, you flip it over. Easy-peasy." I look over at him and smile, happy to see he's back to concentrating on the cooking lesson. "And now for the final piece. How do you like your eggs?"

He's quiet for a moment. I can practically see the wheels spinning in his head. "I've always wanted to learn how to make them with the middle runny but the outside cooked."

I smile again. "Over-medium. That's how I like mine, too, and you're in for a treat. I just so happen to know the trick to making the *perfect* over-medium egg. But." I turn to face him, giving him a serious expression as I point the spatula at him. "If I teach you, you have to swear to keep it a secret."

He smirks. "I had no idea cooking was so serious and secretive."

"You're damn right it is," I continue with a stern voice. "Well, do you promise?"

He nods his head, hand coming up to brush my cheek. "I promise to keep all of your secrets, Firecracker."

Again, this feels way too intimate, and I have a feeling he's talking about more than just my egg trick. "Ok, then...." I brush it off and turn on the last burner. "You want to add a little bit of butter to the pan and let it melt. Then, we're gonna crack the eggs. Oh, can you grab the salt and pepper from that cabinet please?" I point to the one next to us.

"Season with salt and pepper, let the eggs cook for just a bit, and then, the secret to a perfect egg...." I walk over to the sink and pour water into a cup. "Pour a little bit of water into the pan, then cover it and let the steam from the water cook the rest of the egg to perfection without worrying about flipping it or cracking the yoke," I say, pleased.

I turn off the burners except for the pancake pan. "Go ahead and flip the pancake," I say, gesturing and stepping back to allow him space. "And ta-da, you've officially made breakfast."

I glance up to see the cabinet door left open. "I swear," I huff playfully. "What is it with men being incapable of putting things back where they go or shutting cabinet doors? It's like it's encoded in your guys' DNA or something." I move to close the cabinet door when he grabs me by the waist and lifts me onto the island, a little yip and a laugh escaping my throat as he does.

He forces his way between my legs and even sitting on the countertop I have to tilt my head back to look up at him. "Let's get some things straight," he says sternly. "One, you've called me typical, and you've compared me to other men. I do not like being compared to *anyone*. Two, your words insinuate that you've had other men here, in your kitchen, leaving cabinet doors open, and I definitely don't like the thought of you being with *anyone* other than me."

"Are you jealous?" I try and tease.

His hand clamps down on my face and I watch the muscle in his clenched jaw jump. "I'm greedy, possessive, and selfish. I refuse to share or even *think* about you with another man. Do you understand?"

I square my shoulders and try my best to be defiant in his crushing hold. "That's quite the double standard you've got there, *Wonderboy*." I say the nickname sarcastically.

"How do you figure?"

"Well, first there was the little blonde barbie, *Jennifer*," I seethe, still pissed at myself for remembering her name. "Then sheer dress, and the one you escorted just tonight—"

"I didn't sleep with the blonde and you know where I've been after every fight. Which is right here, with you. Not sheer dress or the girl from tonight. I'm here with you, Firecracker. And when I'm not, I'm thinking about being with you. Is that what you want to hear?" His blue eyes dart back and forth between mine, his hold never wavering, making me see the truth of his words.

"I...." I swallow, forcing down the emotion his words want to bring out of me. I shouldn't ask for more. I shouldn't even let him be here right now. But I can't stop the words from leaving my mouth. "So, you're saying you want to what? Be exclusive?"

"I don't want another man to look at you, much less touch you. So, whatever the fuck you want to call that."

"Well, I don't want other women touching you either," I admit.

"Done," he agrees easily. "I told you; I don't want you jealous and I meant it. For as long as I'm here, I'm yours and you're mine."

As soon as my heart starts to soar at his admission, it sinks just as quickly. "What do you mean, as long as you're here?"

"I told you on night one, don't mistake this for something that it's not. Don't mistake me for something that I'm not. I'm just passing through. I never stay in one place very long, it's not who I am. But as long as I'm here, I want it to be with you. Take it or leave it, Firecracker, but that's all I can give you."

I feel the swell of tears building behind my eyes and my throat burns at the effort it takes to force the sadness down. To not let him see how much his words devastate me. Because even though this is more than I ever expected, it's bittersweet. What did I think? That this gorgeous stranger just waltzed into my life out of the blue to be my happily ever after? That he would take me away from this place? That he would *save* me? How fucking naïve can I be?

Raymond would never allow me that happiness anyway. And I belong to him. He *owns* me.

It doesn't matter how good of a fighter Jett is, he's no match for the God of the Dead. So, even if he did want to be with me, I could never give him what he wanted anyway. I could never *be* his. How quickly I lost sight of that dreaming of a happily ever after. A fucking fairytale.

"Let's eat," I say, forcing a weak smile on my face, the thought of food now turning my stomach.

Jett caresses my cheek softly, his sharp gaze no doubt seeing everything I'm trying and failing, to hide. But he doesn't say anything. He just nods, easing me off the island, allowing me to pretend like this is all ok. Like I'm ok. When my heart is already breaking a little inside my chest.

Chapter twenty-two

Fix by True North

The days and nights I'm not with her have turned into a blur. It's like I'm going through the motions, training with Phil and Mordecai, physically present, but a million fucking miles away. When I'm with her, nothing else matters; not the tournament, the money, or the reason why I'm even fucking here.

And when I'm not with her, I feel…disconnected. The thoughts in my head are more chaotic than ever, thoughts of her consuming me. Her body in those skintight dresses. Her naked body at my mercy. The beautiful sounds she makes and the glowing of her skin as I make her cum. My T-shirt hanging off her body, leaving only her thick legs on display. Every version of her sexier than the last.

I've had her in so many different ways sexually, and though I'm extremely satisfied, I'm also yearning for more. I have yet to fall asleep with her in my arms or wake up with her next to me. Those acts are far too intimate, and yet, they're the ones I crave the most. They're the ones that I've been deprived of since I was way too young. They're the feelings I've simultaneously been chasing and trying to deny my entire life. I've never even felt close to wanting these things before, like I do with Meg, but giving in to those temptations will only cause her more pain when I leave. Hell, who am I kidding? It's going to hurt me to leave her too. So, why torture ourselves with things we want but can't have?

These truths have sunk their claws into me, causing me to be more agitated, and angrier. My last two fights have been brutal and not in a good way. Only Peggy's connection to me has kept me from killing my opponent. Much like the night I killed Tiberius, the world around me simply disappears. I don't hear the crowd. I don't hear Phil yelling at me from feet away. Only Peggy, a voice and feeling inside of me, has pulled me back from the brink of madness.

Déjà vu flashes through my mind as I sit in the locker room, looking down at my blood-stained hands. There's only one the fight between Mordecai and Nessus left to find out who will be joining me in the championship fight. Even though I've been training with Mordecai, and I like the guy, I don't really have any feelings one way or the other about fighting him if he wins. And, surprisingly, Nessus is fierce in the ring, but I think Mordecai will come out on top.

Someone punches my shoulder. "Hell of a show you've been putting on out there, T! Man, it's amazing how you—"

"Joey," I interrupt, "what the hell are you doing here? I told you—"

"I know what you told me, T, but you're not my dad. I want to be here. I want to watch you and support you. Isn't that what brothers do?" He squats down to pet Peggy where she's lying next to me, mumbling his next words. "I mean, brothers like in training brothers, I'm not saying that—"

"Yeah, Joey," I ruffle his hair, "that's what brothers do." He looks up at me with big, brown eyes, and a huge grin on his face. As much as I want to scold him and be mad at him, I can't.

"I won some money betting on you." The grin widens. "Not much because I didn't have much to bet." He shrugs. "But I knew you'd win."

I can't help but sigh. "Joey, you can't be betting and getting into that kind of trouble. I mean, who the hell lets you bet anyways?

You're not even eighteen.

He laughs. "That doesn't matter down here. Money is money. No matter who's holding it, it's always up for grabs. It wasn't a risk, T. I *knew* you'd win."

I start to rub my hands down my face but stop short as I remember they're covered in dried blood. "Just promise me you're not getting into anything like before." I dart a look around. There were quite a few smaller fights leading up to the two main ones, so several fighters are using the locker room. Afterall, they gotta keep the crowd entertained and give them what they want. A bloody show. I lower my voice. "You know what I'm talking about." I spear him with my gaze. "Promise me."

He nods. "I promise."

A loud whistle, and some heckling, grabs my attention.

"Hey, doll. You looking to have some fun?"

"The fucking rack on her."

"Mm, I would destroy that ass." This comes from a fighter stepping out of the shower completely naked, stroking himself as Meg walks by, causing the blood in my veins to boil. I'm on my feet instantly.

She stops in front of him, looking down. "For your sake, I hope you're a grower because you sure as hell ain't a shower. You won't be destroying anything with that pathetic toothpick." As she starts to walk away, he grabs her arm and all I fucking see is red.

A feral roar escapes my lips as I lunge for him, grabbing him around the neck and slamming him into the wall. My free hand reaches down and grabs ahold of his balls, squeezing them tightly. He whimpers and tears fill his eyes.

"If you ever lay your filthy hands on her ever again, I swear to God, I will rip off your tiny little balls with my bare fucking hands and shove them down your goddamn throat." I start to pull, letting him feel the strength in my grasp, his face turning beet red from the pain and the lack of oxygen. It doesn't satisfy me one bit. I need to see blood.

I slam my forehead into his nose, breaking it, causing blood to gush down his face and spatter onto me. The rage running through my body is hot. I feel like I'm going to fucking explode with it, like a goddamn volcano, burning everything in my path.

I feel Peggy's presence in my mind before she nudges me with her head. I release my hold on the man, and he drops with a hard thud to the floor. He curls in on himself, one hand feeling his nose and the other grabbing his sensitive balls. He's choking on sobs and blood, his body racked with pain, and it still doesn't satisfy me. All I can see is his hand on her body.

Peggy's wings shoot out, effectively blocking my line of sight and I snap out of it. I take a deep breath and turn to face Meg, not sure what expression I'm going to see on her face after that brutal display. It's one thing to see me fight in the ring, it's another to witness my cruelty up close.

When I meet her eyes, I don't see any of the emotions I thought I would. Disgust. Fear. Shock. I see what I always see when she looks at me. Desire. Her chest is rising and falling a little too rapidly and she licks her lips before taking a slow step toward me.

Peggy moves to stand in front of me, her ears pinned back, and a low growl on her lips. I can feel not only her possessiveness but also her caution. She's unsure of Meg and I can't fathom why.

Meg's eyes fall to Peggy. "I don't think your Pegasus likes me very much."

"She's just protective," I say, petting Peggy's head and sending soothing thoughts her way. "And she just doesn't know you." Meg nods but makes no move to get closer to me. "What are you doing here, Firecracker?"

"Oh, umm…." She clears her throat. "Mr. Harris has asked to see you. I'm here to take you to him."

Mr. Harris. Hades. "Why are *you* bringing me to him?" I ask curiously.

A look of shame passes over face, but she holds her head high and never wavers. "I work for him."

Our first encounter comes back to mind. She had been trying to make a deal of some kind with Nessus. She had mentioned being a part of someone's empire and Nessus had threatened that Mr. Harris wouldn't be pleased with my interference. I just didn't have a clue back then who exactly Mr. Harris was, and to be honest, I had forgotten all about it once I did find out.

"Why?" I narrow my eyes.

"Why what?" She crosses her arms over her stomach, pushing her hip out in a defensive stance I clearly remember from our first meeting.

"Why do you work for him?"

"Why wouldn't I work for him? He's the most powerful man in The Underworld."

"I didn't take you for someone who's power hungry," I counter, my voice dipping low with frustration at her attitude. She hasn't been like this with me since we started seeing each other and I don't like the change.

"And you know me so well?" She scoffs. "Come on, he doesn't like to be kept waiting." She turns and walks out of the locker room, not even bothering to make sure I'm following. I have no idea what the fuck just happened, or what changed, but I don't like it. I look down at Peggy. "Take care of Joey and make sure he gets back to Phil's safely."

Joey scoffs. *Great, more attitude.* "I can take care of myself, T. I don't need a babysitter."

"Well, then, you take care of Peggy for me, ok?"

He looks annoyed but he rolls his eyes and nods. "Fine."

I catch up to Meg as she's stepping into the elevator. There's another girl already inside. I hold my arm out, keeping the doors open, and speak to the other girl. "Out."

"Excuse me?"

"Get. The. Fuck. Out," I seethe. She scoffs but scurries out of the elevator, cursing under her breath as she does, leaving me alone with Meg.

"Wow. That was real gentlemanly of you. You sure know how to woo the ladies."

I'm in her space before she can say another word. I tilt her head back, forcing her to look at me. "I thought you wanted me to be a dick to other women. Besides, I'm only interested in *wooing* one woman, and she's got an attitude that's going to get her spanked if she's not fucking careful."

"Don't threaten me with a good time."

"Firecracker," I growl in warning, pushing her up against the wall. "I don't know what's gotten into you, but if you keep this up, we're going to have a hell of a time in this elevator."

Her hand brushes over my shorts, feeling my already hard cock. The material is thin, and I feel the heat of her hand intensely. I close my eyes for a few seconds, relishing in the feel of her hands on me before I grip her wrist, holding it hostage. She's deflecting on purpose. I loosen my hold on her face, and I feel her defeat like it's my own.

"Tell me what's wrong," I ask. "Is it what I did in the locker room?"

"What? No, of course not. I mean, I didn't need you to save me, *Wonderboy*." She smiles softly, but it's a swift smile. "I just...." She lets out a heavy sigh. "I don't really wanna talk about it right now, ok?"

I brush my thumb over her cheek. "Ok."

I shouldn't let myself get distracted by her, especially when I'm on my way up to see Hades, but I can't help it. I need to taste her like I need oxygen to breathe. I lower my lips onto her, claiming her mouth greedily. She bunches her hands in my T-shirt, pulling me closer. I can feel her need for me as much as I feel my own. All I want to do right now is take her to bed and make her forget whatever it is that has her so worried and unhappy. Unfortunately, we don't have that luxury.

She pulls away from me as the elevator dings and the doors slide open. She adjusts her dress, pulling it down and fussing with her hair. She doesn't spare me another glance as she walks into the lobby of Hades' office. I'm left to follow in her wake, unsure of everything that's just happened within the last ten minutes.

The blonde from the first time I was here sits behind a desk, wearing clothes this time, and doesn't seem to be high out of her mind. She nods at Meg who nods back as we pass the desk and walk to his office. The doors are open, but Meg stops in the doorway and knocks, announcing us.

"Mr. Harris, Jett Stephens, per your request." Her voice is monotone, her expression blank. This version of Meg is so different than the sweet, soft, and loving Meg I've come to know behind closed doors. It's jarring to see, and it makes me wonder which one is real.

"Ah yes, Jett. Please, come in."

I stop in front of Meg before I enter his office. The movement is automatic as I grip her chin and force her head back. Her eyes are wide, scared, as she peers up at me. My heart hammers in my chest, desperate to understand what the fuck is happening and why she's practically shaking in my arms.

"Wait for me," I whisper. I wait to see an acknowledgment. A nod of her head. A whispered agreement. But all she does is look down and pull out of my hold, closing the door between us.

I clench my jaw and turn to the god sitting behind his desk. I barely manage to keep the snarl off my lips as I make my way to the chair in front of him. "What do you want?"

He quirks an eyebrow. "You're either ignorant or stupid, and I don't think you're stupid, so I'm going to chalk up your blatant disrespect as ignorance. I don't know what you know of me but let me be fucking clear." He steeples his hands together, leaning onto the desk. "Do not mistake my tolerance for weakness. I've put up with your attitude but I'm losing my patience."

"Then, by all means, get on with it. What the fuck am I doing here?"

He smirks and chuckles. "So very brave, aren't you, Jett?"

I don't dignify that with a response as I continue to stare at him with all the anger and frustration I feel.

"You're angry. I can see that. Good, I can use it too. I'm not sure how much you know about my world...," he leans back in his chair, smoothing his tie, "but I recently lost a very important fighter."

He pauses, staring at me, waiting to see how I react. I'm happy to disappoint him when I remain cold and blank. I have no guilt or remorse to show for what I did. "And?"

"And that means I need to replace him. I want you to take his spot and fight for me as one of my Titans."

"No." The answer is immediate and final. I don't even have to think about it.

"Hmm," he hums in his chest, watching me closely. "You still have one fight left, and if you lose, I'll be offering the spot to the victor. But I highly doubt that's going to be the case."

I know it won't be the case. I don't care who I'll be fighting in the championship round, I *will* be the victor, and I'll be damned if I ever fight for Hades.

"I want you to remember what I said, Jett. I'm out of patience, and I will get your cooperation one way or another. I have the means to be very motivating."

I stand. "Are we done here?"

"For now," he says with a devious sparkle in his eye. If I knew more about this world, more about *gods*, perhaps I'd act differently. But I don't. And he has nothing on me. Nothing to threaten me with.

I storm out of the office. Meg jumps up from where she was sitting on the couch. Her eyes land on me but quickly dart over my shoulder.

"Meg, my dear, my sweet. Do join me." His voice sings sweetly but there's no denying the nasty gleam in his eye as he approaches the doorway.

"Don't wait for me," she says as she walks past me and disappears into Hades' office.

He smirks once again then shuts the doors to his office, cutting off my view of Meg where she stood, still as a statue in the middle of his office, with a look I never want to see on her face ever again.

I don't know what the fuck is going on here but I'm sure as hell going to find out.

Chapter twenty-three

Dismantle by Icon For Hire

I somehow manage to slow my racing heart as Raymond walks calmly to the bar, getting himself a drink. I never can tell what kind of mood he's in. Twenty-one years of this shit, these games, and you'd think I'd be able to predict what would happen. But when it comes to him, there really is no telling.

Drink in hand, he turns, eyes slowly raking down my body before coming up to meet my eyes. "You look good, pet. You've got quite the...*glow.*"

Damn me and my fucking nymph skin. Still, I try to deny it. "Just doing what you asked and getting close."

"Mm-hmm...." He sips his drink, never taking his eyes off me. "And what have you discovered?"

"Not much. He, uh...well, umm...his skin is different," I finally get the words out. "The hydra bit him yet he had no wounds. Just about anyone else would have had their arms shredded and bones snapped in those jaws, but he only had red marks hours after the fight."

"If you want to continue being useful to me, you better give me something I can *use.* That is the key word in useful, isn't it? I know about his strength and his skin simply from watching the fights. Anyone could have told me this information." Another sip. "I need to know more. Who is he? Who are his parents? Why is he here? What does he want? Who is he close to? Who does he care about? I shouldn't have to remind you what I need, pet. You're the best at playing this game."

I swallow. "There's not much else to know. He said he doesn't know his history or what kind of Mageía he is. He doesn't understand magic or how The Underworld even works. He may as well be human. I don't know what you think I'll find but I don't think he's whoever you think he is. I think—"

Again, he's on me before I even seen him move. A sharp pain erupts across my cheek, and I barely register the floor under my hands before I'm yanked back to my feet.

"I don't keep you around to think!" His grip on my face is crushing. Scorching flames have replaced his black eyes and I feel the heat of his fire licking against my skin, burning me. "I keep you around to get information! And if you can't do that then you're no fucking good to me. Do you hear me?"

Tears run down my cheeks, and I have no hope of stopping them. Raymond seems to notice them at the same time I do. He releases me abruptly and I stumble, falling to the floor. I see his shoes pace back and forth in front of me a couple of times before he kneels down, lifting my face up to meet his. His eyes are back to being the black, fathomless pits they always are.

"Look what you made me do, pet." He softly caresses my cheek. It's exactly the way Jett does, but this caress sends cold shivers of dread down my spine. I physically shiver at his touch, unable to rein in control of my emotions. "I'll only tell you this one more time. Get me the information I want, or I'll give you to Nessus to do with as he pleases. And once your body is broken, I'll drag you to The Pit and break your soul when I force you to watch as I toss her in." Another gentle caress on my cheek before he gets up and leaves the office.

Once I'm sure I'm alone, a sob escapes my burning throat.

And once I hear that one lonely cry, all the others I've bottled up inside come rushing out. I clamp my hand over my mouth, desperately trying to quiet my cries as I sit on the floor and break.

Chapter twenty-four

"That's enough, Mordecai. Let him up," Phil instructs, sounding as exasperated as I feel.

The last fucking thing I want to be doing right now is training. What more am I going to learn at this point? Mordecai and I are at a stalemate, neither one of us wanting to reveal too much considering we're fighting each other in the championship fight in a few days.

"Look...," I run a frustrated hand through my hair, "this is fucking pointless. Mordecai isn't going all out, and neither am I. We already know most of each other's moves and everything else we're saving for the ring. So, why the fuck are we even here?"

"He's got a point," Mordecai agrees.

"Just because ya ain't going all out doesn't mean it ain't still needed. You've gotta keep your body in shape. Keep your mind focused, which one of ya sure as hell could use some help with. This is big, kid. This fight needs to be your priority. No offense, Mordecai, but he's my fighter and of course, I want him to win."

"None taken. Though I'm not gonna roll over and give it to him. It's gonna be one hell of a fight."

"That it is, kid. That it is."

"Well, let's save it for the ring then," I say already walking off the mat. My mind is on Meg. I waited for her outside her suite for hours before finally giving up and going home. I have questions and I need answers. Not to mention the fear that flashed in her eyes as the door closed between us has had me uneasy ever since.

"I didn't dismiss you." Phil's voice is hard and authoritative. A voice I don't hear much from him even when he's coaching.

"I didn't realize I needed your permission," I snark back. I don't have the time or the patience for this right now.

"I know where you're going, kid. I know who you've been seein' and I'm tellin' you right now because I care about you; she ain't no good."

I spin on my heels, charging toward him, my anger quick to rise to the surface. "You don't know shit about her," I snarl through clenched teeth.

He scoffs. "What? And you do? In the few weeks you've known her?"

"I know she's a good person and that's all that matters."

"It ain't all the matters, kid. Everything she does, she does for him. She's no more than a tool, Raymond's whore—"

Before I have time to process my actions, Phil stumbles, catching himself before he falls to the floor. He slowly rises, wiping blood off his lip with the back of his hand. My chest is heaving, fists clenched at my sides, but the sight of his blood penetrates my red haze.

"I'm...I'm sorry. I didn't mean to...." I pinch my eyes shut and take a deep breath. When I open them again, Phil's expression is blank. "I'm sorry," I repeat. "But I won't let anyone talk about her that way."

I turn to leave but Phil's voice stops me. "If you walk out right now, I'm done, kid. You fight the rest of this battle without me."

I hear him loud and clear. His words slice through me, more painful than I thought possible, but the need to see her, to make sure she's safe, is stronger than the twinge of pain working its way into my chest.

I don't turn back around.

I don't say a single word.

I let my feet carry me away from the only person who's shown they care about me. I do what I'm so incredibly good at; I abandon him. I leave what I know to be true behind, as I walk toward the unknown. Is Meg using me? Has she been spying on me for Hades this whole time? Or is what I feel when I'm with her real? Does it even matter? I've already told her I'm not going to stay, so why the fuck do I even care if it's real or not?

There's no logical reason why I'm in the elevator, heading to her floor. There's no logical reason why my heart is pounding so anxiously. There's no logic, no common sense, no thinking whatsoever. My body is simply acting on impulse, as I bang on her door so fiercely, they shudder under my fists.

"Firecracker!" I yell. "Let me in or I'm breaking down these fucking doors." I continue banging until one of the doors opens, allowing me entry.

"Gods, Wonderboy, what in the hell is going on? Is everything ok?"

I freeze in the doorway, all my internal madness utterly seizing as my eyes take her in. The first thing I notice is her hair is down. I've only ever seen it in a ponytail, pulled away from her face. This…this is a completely different woman. Her dark brown hair cascades around her shoulders, all the way to her waist, in waves that look like silk. Her face looks softer and sweeter than ever. I swear to whatever god is real, she's a fucking angel sent from Heaven, or Olympus, or where the fuck ever.

She's absolutely beautiful and steals the air right out of my lungs.

Then I notice the discoloration on her face. It's hard to make out at first in the dim lighting of her entryway and she's doing a decent job of using her hair as a shield to hide behind. But once I see it, I'm immediately furious.

Walking up to her, I push her silky hair back behind her shoulders and gently cup her face in my hands. My eyes take in every inch, noting the purple around one eye, a swollen red cheek with a small cut, a busted lip, and on each side of her jaw, burn marks in the shape of fingers.

My fingertips gently touch her injuries, shaking with the absolute rage running through my veins. My eyes finally meet hers, red and puffy from crying. My heart feels like it's going to explode in my chest from the anger pounding inside me.

"Who did this to you?" My voice is low and dangerous, promising pain. I fight the urge to clench my fists and put them through the fucking wall. I don't know why I even ask. There's only one motherfucker who would dare put his hands on her. "Hades," I growl through clenched teeth.

She's stubborn and tries to hold on to some of her self-righteous pride, tipping her chin up in defiance. "I can take care of myself."

"I know you can, but you shouldn't always have to." I see some of the fight leave her eyes as her shoulders sag.

"I'm fine, it's fine," she rushes out. "It's not as bad as it looks."

She tries to turn away from me, but I don't let her take a single step, grabbing her around the waist, pulling her into me, securing her place in my arms.

"You're not fine, and this is most definitely not fine. I don't care if it's not as bad as it looks, Meg, that's not the point." I caress her uninjured cheek, my eyes passing over her injuries again. "Any man that lays his hands on a woman is the weakest fucking monster and will get what he deserves. But I'll be damned to fucking Hell if anyone gets away with putting their hands on *my* woman. I don't care if he's a god or what kind of power he has. He will pay for hurting you. Mark my words. I'll fucking kill him."

The one thing I've never wanted to be is a killer. The one thing I told Phil I'm not. The one thing I've been adamant about is gone, thrown out the damn window as I look at her bruised face. I will kill for her without a second thought.

"No, he'll kill *you*, Jett. But not before destroying you. He—"

"He can fucking try."

"Jett, please, listen to me." The desperation in her voice makes me hesitate. The tears gathering in her eyes make me push past the anger. And when they spill over, running down her cheeks, they completely wash it away. "Promise me you won't go after him, please. I don't want to lose you. Not that way," she whispers. "Not that way."

I cradle her face in my hands and gently brush the tears from her cheeks, careful not to cause any more pain. The tears stop flowing as she tiptoes, reaching for me. I lower my head to hers and let her control the kiss. Tonight, I'll follow wherever she leads. Tonight, I'll give her whatever it is she needs. All thoughts about getting answers seem unimportant as her tongue swipes my lips, seeking entry.

I push my hands through her hair, relishing the way it slips through my fingers before I grab a fistful at the back of her head and gently tug. She moans into my mouth, her hands sliding under my shirt to graze my abs before sliding up to my chest.

I break the kiss and look down at her. I swear she's never looked more beautiful than she does right now, open and fearless, looking up at me like I'm the goddamn sun in her sky. How can this not be real?

"What do you want, Firecracker?" I ask, still clutching her to me tightly, not wanting to let her go, but will if she asks me to.

"I want you to take me to bed but I don't want you to fuck me like you hate me this time. I want—" She swallows and drops her eyes from mine. She may not be able to say the words, to express the desire to feel loved right now, but she doesn't need to. I see it in her eyes. I feel it in her touch. I feel it in her kiss. My words from the first time come back to me.

I don't do soft. I don't do sweet words.

Those words weren't a lie. Then again, I've never felt like this before either. Like my insides are liquid heat. Like my heart has been skinned and is raw and aching. Like I need to taste her again or else I might lose my sanity. Like I need to slide inside her again or else I might fucking die.

I grab under her ass, picking her up. She wraps her beautiful legs around my waist, and I carry her into her bedroom. We stare at each other, neither one of us saying a single word, as I set her down on the edge of the bed. My hands find the bottom of the purple silk nightdress bunched up around her thighs and slowly lift it. She raises her arms in the air, allowing me to take it off her.

"On the bed." I lift my chin, indicating I want her to lie down.

She scoots back until she's in the middle. I quickly get out of my shirt, shorts, and shoes, but before climbing onto the bed with her, I take a few seconds to look at her. She's propped up on her elbows, looking at me the same way. Some of her hair has fallen over her shoulder, her skin shimmering under my gaze as it travels across every curve. I want to explore every single inch of her skin. I want to know all her tastes and textures. I want to know every single spot that makes her moan and whimper. I want to know her, completely.

I climb on top of her, but I don't settle between her legs. I prop myself up on the side of her, tracing first her arched eyebrows, her dainty nose, and down to her parted lips. I press mine into hers, sinking into the softness of them, before sliding my tongue against hers. It's a slow and languorous kiss, unlike anything we've ever shared before. I take my time kissing her, loving the feel of her lips on mine and between my teeth as I gently bite down on her bottom lip before releasing it and kissing her again. Her hands are in my hair, holding me gently but with no hesitation in her touch.

I finally move from her mouth and glide my lips along her jaw. She moves her head back and to the side as I kiss her neck. I softly suck, letting my tongue caress her sensitive skin. Her moans let me know just how much she's enjoying this. I continue my slow descent, trailing my lips and tongue across her collarbone, kissing my way down her chest and between her breasts. I use one hand to cradle a breast, gently squeezing and teasing her nipple, while my mouth finds the other one, softly sucking and caressing the same way I explored her neck.

She arches her back and pulls harder on my head, her fingers gripping my hair. As I move to kiss a trail down her stomach, it's rising and falling with her heavy breaths. I continue dragging my lips and tongue lower, but instead of going straight for her pussy like I did the first time, I take my time to kiss and grip her thighs, sucking in a large chunk of skin before letting it go with a pop.

"Fuck," I say as I sink my fingers into her skin, looking up at her body from between her legs. "So. Fucking. Beautiful."

I finally settle, sliding my hands under her legs, gripping her small waist. Her sparkling eyes meet mine as I drop a line of spit on her clit, letting it slowly trickle down. Then I slide my tongue up her slit. I can't help but close my eyes and moan as the taste of her washes over my tongue. She echoes my moan and throws her head back, hands still in my hair, resting there more than anything else as I begin to devour her.

I kiss her pussy just as slowly as I did her mouth, taking my time exploring her with my tongue and lips and teeth. Every time my tongue caresses her clit she whimpers and clenches her fists in my hair. I know it's what she wants. What she needs to find her release. So, I stay on her clit, massaging it in slow, deliberate strokes. I'm so fucking intensely satisfied as I watch her body begin to move against me. She's rocking and rolling her hips seductively, but what really fucking turns me on is when she gets vocal.

"Oh yes, your tongue on my clit. Just like that." Her voice is breathless and sexy. I focus on the way it sounds, desperate to remember it just like this the next time I'm jacking off to memories of her. "Gods, Jett, that feels so good. Please don't stop."

My name on her lips is my undoing every goddamn time. I will worship her body for eternity if I get to hear my name on her lips like this. I know she's close to cumming when her body starts to jerk and shudder, and her hands grip my hair with strength, practically shoving my face in her pussy.

Doing what I know will set her over the edge, I slowly slide two fingers inside her as I suck her clit into my mouth and continue stroking it with my tongue.

"Oh fuck! Yes, right there. Just like that. You're going to make me cum. Oh gods, Jett!" She screams my name as the orgasm crests. I growl my own satisfaction into her, holding on to her bucking body, riding it out with her as her body pulses and glows around me.

She's still shaking as I move to my knees, griping my hard dick as I line it up at her core, ready to enter her. Her eyes are on my dick as I stroke myself, her body tensing just slightly, preparing for what's to come.

"Give me those eyes, Meg," I order, placing my palm on her stomach. She does and I swear I can see her soul shining through. I don't see one hateful or devious thing when I look into them. I've met a lot of selfish and evil people, and I refuse to believe she's one of them, no matter what Phil or anyone else says. "I need you to do me a favor, ok?"

She nods. "Ok."

"I need you to just breathe. Take a deep breath."

She swallows and then nods again. As she sucks in a large breath, I push down on her stomach and slide inside of her in one long, hard thrust. She cries out as I sink deep inside her. Then I start to pump my hips, still maintaining the pressure on her lower stomach as I give her all of me in each stroke, pulling out to the tip before pushing back in. It only takes a minute before I feel her pussy tightening on my dick.

"Oh. my gods, what the fuck." She looks shocked and delighted as the pleasure builds inside her. "This is going to make me cum again. Fuck, Jett, it's coming, it's coming!"

The pressure of her orgasm makes me pull out of her as she squirts on my stomach. Her hand moves to her clit, stroking it and screaming her pleasure to the ceiling.

"Where are you going?" Her eyes widen and her voice is desperate as I climb off the bed. I pull open the drawer of the nightstand and take out the bright pink vibrator, bringing it back to the bed with me. "What are you doing?" she asks nervously.

"I may be a lone wolf, but I know when to be a team player. Tonight is all about you, Firecracker. I'm going to make you cum until you see stars. Until every other thought in your mind is reduced to nothingness." I turn on the vibrator and hold it against her clit as I slide my dick back inside her. The deep guttural groan that graces my ears makes me smirk, but it's gone quickly as I lose myself in the feel of her. "Fuck, you're so fucking wet."

My eyes never leave her face as I continue to fuck her. I can feel the vibrations of the vibrator on my dick, and it only adds to the pleasure building between us. She pinches her eyes closed tight and it looks like she's in pain as she's preparing for another release.

"Meg, I need you to breathe," I remind. She lets out a whoosh of air, her eyes opening to find mine. "Hold this." I lead her hand to the vibrator and once she has it in place, I grip her hips and pound into her harder. She lifts her hips up, meeting my strokes in a sexy rhythm that has me gritting my teeth, fighting against my own orgasm.

She starts to scream again, but it's cut off, and she's left with her mouth hanging open and her eyes pinched shut again as the orgasm grips her. I have to force her legs open to remain pushing inside her. Once the orgasm fades, the vibrator is thrown to the side and I lower myself between her legs, claiming her mouth with mine. I force myself to slow my strokes and kiss her just as slowly. Her legs wrap around my waist, her arms around my back, clinging to me.

I break the kiss and hold her stare as I continue to slide in and out of her achingly slowly. We're both panting and moaning, lost to the pleasure, lost in each other.

"Fuck, Meg, you feel so good." I can feel my orgasm breaking through.

Her hand finds my jaw and her thumb moves over my cheek. "Jett," she whispers, and I break. I sheath myself as deep inside her as I can get. My forehead drops to hers and I close my eyes as I cum inside her. In this moment, all that's left in the world is right here, in this bedroom.

Her body underneath mine.

Her breath mingling with mine.

Her heartbeat pounding in sync with mine.

I roll off her, laying on my back, bringing her with me. She follows, wrapping her arms and legs around me. One hand holds her tightly against me, the other moves tenderly against the leg that's thrown over my stomach. We lay in comfortable silence for a long time. Then I hear a soft snore. I swallow down the fear threatening to make me bolt as I'm left with only my thoughts.

What we just did *wasn't* fucking.

And I can lie, tell myself I only did what she needed in this moment, that it meant nothing to either of us, but I *know* it's a fucking lie. I cherished every kiss against her body.

Every look.

Every touch.

Every moan.

Every single thing that clearly said what neither one of us can bring ourselves to voice.

And now, laying here with her asleep in my arms, is the nail in my fucking coffin. Because as much as my fear wants me to leave as fast as I possibly can, I won't. Because this feeling of her asleep in my arms…*holding her like this*…is everything I've been craving my entire life.

I hold onto her just a little tighter as I lay a soft kiss on her head, inhaling her sweet scent deep into my lungs.

This changes everything.

She's changes everything.

And I'm fucking terrified.

Chapter twenty-five

Craving You by Thomas Rhett, Maren Morris

The world comes back to me slowly as I surface from a deep, dreamless sleep. It doesn't feel like I have a body at all. I'm so relaxed and so...satisfied. My body feels like it's floating on clouds; if clouds were warm, and hard, and pressed against me.

As soon as I register the large body behind me, the previous night's events come rushing back. Jett threatening to break down my door like he was the damn SWAT team, the anger in his eyes as he saw my injuries, and then the incredible gentleness he showed when he focused all his glorious attention on me.

Just remembering all that pleasure has my body reacting. My heart starts to race, my body fucking tingles in anticipation as if it knows what pleasure is to come, and heat pools between my legs as I feel Jett's impressive dick begin to harden against my still very naked ass.

His voice is filled with heat and gravel as he whispers against my ear. "You have two seconds to leave this bed before I take you again."

I pull away from him and he growls in frustration, but he lets me go. I turn to face him, his beautiful skin glowing in the light streaming in through the windows, the curtains left open from the day before. The Underworld has light, even if it's not actually from a sun in the sky.

He looks like a god, sprawled across my bed, hands behind

his head, deliciously sculpted body on full display. Not one centimeter of skin has a flaw. He's absolute and utter perfection.

The light shining in his eyes makes them look lighter than I've ever seen them. A brilliant arctic blue that floods my body with warmth from my head to my damn toes.

A smirk pulls at his lips. "As much as I love the way you look at me, you can't look at me like that and get away with it. If you're still within my reach when I'm finished talking, you're not going to get a chance to leave again."

I get to my knees, but instead of getting off the bed, I throw a leg over him. I grab a hold of his hard dick and hold it up as I slide my pussy over the tip.

"Do you feel how wet I already am for you?"

His jaw clenches but he remains still, hands still tucked behind his head as he watches me intently. "Well…," he finally says, "what are you going to do about it?"

"I'll make you a deal," I say as I slowly sink onto the tip, causing him to hiss, before pulling off again. "I'll take care of both our needs this morning, but you can't touch me."

His jaw ticks again, and he narrows his eyes at me, thinking about my offer. Finally, he says, "Do your worst, Firecracker."

I grin and slowly sink onto him. I can't help but moan at the delicious feeling of him stretching me open to fit him. Once I'm seated all the way down on him, I get my feet under me, so I have more control and more room to move, then I start to ride him. I move up and down the length of him at a slow but steady pace.

"Fuck, yeah, ride me slow. Just like that," he says as he watches. "I love seeing my dick disappear inside of you."

Since I told him he can't touch, I'll be damned if I don't at least give him a show. I ride him until my legs start to burn, then I drop to my knees and continue sliding up and down his dick, though I can't get as much in each stroke. My hair is still loose and falling over my shoulders, so I move it back, giving him a clear view of my body and what I'm about to do. I put my fingers in my mouth, gathering saliva, then start to rub my clit. His eyes darken even more, and I can see the restraint in his muscles as he keeps his arms locked behind his head.

I continue to rub my clit and massage my breast with the other hand, pulling and tugging at my nipple. I close my eyes and get lost in the pleasure of my hands and the satisfaction of knowing that he's watching every single move I make.

His hips start to thrust up, meeting my strokes, driving himself deeper and harder. "Are you gonna cum for me, Little Firecracker?"

"Yes," I moan. "Yes, I'm going to cum." I rock my hips faster, back and forth, back and forth, as I continue to rub my clit, until I feel the release deep inside of me. I steady myself against his stomach and throw my head back while he continues to plow into me. I can feel my pussy clenching around him, drenching his dick in my cum.

"Fuck, Meg. So goddamn beautiful."

Opening my eyes, I find him drinking me in, his fists clenched tightly to the pillows on either side of him. It's thrilling to be in control. To know that he's aching to touch me, making his desire even more wild and uncontrolled, forcing him to focus solely on the feeling of me bouncing on his dick.

"Goddamn, I'm gonna cum," he says through gritted teeth. I reach behind me and caress his balls, causing him to cry out in a sound I've never heard before. I feel his dick get harder seconds before he pulses his release inside of me. I continue to ride him until his hands slam down on my hips and he stops my movements. "Stop, stop, stop," he begs, eyes closed and chest heaving.

We stay like that for a few seconds, both catching our breath, when he finally opens those vivid blue eyes. That genuine, stunning smile splits across his face and my heart fucking tumbles out of my ribcage and into my stomach.

"God, you're a devious little tease," he laughs brightly.

Then I'm on my back as he leans over me, his mouth landing on mine in a deep, yet unhurried kiss. When he pulls away, I'm left breathless once again.

"I don't know about you but I'm starving," he says, brushing a gentle thumb over my injured cheek. "Let's make pancakes again."

I echo his laugh. "Ok, but first, we both need a shower. We smell like sex. Like...a lot of sex."

"Mm." He runs his nose across my neck, making me giggle and goosebumps race across my skin. "Better get used to it, Firecracker, because I am never going to get enough of you. C'mon." He slides off the bed and walks toward the bathroom, giving me a glorious view of his ridiculously sculpted back, ass, and legs. "I'm starving," he repeats.

Sitting down at the island, Jett moans his pleasure around a mouthful of pancakes. "This almost tastes as good as you. Almost." He winks at me with a smirk that has my cheeks heating.

I clear my throat and change the subject, asking a question that's been nagging at me. "Not that I'm complaining, because I'm not," I insist, "but you've never stayed over before. Aren't you going to get in trouble or miss training or something?"

He looks down at his pancakes, cutting another bite with his fork. "Phil and I had a bit of a...disagreement. I'm not going to be training with him anymore."

"Oh." I wasn't expecting that answer. "What happened?"

He levels me with a stare, his eyes taking in my injuries again before holding my gaze. "I don't do well with anyone telling me what to do or giving me ultimatums."

I nod, looking down at my plate, sensing there's more to it than that but not wanting to push.

"I need to ask you something, and you need to be clear and honest."

I nod again. I already knew this was coming but it doesn't mean I'm prepared for it. I drop my fork and push my plate away from me. I sit back, arms crossed, and face him. "Ask your questions."

"Why do you work for Hades?

I blow out a heavy breath. "I don't just work for him. He owns me."

He scoffs. "No one owns you, Meg. He—"

"He *owns* me, Jett!" I snap. I close my eyes and take a deep breath. "I know you don't know much about the Mageía, or The Underworld, or magic, but it's all real. Raymond is a god, Jett. He is Hades. I know that doesn't mean anything to you, but he has power. *Real* power."

"Alright." He pushes his own plate away and sits back in the barstool seat. "I'm listening. Explain it to me."

I sigh. "Gods, where do I even start." I'm quiet for a minute as I try and gather my thoughts. "Ray is known for his deals with humans and Mageía. People who are desperate seek him out all the time. Unfortunately, my mother was one of them. She wanted nothing more than to be a famous singer. She wanted the world to know her name. So, she came to Raymond. Of course, he never makes a deal where he doesn't get something out of it. He agreed to help my mother under one condition. He wanted her firstborn child." I laugh sarcastically. "What in the fuck did Hades, God of the fucking Dead, even want with a damn child? I never understood the bargain. And I'll never understand why she agreed. But here I am so...." I shrug my shoulders.

"Why can't you just leave?" he asks.

"Every contract is signed and sealed with his hellfire. A contract can only be broken by death."

He rubs at his lips, brows furrowed, as he mulls over my words. "Ok, but I still don't understand why you're caught up in it. Why do you have to do his bidding? Do you have your own contract with him?"

I shake my head. "No."

"Then why do you stay? Or at least, why do you let him use you and manipulate you?"

"For her," I whisper. "I do it for her because if I don't, he'll kill her." I feel the tears quickly building behind my eyes. "He'll take her to The Pit of Souls and her soul will be trapped there forever. She'll never find peace. And I know what you're thinking." I swipe at my tears. "She gave me up, why do I care what happens to her? I've asked myself that same question a million times. I don't have an answer, I just do. She's my mom," I choke on a sob. "I hate him."

Jett's arms are around me, pressing my head into his chest. I cling to him, letting so many tears I've suppressed in fear finally flood down my cheeks. "The worst thing you can do is hate. So, you can cry, and you can scream. You can feel the hate for a moment, but you have to let it go or else it will consume you. You leave the hating to me."

He holds me tightly, letting me soak his T-shirt with my tears, stroking my hair, and giving me all the time I need to be in my feelings. When my sobs have quieted, he finally speaks again.

"I lost my mom when I was six. My father too. I know what it's like to love a mother you'll never have. But your situation is different. There's still hope. She's still out there, Meg."

I shake my head against his chest. "I don't know where or how to even find her. I don't even know her name or what she looks like. Ray has kept it all from me." I pull back, looking up at him. "I'm sorry about your parents. What happened?"

"A home invasion and robbery gone wrong. Just a hateful crime done by hateful people living in an evil world. The only reason I survived is because of my skin, because the fire didn't burn me, and I was able to get out of the house." He's quiet for a minute, a faraway and haunted look in his eyes before he continues. "I don't know why I'm different than my mother or father. If I'm Mageía, then they should have been too, right?" He shakes his head. "I don't have any answers and that's why I'm here."

"You're trying to find out who you are," I say, and he nods. "I was wrong."

"About what?"

"When we first met, I accused you of basically being a spoiled brat who had everything handed to him." I scoff. "Gods, I was such an idiot. I'm sorry."

He smirks. "I don't blame you. I did come on a little strong."

"A little?" I laugh. He chuckles, too, but it dies quickly. "Do you have any answers yet? Any idea about who you are?"

He shakes his head, looking down at his arms. "I've always had this strength, this impenetrable skin, and when the time came to use it, to help them, I froze. I was so scared. I watched my parents and my only friend, who was staying over that night, burn. I was scared for a long time after that too. I lost someone else because of my cowardice and that's why I refuse to be afraid anymore. That's why I won't ignore what's happened to you. It's not in me to walk away."

"You have to, Jett," I plead.

He releases me and rubs his thumbs over my cheeks, drying them. "I should go."

I grab his arm as he turns to leave. The panic I feel racing through my body is almost paralyzing. "Stay," I almost shout. "Please, stay with me. Let's just...." I shrug and laugh nervously. "I don't know, watch a movie or something."

He smirks and lifts an eyebrow. "A movie?"

"Yes. No." I laugh again. "Hell, I don't care what we do, I just know that I want you to stay. Please."

He pushes himself between my knees and places his fingers under my chin, tilting my face up. Gods, why do I love when he does this? Why do I love looking up at his arrogant, but gorgeous, face so much?

"If I stay, I can't promise I won't fuck you again. And if you keep looking at me like that, I absolutely *will* fuck you again."

"Looking at you how? I don't even like you."

"Ditto," he says as his lips land on mine. It's a quick kiss and he pulls away with his brows furrowed. "What kind of movie?"

Chapter twenty-six

Slow Burn by The Word Alive

We clean up the kitchen and settle on the couch. I have no idea what to expect from this movie she's picking out for us. I don't know much about movies or TV, period. I didn't watch TV in the foster homes I was sent to, and there sure as hell aren't people playing movies on the streets. But the giddiness radiating off her as she throws herself down on the couch, dragging me with her, is all I need to be satisfied. Anything to keep tears out of her eyes.

"Ten things I hate about you," I read the title out loud as she selects the movie on her enormous TV. "Are you subtly trying to tell me something, Firecracker?"

"Maybe." She shrugs, a sly smile playing on her lips. "Here." She places a pillow in her lap. "Lay down."

"Why?" I ask skeptically. I don't mean to sound questioning but all of...*this* is new to me.

She laughs and rolls her eyes. "Because I want you to. Not everything needs to be a fight, Jett."

She's right. Besides, we've already crossed every goddamn line I said I'd never cross with anyone, what's one fucking more? I lower myself onto the couch until my head is resting in her lap. She hits play and starts rattling on about how this is one of her favorite movies, and this and that, but I don't hear a word.

Her fingers move through my hair, gently scratching and

caressing my scalp, and my entire body melts under her soft touch. I'm a fighter, physically, mentally, and emotionally. My entire life has been surviving one hit after another, but I've never felt such savage hands. Because when she touches me like this, it penetrates my impenetrable skin and sinks directly into my fucking soul.

I may as well have died and gone to Heaven because this is the best thing I've felt in years. As much as I want to fight it, whatever is happening between us, my resolve is pretty much shit. With every tender stroke of her fingers, it's a punch to my chest, wearing me down.

"What's your favorite color?" she asks out of the blue.

"Don't have one."

"What?" She playfully slaps my shoulder. "Everyone has a favorite color."

I turn to face her, my head still in her lap, and she's smiling down at me. Fuck, I'm so goddamn screwed. Just the simple sight of her smile and those eyes has me as weak and pliable as putty in her hands. I've known it was happening since the first time I saw her but it's like a sucker punch to my gut right now.

I'm falling so fucking hard.

"I've never had the luxury of sitting around to think about something so…unimportant," I explain.

"Well, think about it now. Think of all the colors out there. Come on, close your eyes." She closes hers, that beautiful smile on her face. "What do you see when you close your eyes?"

I don't have to close my eyes to know what I see. Eyes wide open or eyes shut tight, I only ever see one thing. "Purple."

Her smile falters, and she opens her eyes, locking them on mine, so many emotions swimming in their depths. She's been used her entire life, a pawn in Hades' schemes, and has never once been in control of her life. Which means, this is no different. Her, here with me now, it's not her choice. I know this logically, but I can't help but question it. Because I swear everything I feel, I also see reflected in her eyes. Or maybe what I see is wishful thinking.

I close my eyes so I'm not forced to see what's in hers and so she won't be able to see what's in mine. Her fingers continue to slide through my hair. I can hear the movie playing behind me, but it's obviously been forgotten.

Then, it dawns on me.

Even with the uncertainty of everything happening between us, everything I'm going to do going forward, the championship fight and what comes after, my mind is utterly quiet.

I feel the same type of peace with her touch that I do when I'm fighting. I don't even remember falling asleep in her lap. The last thing I remember is one simple word.

Home.

Chapter twenty-seven

Cold-Blooded by Zayde Wolf

I don't want to be here. In this fucking glass box. With him watching my every move. The last few days I've spent with Jett have been nothing short of perfection and I want nothing more than to stay locked up in my suite with him for the rest of my life. Unfortunately, that's just not my reality. What happens when Raymond sends me to someone else? Jett already said he won't allow another man to touch me, and in this world, where I have zero control of my life, men *do* touch me.

This is all just a disaster waiting to happen.

It's not fair to me.

It's not fair to Jett.

Life absolutely fucking sucks ass.

I sigh and push out of the chair, my restless energy not allowing my mind or body to relax. I end up exactly where I've been every single time I've watched him fight, standing with my nose pressed up against the glass and my heart in my throat.

Ladies and Gentlemen, the Raymond Harris Arena welcomes you to the championship fight of the annual Titan Tournament!

Oh gods. My heart rate spikes even more as the announcer starts his welcome speech. In just minutes Jett will be in that ring, once again fighting for the win. Again, my only sense of relief is knowing Mordecai won't go for the kill. His father was a big part of the fighting community before he died, and he was one of the few who had honor.

I know Mordecai follows in his father's footsteps. I also know that means he's one hell of an opponent. I mean, he made it here to the championship fight. That says enough.

"...Mordecai, The Menacing Minotaurrrrr!"

The speakers boom with Ludacris' voice followed by Carrie Underwood as the song, *The Champion*, blares to life. I scoff. That's pretty presumptuous and really fucking arrogant of him to choose that song to walk out to. Then again, I suppose it's all about believing it, right?

I watch as Mordecai and a small group emerge from the tunnel, arms in the air, hyping up the crowd as they make their way toward the ring. Mordecai is massive and he knows how to use his size and strength, not to mention those dangerous horns on his head, and the tail that can trip anyone up. This is going to be one hell of a fight. I let out a shaky breath, my nerves really screwing with me.

"...and our new, favorite underdog, Jett Stephenssss!"

Once again, Jett walks out of the tunnel by himself with no music to accompany him. Only this time, the crowd goes wild, cheering and chanting his name as he walks to the ring unfazed by any of it. His sole focus is on Mordecai, but his face is blank, giving away no indication that he's nervous, anxious, or even excited about this fight.

I blow out a heavy breath as he steps into the ring and the gate is closed behind him.

"Let the fighting and bloodshed begin!"

I don't know what I was expecting but I wasn't expecting them to calmly walk to the center of the ring, exchange words, and then bump fists. There's a long, hushed pause as the crowd seems to all hold their breath at the same time, waiting on the edge of their seats for the fighting to begin. Then, it's as if my ears pop, and the world around me bursts.

Jett and Mordecai clash together.

The impact is so powerful I hear it all the way up here. They attack each other with everything they have, the sound of flesh hitting flesh making me wince. It looks like neither one is even trying to protect themselves. They're just doing everything they can to land hit after hit, oblivious to the hits they're taking. Blood runs from Mordecai's eyebrow and mouth, and even though Jett's taking equal punches to the face, there's no blood to be seen.

What in the hell are you? I've never seen a Mageía of any kind so...powerful. I'm knocked out of my thoughts as Jett lands a vicious punch to Mordecai's face, causing him to stumble backward, but he's only dazed for a second. Unlike Laszlo, it appears Mordecai can take a punch and he's charging at Jett as soon as he recovers, head down, horns angled right for Jett's stomach.

Jett sidesteps at the last second, grabbing onto his horns and using his momentum to flip him, body slamming his back into the mat. Then Jett is on top of him, delivering punch after punch to his ribs. I swear I hear the crack of bones before Mordecai's roar rips through the arena.

His tail wraps around Jett's neck, pulling him off his body. They both get to their feet, but Mordecai is leaning slightly to one side, cradling his ribs. *Oh gods, please let this be over soon.*

Jett takes advantage of the injury and rushes him again. He leads with a punch that Mordecai's tail stops, but it was just a distraction as his leg comes up, smashing into his injured ribs with immense force. Mordecai falls to his knee, cradling his side, and Jett's foot is there slamming into his chest, sending him flying back into the electric fence.

His entire body jerks as the electric current run through his body. He pushes off the fence and falls, facedown, onto the mat.

"Stay down, stay down, stay down," I whisper chant.

He doesn't. He slowly climbs to his feet and Jett lets him. They speak to each other again and I wish I knew what they were saying. Mordecai shakes his head. Jett nods, a frown pulling at his lips. Then he's airborne. He takes two steps and launches himself at Mordecai, his knee connecting with Mordecai's chin, sending a loud *crack* echoing through the arena. Mordecai's body flies back, slamming into the fence again, about five feet off the ground, before plummeting to the ground.

Jett wastes no time allowing him to get up again. He rushes over, flips Mordecai onto his back, and then slams his fist into his face.

Once. Blood goes flying.

Twice. A broken jaw.

He's about to punch again but stops himself short. He stands straddling Mordecai's body, looking down at him, chest heaving, bloodied fists clenched at his sides, but his face is serene and calm. He finally steps away.

Mordecai is knocked out.

The relief that floods through me is so intense, I have to hold myself against the glass to keep from falling. He did it. He won the Titan Tournament. Now he can stop fighting. He can get back to the reason why he came here in the first place; to figure out who he is.

I'm about to move when his voice over the speakers makes me look back down. He's standing off to the side of the ring where the reporter is, mic in his hand, and he's looking right at me.

"When I first entered this tournament, it was nothing more than to win a few fights, earn some money, and move on. But recent events have made me change my mind. I will be moving forward with title fights. I'm coming for you." He points to the viewing box. "For all of you." The crowd falls deathly quiet at his announcement and threat, all eyes on us.

I swallow against the fear that's quickly rising inside me. Jett, what have you done? He hands the mic back to the reporter and charges back to the tunnel in his *fuck everybody* attitude, and the crowd explodes. They chant his name as if he's the god down here instead of Raymond. I'm terrified to even turn around and see the look on his face. No one defies him. *Ever.* Especially not the way Jett just did. This can only mean one thing.

War.

I try to escape unseen, but I'll never go unseen. Raymond is always here to remind me of that.

"Meg." His voice is taunting, and I stop walking and turn to face him. "What do you have for me, pet?"

I shake my head. "Not much. I found out that he lost his parents at a young age and he's only here to try to figure out who he is. The only people he has in his life are Phil and that boy who's always hanging around. Whatever you're hoping to find, it's not there. He's not a danger to you, Raymond, and I refuse to be a part of this. I won't help you hurt him." I lift my chin in defiance, despite the fear making me want to puke. The feeling of his hand on my face, burning me, makes me squirm but I hold my ground.

I'm shocked when he throws his head back and laughs. "Oh Meg, my dear, my sweet. You've given me so much more than you realize." The evil mischief dancing delightfully in his gaze has my heart sinking in my chest. This isn't good. This is never good. "You may go." He waves his hand, dismissing me.

I'm so shocked at the dismissal that it takes a few seconds to get my feet moving. Once I do, I have to rein in my urge to run. To run from this room. To run from Raymond. To run and warn Jett. Whatever Ray has planned, it's not going to end well if Jett continues to fight against him. He may be insanely strong and hard to hurt, but there are other ways to lose, and the God of the Dead knows this little fact all too well.

I can feel the sand slipping through the hourglass. Time is

running out for everyone to walk away unscathed.

Chapter twenty-eight

Straight Out The Gate by Tech N9ne, Krizz Kaliko, Serj Tankian

A sense of urgency drives me as I head back to the locker room. I have this gut-wrenching feeling that something is wrong. I think it's Peggy trying to send me a message. She's remained at Phil's these past couple of days I've been with Meg. After what happened between me and Phil, I haven't made it back to figure out what's going to happen. I'm sure I don't have a place to stay any longer after what I did. As much as being on the streets doesn't affect me, for some reason, I've been hesitant to face Phil. I don't want to see the disappointment in his eyes and that's a new feeling for me. I've never cared about what anyone thinks of me before.

I don't have too long to dwell on the feeling as I'm confronted by the twins, Tianna and Tillie. Considering I basically just threatened them in front of thousands of people, I'm preparing myself for a fight. I slow my pace, eyeing them warily, fists clenched at my sides.

"Easy, pretty boy," the redhead, Tianna, laughs. "We're not here to fight you."

"We do all our fighting in the ring," Tillie says as she pushes off the wall she was leaning against.

"Forgive me if I don't trust you." I narrow my eyes at them. As far as I know, from what Phil told me, these two ladies harness the power of fire and ice. Since I fought the man with dragon fire, and it did little to my skin other than irritate it, I'm not too concerned about their magic, but I still don't need anything to pop off down here. Not when I have a point to prove.

Tillie shrugs. "You don't have to trust us, but you do need to come with us."

I scoff. "I'm not going anywhere with you."

"I'm afraid you don't really have a choice," Tianna declares. "These orders are from Raymond."

They both look at me expectantly as if just by dropping his name I'm going to jump into action and do exactly as they say. "Well, you can tell *Hades*," I use his real name, "to go suck a Titan dick."

"As much as I find your bravado amusing…." Tianna sways her hips as she approaches me slowly, her red eyes roaming down my body as she stops in front of me. "And would love nothing better than to play with you…." She drags a finger through the blood still wet on my chest and then sticks her finger in her mouth, slowly sucking it clean as she pulls it out. "Mm." She licks her lips. "I'm afraid we just don't have time."

"All the time in the world wouldn't be enough for me to spend one fucking minute with you." I push her aside as I continue down the hallway.

"Trust me, pretty boy," Tianna's voice follows me, "you'll want to see what Ray has to show you."

Something in the way she says it sends shivers running down my spine. Suddenly the only thing I can think about is Meg and what he might be doing to her right now.

I spin on my heels and grit my teeth. "Fine. Lead the way."

The twins link arms and lead me down the tunnel, but instead of heading to the locker room, we head toward the elevator. Once inside, I can't help but look at the number ninety, wishing I was here alone, pressing the number that would take me to her. My heart is beating too hard in my chest at the thought of her being somewhere in pain.

I barely register when Tillie lays her hand flat against the number panel, in a blank space at the bottom, and a hidden compartment is revealed. The button lights up as she hits it and we're suddenly going down. Of course, as if The Underworld isn't far enough underground as it is, we're going deeper into fucking hell.

When the doors slide open, Tillie and Tianna link arms again, leading the way down a dark and eerie tunnel. Much like the feeling I got when I first came to The Underworld, I feel the same sense of dread. I feel the darkness pushing in against me, warning me to turn back. And faintly, I hear distant voices, like murmurs and wails. I can't make out any words, but the message is clear.

Agony.

We step into a huge open cave illuminated with blue flames that seem to simply float in the air above us, giving the cave an eerie, cold, blue glow. Hades stands at the edge of a cliff, his back to me. I stop before getting too close.

"Thank you, ladies." Hades' voice is loud and clear in contrast to the whisper of voices around us. "You may go."

The twins turn and walk back the way we came. I glance around, looking for any signs of Meg, but there's nothing around us but rock walls and what looks like a huge drop on the other end of the cliff. I want to run over to it and look down, see if Meg is somewhere down there being held against her will, but I also am not going to join Hades at the edge of a cliff where he can throw me off either.

"Thank you for coming, Jett. I—"

"Where is she?" I ask, cutting him off. "I swear, if you hurt her again, I—"

His boisterous laugh cuts me off. "You'll do what, Jett? *Kill me*?" he mocks. "I assure you, she's perfectly safe…for the moment. However…." He finally turns to face me.

"Joey!" I lunge forward.

"Ah ah ah," Hades puts up a hand to stop me in my tracks. "Not too fast there, champ. We have some things to discuss."

My eyes are glued to Joey and the hand that's wrapped tightly around his mouth, keeping him from speaking or moving. His eyes are wide, locked on mine, and I can practically feel his fear. I don't know why I open my mouth. I don't know why I continue to lie to this poor boy. But I need to say something.

"It's gonna be ok. Don't worry. I'm not going to let anything happen to you."

And that's when I see it. The hope that fights its way through the fear. Joey believes me when I tell him that I'll save him, and I pray to God that I can. Hades' cruel laugh brings my attention back to him.

"Let him go. He has nothing to do with us," I order, familiar rage rushing through my veins.

"Oh, I do believe little Joey here has everything to do with this situation. Wouldn't you agree?" He looks down at Joey, finally removing his hand so the boy can speak.

"T, I'm sorry! Phil and Peggy tried to stop them but the Titans—"

Hades clamps his hand down on Joey's mouth again. "Now that's enough of that. We can't give too much away now, can we?"

I take another step forward before Hades shoots me a warning glare. "What did you do?"

"You behave and you'll have nothing to worry about. Phil and the others won't be hurt as long as I walk away from this little meeting."

"What do you want?"

"You know what I want. I want this nonsense you're spewing to stop. I want you to join me, be one of my Titans, and let's rule The Underworld together."

"Something tells me you don't share your reign with anyone."

He shrugs. "Well, you can be a prince down here, either way. Rich. Untouchable. I'll even give you *her*."

"She's not yours to give," I seethe.

"She is exactly that. *Mine,*" he growls. "And it's best for everyone if you, and her, remember that. I'm the one in control. Not her. Not you."

"I already told you once, I'm not going to fight for you."

"Well, then I guess Joey here pays the price. After all, he's the reason Tiberius is dead, is he not?" My eyes shoot up to his, and he chuckles, sending chills down my spine again. "Did you think I didn't know? Did you think I didn't know exactly who you are and what you did the first moment you stepped foot in my world?" I wish I could punch the smug look off his face. "I told you, Jett, I'm in control here."

He moves so fast I barely register it. Joey screams as he's held over the side of the cliff. I lunge again but Hades sends a line of blue fire in my direction. The heat is unlike any other fire I've encountered before. This fire will most definitely burn me.

He keeps the fire burning in his outstretched hand, but he motions with his head for me to come forward. "Come on, I know you're curious. Come have a look." He gestures over the side of the cliff where Joey's body dangles.

"No, please, I'm sorry! I can pay you back, please. Let me work for you and pay you back," Joey pleads.

I walk slowly to the edge of the cliff, trying to keep my eye on Hades, on Joey, and on what I'm about to see. Stand a few feet from the edge, I lean forward and look down, an immense lake larger than anything I've ever seen below me. An eerie blue light seems to come from underneath the water, allowing me to see beyond the surface. I can make out shapes swimming in the water. The voices sound louder as I watch them swim aimlessly.

Souls.

"This is The Pit of Souls," I say to myself.

"Bingo! And if you don't want sweet little Joey here to end up in it, I'd suggest you rethink my offer. I'm owed for the money I lost and for the Titan I lost. Either you agree to repay the debt, or I take what's owed."

"T, please!" Joey looks up at me, tears running down his face. "I don't want to die."

I'm suddenly pulled back to my childhood home and the intense fire blazing all around us. Jonah coughing as he tries to find a way out of my bedroom. Me, crouched down in the corner, scared and frozen. *"T, you've gotta find us a way out. I don't want to die."*

"What's it gonna be, champ?" Hades asks. "Last chance."

I look over at Joey, clinging to Hades' arm, tears running so fast down his cheeks it looks like someone opened a water faucet. "T, please. I'm sorry," he sobs. "I'm so sorry."

"Me, too," I whisper.

I look at Hades, and he sees the resolve in my eyes. He knows I refuse to bend to his whims. I refuse to fight for him. The devilish grin that spreads across his face is almost enough to make me freeze but I lunge for Joey as he releases his grip.

I fall to the ground, hand outstretched, reaching for Joey's falling body. I feel something tickle across my fingers and I grasp at it. Joey's scream as he falls into The Pit slices open my chest and pierces my heart. I watch as his body plummets under the surface, his body continuing to sink, a white ethereal shape stays lingering just under the surface.

His soul.

I swear I hear his voice wailing above the others. My eyes blur and I blink rapidly, trying to clear my vision, as I look down to see a few of his hairs trapped in my grip. Once again, I failed to keep someone safe. I promised him nothing would happen to him. I lied.

Everyone around me always dies. Because I'm fucking no one. I can't keep anyone safe.

My sorrow is quickly replaced by my anger. I let out an earth-shattering roar as I push off the ground to face the God of the Dead.

"Remember," he says, "I walk out of here or Phil dies too. Along with all the others in the gym."

"You're going to pay for this. You're going to pay for all of this." My body physically shakes with the effort it takes to remain in control when all I want to do is rip his fucking head from his body.

"No." He grins. "I'm not. Because this is what I do. This is who I am. And you…." He looks me up and down. "Are no one."

He turns his back on me and strolls out of the cave, leaving me to fume in my hatred alone. I turn back to The Pit and look down, no longer sure which soul is Joey's as they all mingle and glide under the surface. This image, and the sound of Joey's pleas and screams, are going to haunt me forever. Just like all the others, I couldn't save him.

What the fuck am I even doing here?

I'm not a savior. Never have been. Never will be. But I am a fighter. I can fuck his life up. I can fuck his world up. And that's what the hell I'm going to do.

"It doesn't end here, Joey. I'm just getting started."

T
Chapter twenty-nine

Since walking through the city half-naked, covered in blood, doesn't sound like the best choice, I stop at the locker room to throw a shirt on before heading to Phil's. As I approach his gym, I stop in my tracks. Glass litters the sidewalk, the glass door and all the windows shattered. To say I'm fuming is an understatement. It's one thing to come after me, but to hurt innocent people to get to me, that's where I draw the line.

This ends now.

I walk into the gym and it's even worse inside. The destruction is extensive, not one part left undamaged. Phil and a few others are cleaning up the mess, but honestly, it's going to take days. Not to mention a hell of a lot of money. Good thing I just happen to have half a million dollars. This is all because of me, so the least I can do is pay to repair it.

A familiar nudge on my fist draws my attention. "Peggy." I drop down to my knees, leaning my forehead against hers. "Are you hurt, girl?" The feeling I get through our bond tells me no, but I still take the time to look her over, only satisfied once I see that she's physically ok.

Seeing no other option, other than running away like a coward, I finally muster up the courage to approach Phil. We haven't seen each other or spoken since I hit him in the training room with Mordecai.

"Phil," I announce my presence. "This...." I look around, my rage still simmering just beneath the surface of my control.

"Well, kid. You weren't kidding when you said trouble finds you."

"This is all my fault, and I will pay for it all."

He heaves a heavy sigh, nodding. "It's unfortunate, but I knew what could happen by taking you in after what unfolded that first night. All of this can be replaced." He finally looks at me, defeat written all over his features, but he asks anyway. "Joey?"

I have to fight to control my emotions. The anger, yes, but also the sadness. The fucking guilt. Even though Joey got himself into trouble by getting in bed with the devil, I still feel responsible for what happened to him. He was a part of Hades' plan to break me down. And once again, I failed. I failed to save him.

I shake my head. Phil nods, blinking back tears. He knew it wasn't a hopeful outcome but having it confirmed is that last blow that finally breaks his heart. I think we're programmed to hold onto hope in order to survive, to remain sane, but once that hope is officially gone, we're forever changed.

"I won the tournament. I'm going after them. All of them. I'm going to end it. Their reign. Their power. *It. Ends,*" I say definitively.

Phil shakes his head. "I would try to talk ya out of it, kid, but I know better. You're gonna do what you feel you need to do. I won't stand in your way, but I won't be by your side either."

All I can do is nod in return. I knew Phil was a man of his word and his principles. I knew that walking away from him that day would seal my fate. I knew that he wouldn't accept me back under any circumstances. And yet, that godforsaken fucking hope. A small sliver of hope still lingered, a small part that thought just maybe I hadn't lost him. But now that it's confirmed, it's the final blow that cracks my heart.

"I'll grab my things and be on my way." I extend my hand to him and see the hesitation in his eyes. "Thank you, for everything.

Take whatever you need from the winnings to get this place fixed. Promise me." I grip the hand he finally offers, not letting it go until he says what I need to hear.

"I promise, kid."

I nod, letting go of his hand. I've never had anyone like Phil in my life. I've never had a sense of belonging or family since mine was taken from me, but I felt it here, with him. And I fucked that right up. It takes all my effort to keep the tears from welling in my eyes and to walk away from him. But I do.

I climb the stairs one last time. I enter the small bedroom one last time. I throw all my belongings inside my backpack, barely fitting it all in. I still don't have much, a life lived with the bare minimum is a hard habit to break, but I have more than I've had in a long time. The most important things I've found since getting here aren't things I can just pack away and take with me though.

I linger in the broken doorway of the gym, looking back at a place that had become a home. A family I had found. Far from perfect and not ideal, but found, nonetheless. And now, one I have to let go. The ache in my chest betrays my hard exterior.

"Come on, Peg. Let's find another place to lay our heads until this war is won and we can leave this wretched city."

I manage to get my feet moving, every step feeling heavier than the last. The weight of the world is on my shoulders, but if anyone can carry it, it's me. There's still one person counting on me, whether she wants to admit it or not. And I *will* save her.

Or I'll die trying.

Chapter thirty

Stay by Colorblind

A knock on the door has me running to open it. I don't know how I know it's him, I just do. When I tried to find him after the fight, he wasn't in the locker room. I even went to the stupid afterparty, thinking I might find him there even though we both hate those things. Of course, he wasn't there. So, I've been home, pacing for the past two hours, not knowing what else to do but wait and hope he shows up.

"Jett." I fling the door open and throw myself into his arms. "What happened? I couldn't find you."

"Worried about me, Firecracker?" His words are teasing, but there's none of the usual lightness or arrogance in his tone. Stepping out of his arms, I notice the backpack slung over his shoulder and the Pegasus by his side.

"I was hoping we could stay with you for a few days, just until we can—"

"Absolutely," I cut him off. "Of course, stay as long as you need." I move to the door, gesturing for them to follow me. The Pegasus firmly sits on her haunches, wings tucked in close to her body, with a slight snarl on her lips as she glares at me.

"Give us a minute?"

I nod. "Sure. Come on in when you're ready."

I walk just out of eyesight but linger close enough to hear, curious what Jett has to say.

"Peg, we talked about this. We don't have anywhere else to go and we need to keep an eye on her." A pause. "No, this is not up for debate. You mean a lot to me, Peg, but she does too. I need you to be with me on this and I need you to be nice." Another pause.

I mean a lot to him. I bite my lip, trying and failing to fight the smile spreading across my face. I thought I might mean something to him, but he's so hard to read, I wasn't sure if I was simply making shit up in my mind.

"It's only temporary," he continues.

And just like that, the smile is wiped from my face. I mean something to him, but I guess not enough to stay. Well, that blows. I shouldn't be surprised. He's been talking about this not being anything serious or permanent since day one. I guess I had just hoped he'd change his mind. I hoped that *I* would change his mind.

"Good girl," he says, and I walk a few feet away, acting like I'm busy with something at the bar as they walk in.

"Got it all settled?" I manage a small smile.

"Yeah." He sighs and dumps his pack on the couch before falling down alongside it. Peggy lays on the floor by his feet, her eyes never leaving me as I slowly make my way to the couch and sit down beside him. I tuck my legs underneath me and sit sideways, facing him.

His head is thrown back and he's looking up at the ceiling, but I know he's not actually seeing anything in this room. I've only seen this look in his eyes once before when he was talking about his parents, so I know it can't be good.

"What happened?" I ask as I gently rest my hand on his leg. I want to climb into his lap and kiss him until that look vanishes from his eyes. I want to ride him until pleasure is the only thing he's focused on. But sex isn't what he needs right now. He's quiet for a long time, not looking at anything except the ceiling. "You don't have to tell me, but I'm here, Jett. You don't have to fight this battle alone. I'm here, ready to fight with you. Ready to fight *for you*. Because sometimes, the fighter needs to be fought for."

He keeps his eyes locked on the ceiling, but his hand wraps around mine, holding it tightly. "On my first night here, I killed Tiberius." His voice is hollow. Expressionless.

"I know," I whisper my confession.

His eyes dart to mine, confusion written all over his face. "How? Did Hades tell you?"

I shake my head. "I was there. I witnessed it."

A pained look washes over his face, but he clenches his jaw, fighting against it. "So, you know what I am then."

"I know what you're capable of. What we're all capable of. But if you think for one second that I'm afraid of you, or think you're a killer, you're wrong. Maybe it's naïve, but I know you, Wonderboy," I tease lightly. "You're not like him or them. You're not a killer."

"That's literally what I am, Meg," he says angrily.

"You saved that boy. If you hadn't—"

"That boy is dead," he snaps. "I couldn't save him. Just like I couldn't save my parents, or Jonah, or Stacey. Just like I can't fucking save you, Meg. Because the only thing I've ever been good at is hurting people and failing the ones I care about."

His voice is so cold and angry, but the look in his eyes is anything but. They're shining with unshed tears that he's fighting to keep from falling, and it breaks my heart.

"You were just a kid, Jett. Gods, you were six years old! There was nothing you could have done. And the boy now—"

"Joey."

"Joey," I say his name softly. "Joey's fate was sealed the second he signed a contract with Hades. There's literally nothing you could have done to save him. What you did is extend his life. Even if it was for a short time, *you* gave him that. I know you don't think it's much, and this isn't what you want to hear, but it isn't your fault. None of this shit is your fault. It's been this way long before you got here, and it will be this way long after you leave."

"No, it won't," he says definitively.

"Yes, it will. Because you can't fight him, Jett. You can't win against a literal god."

He looks me dead in the eye, his blue eyes blazing with fire. All traces of the tears that were just there are gone. "Then I'll die trying."

"Gods!" I throw my hands up in the air and then slam them into his chest repeatedly. "Why? Why are you all like this? That's what Perseus said too! Why do you feel the need to save everyone?"

He grabs my wrists, holding them tightly as he pulls me close. "I don't give a fuck about saving everyone. Just you."

"And you think dying will save me?" I ask as the tears start to fall down my cheeks. "Huh? What do you think your death is going to do to me, Jett?"

He releases one wrist so he can wipe at my tears. "Nothing, Firecracker, because you don't even like me." He smirks weakly.

A choked sob escapes my throat as I try to laugh and fail. "I really don't like you right now."

"Is that right?" He pulls me onto his lap. "Then maybe you should fuck me like you hate me." His hand forcefully pulls my head down, and when his lips meet mine, there's a hunger in his kiss like I've never felt.

It's desperate.

And I match that desperation with my own because if he plans on fighting the Titans and facing Raymond, this may be the last chance I get to be with him.

His hands glide under my shirt and skim my skin before sliding up my back and gripping me firmly. His fingertips sinking into my skin, almost bruising, makes me moan into the kiss. I feel his dick getting hard between my legs and I grind against him, already slick with the promise of his punishing thrusts.

He's about to take my shirt off when I stop. "Wait," I say, already breathless from the kiss. "What about Peggy?"

"What about her?" he asks, nipping at my neck.

"She's right here, I dunno, like, watching us."

"Peg, go wait in another room."

A low growl has me looking over my shoulder at the massive teeth on display, but she gets up and walks out of the living room.

My shirt is practically yanked off my body and then his mouth is on my breast, biting my nipple through my thin lace bra. I cry out and arch into him, the warmth of his mouth and the sting of pain both bringing a different kind of pleasure.

My hands tug at his shirt and he stops to allow me to pull it off him. My eyes fall to his chest and stomach, spattered with dried blood from his fight. The image of him crouched over Mordecai, slamming his fist into his face, flashes in my mind.

"Does this bother you? I can go shower first if—"

"No." I shake my head. "It doesn't bother me. Watching you fight is...*difficult*, but it's one of the sexiest things I've ever seen." I pick up his hand, practically covered in dried blood, and bring it up to my neck. His eyes flash as his hand clamps around it. "Use me, Jett. Give me all that lethal grace. Show me what it's like to be at your mercy."

He growls and throws me down on the couch. His hand never leaves my throat while the other deftly pulls his shorts down and unleashes his hard dick. That same hand then grabs my panties, roughly pulling them down my legs. I lift my hips and help him as much as I can, eager to feel him inside of me. Once they're gone, my legs spread open, and he kneels before me. I have no warning and there's no easing into it as he slams into me in one hard thrust. I'm wet, but my body is not ready to accept all of him. I cry out as a shot of pain rockets through my core, but it's cut off as his hand starts to squeeze.

His other hand takes one leg and pushes it up, holding onto my inner thigh, spreading me wide as he fucks me with no remorse. It's hard and deep, little lightning bolts of pain radiating through me as he sinks in, but the pleasure is building quickly behind the pain. My nails dig into his upper arms as I hold onto him through it all.

"Fuck, Meg. You look so good taking all of me," he says as his eyes watch where our bodies collide. "So fucking beautiful."

My vision starts to spot, and I feel lightheaded. I'm close to cumming and close to passing out and not getting to enjoy it. But before I do, he releases my throat, and I suck in a huge breath of air. Then, I see stars. The world goes black, and bursts of color explode like fireworks as the orgasm rocks through me.

When I finally open my eyes, the world coming back into focus, I only have a few seconds to register Jett kneeling between my legs, his fingers pumping inside of me, curled up to hit the spot he loves so much. The spot that makes me squirt like a damn geyser.

"Come on, Little Firecracker," he urges me on. "Detonate all over me just the way I like."

"Oh, my gods. Yes! Jett!" I scream as the orgasm rushes out of me with a force I've never felt. It coats his abs, and he grins like an animal at the sight. His hand comes down in a loud, wet smack on my clit, sending a shock of pain through me and I cry out. He slaps my sensitive clit a few more times in rapid succession, the pain becoming almost unbearable, but then his head is between my legs, his soft tongue easing the pain as he laps at me like I'm his favorite fucking flavor.

I'm so sensitive, the slick press of his tongue is almost too much to take as he finds my clit and begins to stroke and suck it with the same desperation he kissed me with. I asked to be at his mercy, and he shows no signs of giving me a reprieve as he slides two fingers into me while his tongue continues to unravel me.

The third orgasm finds me seconds later, my body shaking uncontrollably, and I feel like a damn bowl of Jell-O trying to survive an earthquake. I barely register being flipped onto my stomach. He lifts my hips, placing one of the many pillows underneath me, and then I feel the delicious pressure of him sliding inside of me again.

His hands grip my ass, holding me wide open as he slides into me from behind. They're slower strokes now but just as deep and I moan into the couch at the sensation. Then a heavy hand falls onto my ass, a loud smack echoing through the room. I push my hips back, meeting his thrust.

"Again," I plead. "Spank me again."

His hand falls onto my ass again, and again, the sting of it making me cry out. I feel his hand on my ponytail and then the hair tie is pulled free, my hair cascading around me like a waterfall. His hand slides through it, gripping a handful at the base of my head, and then pulls.

My back arches, and my head is pulled back until I'm looking up at him where he's leaning over me from behind. "Give me those eyes, Meg." I barely manage to hold his gaze through the punishing thrusts as he brings me to yet another orgasm.

Then, he's flipping me around again like I'm nothing more than a ragdoll in his hands, letting him do with as he pleases.

"Is this what you wanted?" he asks, slapping my cheek. I cry out at the shock of it. My eyes focus and land on his.

"Yes," I breathe.

"You still want to be at my mercy?"

"Yes," I repeat.

He climbs up my body, straddling my chest as he slaps me again. "Open your mouth." I do, and he pushes inside, just as roughly as he did to my pussy.

He slides down my throat and I gag, not ready for the intrusion. He pumps his hips, fucking my mouth, giving me no relief. "Let me see those eyes," he orders.

I look up at him. He's so fucking massive. His body is huge and feels even more overwhelming literally on top of me. I can feel the strength in his legs as they straddle me. I can feel the strength in his hands as they grip my hair. I can feel the intensity of his gaze as he watches me. All of this, all of him, given to me, lights a fire so deep inside of me, there's no chance of ever putting it out.

This is who I want. The merciless fighter and lover.

This is who I want. The selfless lover who puts my needs first.

This is who I want. The man who eagerly wants to learn how to make pancakes.

This is who I want. The man who only has eyes for me.

This is who I want.

I feel the tears running down the sides of my face, and I'm not sure if it's because of his punishing dick being forced down my throat or the realization that I'm so fucking in love with him. He pulls out and I gasp. His hand grips my face.

"Do you want me to stop?" he asks, and I shake my head. *I don't ever want you to stop*, I think, but can't manage to say the words. "Good girl. Open." I do and he pushes two fingers inside my mouth aggressively. "Let me feel that tight little throat. Suck," he commands. He slaps my cheek again as I suck on his fingers, tasting myself.

He replaces his fingers with his dick and continues to fuck my mouth, moaning his pleasure and cursing about how fucking beautiful I am and how good it feels. I want to remember this moment forever and I try to capture it like a picture in my mind.

"Fuck, I'm going to cum," he mutters, seconds before his dick hardens even more. His hand starts to stroke his dick as he keeps the tip in my mouth. He spills inside me with a loud groan. I swallow it down, licking and sucking as his dick pulses. He holds himself up on the back of the couch and hangs his head with a content sigh.

He pulls out of my mouth and moves to the side of me, propping himself up on an elbow, the other hand reaching up to cradle my face. He wipes at the tears, a crease forming between his brow as he looks at me.

"Did I hurt you?"

I shake my head and smile. "No, I promise. That was...."

"Good?" he asks hesitantly.

I laugh. "Good? I mean, was it *just good* for you? That was...." I still can't find words.

He chuckles. "That was fucking mind-blowing for me."

"I saw fucking stars," I admit, laughing. "Literal. Fucking. Stars."

"Meg," he says, voice deathly serious. I give him my full attention. "I mean it every time I say that you're beautiful." He caresses my cheek as his eyes roam over my face, taking in everything before meeting mine again. "I don't deserve you."

I open my mouth to protest, but he kisses me before I can. All the previous fight and desperation is gone, replaced by a gentleness that threatens to break my fucking heart. Because I know this is him saying goodbye. One way or another, whether he leaves by choice or by death, he *will* leave.

It may not be today.

It may not be tomorrow.

But he will leave.

Chapter Thirty-one

Rise by League of Legends, Mako, The Word Alive, The Glitch Mob

I tried to talk him out of it until I was blue in the face. I may as well have been talking to a wall for all the good it did. He refused to change his mind, and now here I am, once again standing in this glass prison, preparing to watch him fight. Only this time, I'm watching him fight for his life.

"Ladies and Gentlemen!"

As soon as I hear the announcer's voice, my stomach flips. *Gods, I'm going to throw up.* I don't think I can do this. I don't think I can stand here and watch if he dies, and I'm beyond caring what Raymond will see or how he'll choose to punish me for it.

"...there hasn't been a title fight in three years, since Perseus tried to..."

Perseus. The last guy I actually dated. The only one I've ever let myself catch feelings for. He came in like a damn hurricane too. Winning fight after fight, until finally, he was able to challenge the Titans. I begged him not to. I begged him to let it go. I understood the love he had for the ring and the fights, but I begged him to let it just be that. Of course, he couldn't. He died at the hands of Tiberius, his first title fight.

And I was forced to watch.

It didn't matter that I loved him. It didn't matter how his choice would affect me. He did what he wanted because all fighters are selfish. All fighters only care about the win, the rush of the applause, and the worship from the crowd. That's what they truly love. And even though I haven't seen the same type of behavior from Jett, he's still being selfish in his way. He knows what's at stake, and if he loved me, if he cared about me at all, he wouldn't leave me.

I scoff internally. The only thing he's ever told me is that he'll leave. I don't know why I'm even surprised. We've only known each other for a month. Just because I fell for him, doesn't mean he fell for me too.

"...our favorite devious duo, Tianna and Tillieeee!"

The song, *Fire & Ice by the Nova Twins*, booms through the speakers as they run out of the tunnel, Tianna is shooting sparks out of her fingertips like miniature flashes of fireworks while Tillie showers the front row with tiny, delicate snowflakes. They're toned bodies are on display in little metallic shorts and sports bras that gleam underneath the arena lights, red for Tianna and blue for Tillie. Tianna's fiery red hair is pulled back in a ponytail and Tillie's is in a singular French braid down her back.

These two may look beautiful and harmless, but they're Titans for a reason. They're just as fucked up and depraved as the others. Their personal preferences lean towards sex, but I wouldn't want to be the one under their cruel hands. That being said, they're obviously good fighters as well. Not as good as Tiberius was, or Tison, but they can hold their own. Their magic plays a huge role in their winning streak though, and I'm nervous how that will play into tonight's fight with Jett. I've seen what his body can withstand, but I don't know if it can hold up against these two.

"...and the man sweeping through The Underworld, stirring up a storm, the undefeated champion of the Titan Tournament, Jett 'Wonderboy' Stephenssss!"

For the first time, the speakers come to life as he's

announced, playing *Rise by League of Legends*. I may or may not have given the nickname and song to the announcer before tonight's fight. My heart hammers in my chest as I watch Jett walk out of the tunnel. He's still reserved, not catering to the crowd, but his eyes look up. I know he can't see me behind the glass, but it feels like he can. I swear his eyes lock with mine as he subtly taps the band of his orange shorts where 'Wonderboy' is stitched in big, bold black letters, and he smirks.

He knows it was me.

I bite my lip, trying to contain my smile and utterly failing. That smirk, and that look, along with the combination of my nerves for what's about to happen, are not good for my heart.

He enters the ring like he always has, and the gate locks him inside with two psychopaths. The twins taunt him, but he remains looking bored and unaffected. If he wasn't standing in the middle of a fight ring, you'd never guess he was about to fight for his life. I don't know how he manages to remain so calm while I'm practically vibrating out of my skin.

"...this is a fight to the death." The announcer's voice is serious, reminding the crowd what's at stake. "Let the fighting, bloodshed, and killing begin!"

Without a second of hesitation, Jett is runs toward Tianna. Just as quickly, she sends a jet of fiery, red flames his way. If he feels anything, he doesn't show it as he runs head-on into the flames and plants a firm kick to her stomach, sending her flying into the fence.

Tillie shoots sleet from her fingertips, sending the shards hurtling at his body. Again, he acts like he doesn't even feel it as he approaches her. She's expecting him though and puts up a fight. She's fucking and dances out of the way of his blows, sending icicle shaped daggers, flying through the air. Red marks form on his skin as he takes the onslaught of hits, but his skin refuses to break.

Tianna re-joins the fight and they both go at him with

everything they've got. It's hard to actually see what's happening behind the bouts of fire and torrents of ice, and at one point he disappears from view completely and my breath sticks in my chest. Then Tillie's body flies through the air, slamming against the fence before dropping to the mat in an unconscious heap.

As the ice and flames clear, I see Tianna on Jett's back, holding on for dear life before he grabs her and pulls her off, slinging her over his head and slamming her body down hard onto the mat. It's clear she loses the air in her lungs, and she's completely dazed as he goes to his knee behind her. He lifts her back off the mat and holds her head in a grip that threatens to snap her neck.

His eyes once again travel up to the glass box, but this time, I know who he's seeking out as he shouts, "Is this what you want? Her death?"

The crowd goes wild, chanting.

Death!

Death!

Death!

His arms tense, preparing to end her life, and I squeeze my eyes shut. I couldn't fathom watching him die, but I also can't stand to watch him murder someone like this. In cold blood. For the fucking entertainment. Achingly slow seconds tick by, and I'm suddenly drowning in the sound of blood rushing through my ears and my heavy breathing.

The crowd has gone silent.

I open one eye cautiously, then the other. Jett stands in the middle of the ring, a live Tianna at his feet, clutching at her chest. Tillie stirs from her spot a few feet away, slowly regaining consciousness. Jett lifts his chin defiantly, still staring at the booth, a direct fucking challenge to Raymond, and my blood runs cold. He's refusing to kill. I know it's to deliberately defy Ray, but I also know it's because that's just not who he is. He isn't like them. He isn't a killer.

He turns his back on us, turns his back on the twins, and walks to the gate, demanding to be let out. The guard looks up nervously, seeking approval, to where I know Ray is sitting behind me, watching everything unfold. The guard clearly doesn't know what to do. Jett won but he didn't complete the task.

When he refuses to open the gate, Jett grabs hold of the door, grits his teeth against the electricity that must be shocking the shit out of him, and pulls the gate off its hinges. He tosses it to the side and storms out of the ring.

My relief as he walks out of that cage is only felt for a brief second before it's overrun by more anxiety. I slowly turn to face Ray. His eyes are glued to the ring, his face unreadable, but blue flames flick at his fingertips, betraying just how furious he is. The thing about him is he won't just knee-jerk react. He'll bide his time and play it all out until he has the perfect plan.

Then, he'll strike.

I use his current distracted state to quietly slip out of the booth and rush home to wait for Jett. Not only do I want to feel his body safe and alive under my hands, I also want to make sure he's really ok. And, most importantly, I want to ask him what in the hell he's fucking thinking!

Chapter thirty-two

Warning by Morgan Wallen

After a solid twenty minutes of Meg trying to decide if she wanted to scold me or pamper me, I finally got her into bed. Honestly, it wasn't that difficult to do. Her desire for me physically is just as strong as mine is for her. And, well, those base instincts are hard as fuck to control, not that I'm trying to control mine.

I know she's worried about me, but what she fails to understand is I'm worried about her too. I can't just sit back and do nothing. Those burns and bruises on her face solidified my decision to take on this fight. I won't let her become another Stacey.

"Mm." Her soft, relaxed moan brings my attention back to her. "I love when you do this. I've never been so incredibly relaxed before. Ever," she mumbles into the pillow.

"I love touching your skin," I admit as my fingertips continue to slide across her naked back.

She thinks I'm drawing lazy, haphazard circles against her skin, when I'm actually writing out my innermost thoughts like unspoken confessions, daring to hope they'll sink IN and become real, just like the snakes and lion did on my skin.

Beautiful. Well, that one's already true.

Happy.

Free.

Stay...

...I love you.

Those three little words absolutely terrify me. I've never really known love, not really. But what else could this be? The pounding in my chest every time I think about her. The somersaults my stomach does when I see her. The way my mind clears and goes silent when I touch her. And when I kiss her, when I slide inside of her...fuck me. The entire world disappears and nothing else matters but her. So, if this isn't love, then I don't know what the fuck it is.

"You're awfully serious for someone who just got laid. *Twice.* What are you thinking about?" Meg teases, rolling onto her side slightly so she can look up at me. The fake light from a magical sunrise with no actual sun is starting to brighten up her bedroom with a golden glow.

I take a few seconds to look at her. Her skin is shimmering more constantly now. Not quite the glow she gets when she cums, but if what she told me is true, then this means she's happy. She's happy being here with me. And if her shimmering skin isn't enough to make me believe it, I see it the beautiful purple eyes looking up at me. There's no mistaking the happiness shining through them. And if that's still not enough, the beautiful smile gracing her lips is more proof. It's not playful. It's not teasing. It's a genuine, happy smile.

I gently trace her lips with my fingertips before I lean down and feel them press against mine. If I never get to taste another thing on this planet but her sweet mouth, it would be enough. And that's exactly the way I kiss her now, showing her with my lips and tongue just how fucking much I love the way she tastes. I'll never get enough.

She pulls away first. "Don't," she whispers.

"Don't what?"

"Don't kiss me like that."

Her strangled voice pulls like barbed wire wrapped around my heart. I tilt up her face, noticing the tears welling in her eyes. "Like what?"

"Like you're never going to kiss me again. Like you're saying goodbye."

"I might die in the ring tonight. You know this as well as I do."

"Then don't do it!" she pleads. "You don't have to do this. You can stop right now. You can—"

"I can't," I say sternly, my tone harsher than I intend.

She clenches her jaw, her own frustration fighting to get through. "I admire your fearlessness but it's bordering on stupidity. I understand your ignorance about this world and about Hades, but there's no excuse when I'm sitting here *telling* you this isn't going to end well even if you survive the ring. Don't you get that? This is a fight you can't win, Jett. It's just not worth it."

"I appreciate your concern, I really do, but I decide which fights to fight, Firecracker. I decide what's worth it," I say, slipping out of bed.

"Where are you going?" Her voice sounds panicked as she sits up, eyes following me as I pull on my underwear.

"I need to train. I need to prepare for tonight's fight and get my head right."

"But you just got here, and you have all day...."

I turn to face her and that fucking barbed wire pulls tighter. I can feel the little barbs sinking into my heart every time I cause her pain. If only she knew that I feel the pain too.

I lean over the bed and cradle her face in my hand. "If I survive tonight against Titus, and tomorrow against Tison, I promise, we'll talk about what comes next for us. But right now, this next fight needs to be my focus." I take just one more second to look at her before placing a kiss on her forehead. I pick up the rest of my clothes and leave her kneeling on the bed, alone, watching me leave.

"Jett!" The pleading in her voice makes me stop, but I don't turn around to face her. "Stay. Choose me."

God, I want to. I want to turn around and fall back into her arms, but if I do, she'll never be safe. She'll never be free. So, I continue walking out of her room without a word. It's one of the hardest things I've ever had to do, but I'll use this moment to fuel myself for the fight tonight and hope that if I survive, she'll forgive me.

Chapter thirty-three

Arcade by Duncan Laurence

I don't have a partner to spar with, but I go through the motions anyway. I pretend I'm listening to Phil, all those hours and hours of instruction making it easy to hear him as if he was still with me.

Move your feet, kid. Stay focused and don't get distracted.

Protect yourself. Arms up. Don't drop your guard.

Gallop. Cross. Hook. Two.

Gallop. Cross. Hook. Two.

I spend the majority of the day going through the motions as best I can, and lifting weights, prepping my body for tonight's fight. There isn't much I can do being solo, but then again, I've gotten this far being solo, haven't I? It's sort of fitting that I finish what I started solo too.

As I'm leaving the training room to head to the locker room to get ready for the fight, I'm approached by my opponent and my body automatically shifts into fight mode. My mind is alert, body loose and relaxed but adrenaline is pumping through at the same time.

Titus stops a few feet in front of me. He's one of the few people I actually have to look up to. He's incredibly tall, pushing seven feet, and his hair blows in a constant breeze that he controls.

"I'd be worried you're here to start our fight early if it wasn't the same old song and dance with you Titans and the *'I only fight in the ring'* bullshit. So, what the fuck do you want?"

"Hades wants to see you."

I laugh sarcastically. "I bet he does. You can tell Hades to go choke on your dick."

Titus smirks. "He thought you might say that." He sends something floating on a breeze in my direction. I hesitate but grab it out of the air as it approaches. It's a lock of smooth, chocolate-brown hair that I'd recognize anywhere.

"That motherfucker," I say through clenched teeth. "Where is she?" I take an aggressive step forward, but a gust of wind holds me at bay.

"She's unharmed, for now, but she won't be if you refuse to go see him. I wouldn't leave him waiting long if I were you. He's patient to a point, but he's also extremely quick to anger."

I clutch her lock of hair in my fist and move to step around Titus. His hold on the wind eases, allowing me to pass without having to fight against him. "I'll see you in the ring," I snarl as I pass by.

"We'll see," he responds with amusement.

All I can do is ignore him and head to Hades' office. One problem at a time and this problem is by far the most important. This is exactly what I was afraid would happen, that he would use her to get to me. I tried to keep what was between us casual, but fucking failed miserably, and now I'm paying the price.

It's easy to fight and throw your own life away, and it's impossible to force someone into doing something when there's no bargaining chip to use. That's why I've always survived so well in the past. I've never had the same weaknesses most people do. Family. Friends. People they love. But now I've already lost Joey to this monster, Phil fucking hates me, and it will break whatever is left of my sanity if he hurts Meg. If he takes her away from me for good, I'll become nothing more than the heartless and evil beast I've fought so hard not to become. Hades will fucking regret it if he does anything to her. Surely, he knows that.

I barge into his office without bothering to knock, the doors slamming into the walls as I fling them open. I'm halfway across the room when I stop dead in my tracks. Hades is perched like a cocky asshole against the front of his desk, a smug fucking grin on his face. But what stops me is seeing Meg sitting in his chair behind the desk, eyes wide with fear, but she doesn't appear to be hurt. She's not tied up or gagged or anything. She's not being held against her will. At least not physically.

"Ah, Jett. So wonderful of you to join us."

I look down at the lock of hair sticking out of my fist, then up to Meg's eyes, before settling on his. "What the fuck's going on here? Why am I here?"

"Why *are* you here, Jett? That's always been the question, hasn't it?" He pushes off the desk and strolls over to his bar cart. "So, let's dig a little deeper into that question." He talks while he pours himself a drink. "Let's start with why you're here right now, in my office. Are you sure I can't interest you in a drink?" he asks, gesturing to the cart. "This is going to be one hell of a story."

The malicious gleam in his eyes makes me clench my fists tighter. I want nothing more than to punch that look off his fucking face. "Let her go," I answer, ignoring his question. "She has nothing to do with this. Whatever this is, it's between you and me. It always has been."

His laugh is pure evil and makes me want to cringe. "Oh, on the contrary, Meghana here, my dear, sweet little pet, has everything to do with it. I'm sure you know by now that she works for me."

"She doesn't *work* for you," I spit out. "You keep her loyal with threats against her and her mother. She's your pawn, but I'm going to fucking change that. She's done being your tool, Hades."

He looks at Meg, a humorous look of pity on his face. "Aww, pet, do you hear that? It's really quite sweet actually," he says as he walks back to the desk, standing beside the chair Meg still occupies. "You got the poor fool to fall for you." He finally looks back to me. "Do you know why she's sitting behind the desk, in my chair?"

I grit my teeth. "Why?"

He laughs. "Because she's the true master behind all of this. She told me about your family and why you're here." My eyes shoot to Meg's, completely thrown off balance by what he's saying. "She told me about your relationship with Phil and that boy." I can't believe she had told Hades everything I shared with her. "But you know what she did the best? She got you to fall in love with her." He chuckles. "Oh, you poor fool, though I can't blame you. She is a pretty little thing, isn't she?" he asks, running a hand down her arm. She flinches at his touch but remains silent. "She only started seeing you because I told her to. You see, she doesn't do anything without my explicit instruction. She's the perfect little actress, isn't she?"

Every new word out of his mouth is poison sinking into my skin. I remember back in the hall when I first spoke to her and how adamant she had been that I would never touch her. Then, the next time I saw her, she had completely changed her tune. All because she was ordered to. And I knew she worked for him, but I couldn't bring myself to believe that what was happening between us was a lie. Fake.

I look at her now, sitting at his desk like the perfect little doll.

"Is it true? You only started seeing me because he told you to?"

She swallows. "Yes, but—"

"Fuck me!" I run my hand through my hair and start pacing, the familiar jolt of anger making me want to run my fists through these walls. I think back on everything that's happened between us. All the words she said to me. "You told me again and again that you didn't even like me." I huff out a sarcastic laugh. "I thought you were being fucking coy, not that you were actually telling me the fucking truth."

"No!" she protests. "It's not like that. It might have started out like that but—"

I cut her off again, not wanting to hear another single false thing fall from her lips. I try to laugh, but it comes out strangled, more of a choke. "You wanted me to choose you when you were never free to give yourself to me. You know, I told myself a million times that I would be the one to break your heart. I never thought you'd be the one to break mine."

"Jett, please! Let me explain!" she begs, tears falling down her cheeks. For once, they don't pierce my heart. Because they're not real. None of it is real. Phil's voice echoes in my mind.

Everything she does, she does for him. She's no more than a tool, Hades' whore—

That's all he was able to say before I laid my hands on him. He was just trying to protect me. He was always the one trying to protect me. And what did he get for it? My fist and my back as I walked out on him. Regardless of what she thinks, I had already chosen her, again and again.

I walk to the desk and toss her hair onto it. "Well, I guess you got what you needed out of me." I turn to leave when Hades' voice stops me.

"We're not done."

This time, I do laugh as I turn around, but it dies in my throat as I see the glint of a sharp blade pressed against Meg's throat, blood trickling down, staining her lavender dress. After everything I just found out, I hate that I'm immediately panicked at the sight. The way she feels about me may not be real, but that doesn't mean that Hades isn't right. I fucking fell for her. I love her. No truth in the world is going to change that.

"What do you want?" I ask, giving Hades my full attention.

"I want to make a deal." He smirks.

"Jett, no!"

Hades' hand clamps down on Meg's mouth, the knife never

once wavering.

"What kind of deal?"

"I want you to give up that impressive strength of yours for the next fight. I want my Titan to have an actual chance of beating you. I want a fair fight."

"If your Titan has magic, I hardly call that a fair fight."

"No magic. Just a man against a man."

I narrow my eyes. "That's all you want? Just a fair fight?"

He nods. "I'll even take the death requirement off the table. Just a fight to see who actually wins when you don't have your power or impenetrable skin to aid you. Nothing more, nothing less."

"Why?" I ask suspiciously.

He shrugs. "Curiosity. I want to see what you're really made of."

"And what happens if I win?"

"If you win, you get to leave The Underworld. You'll have your life to do with as you wish, just not here."

"And if I lose?"

"If you lose, you have to stay and fight for me, as a Titan. You'll have your strength back, but it will be under my control. You'll do whatever I tell you to do."

"I'll agree to this deal under one condition," I say, and he smirks. "Meg goes free. She's no longer yours to use."

"Agreed."

"I'm serious, Hades. Meg goes free, and she's not to be hurt in any way, by you or anyone who works for you. She can stay here if she wishes, or she can leave The Underworld. It's her choice and you will have no say. You will also not harm her mother," I add, remembering how he threatened her with that little detail.

"Done." He steps away from Meg, removing the blade from her throat. She reaches up to cradle her neck, a sob escaping. Hades snaps his fingers, and a parchment appears in front of me along with a pen. "To recap, you give up your strength for this next fight where no magic will be used. Death is also not a requirement for the winner to be announced. Win, and leave. Lose, and you're mine. Either way, Meg is free and never to be harmed from this point on from my hand or any hand that I command, and her mother is safe. Did I get all that right?"

I listen to his words carefully, trying to make sure he hasn't twisted anything, but I can't find anything out of place. I nod. The pen hovers closer to me.

"Then sign our contract and bind our deal."

I grab the pen out of the air. "Jett, don't agree to this! His deals are always rigged somehow. You can't win this!"

Her pleas go in one ear and out the other as I sign my name to the contract. Once it's done, the pen and parchment disappear in a burst of blue hellfire, and I immediately feel whatever power has been with me from birth seep away, as if the blood is being drained from my veins. I stagger under the feeling, catchingmyself against the desk.

Hades approaches and grabs my wrist, turning my arm out. "Just a small nick to see if our deal is in place," he says as he slices my forearm with the knife.

I hiss as the blade sinks into my skin, parting my flesh in a swift slice. Blood immediately seeps out of the wound.

"Wonderful." Hades grins mischievously. "Oh, before you go, I almost forgot to address the second reason why you're here, in The Underworld. You told Meg you lost your family to a home invasion, yes? A robbery gone wrong?"

"Yes."

"Hmm," he feigns contemplation. "That's not actually what happened. Would you like to know the truth? It's the reason why you came here after all, isn't it?"

"You know it is," I say through clenched teeth, finally getting my feet back under me.

"Well, you see, the portal keeping us locked down here, and without our powers above ground, has slowly been weakening. You can imagine my delight." He waggles his eyebrows. "And I plan on once again reigning on Earth. Only, there's this prophecy. I won't get into the details, but basically, it states someone will come along and ruin everything I've worked for."

"What does this have to do with me or my parents?" I ask getting impatient.

"As you can imagine, I'd been seeking this person out for a *very* long time when low and behold, there were whispers of a young boy with inhuman strength living right here in Chicago." He pauses, smiling that wicked smile. "Have you figured it out yet?" My mind is reeling with what he's saying, but I don't quite make the connection. When I don't answer, he continues. "It's clear you haven't, so let me give it to you straight. The prophecy is about you, Jett. I had your parents killed, along with who I assumed was you, but was in fact another young boy."

"Jonah," I whisper to myself, the memories of that night and their screams rushing back full force, staggering me once again. Hades doesn't seem to notice, or at least doesn't care, as he continues.

"Imagine my surprise when you turned up in The Underworld. Of course, I had to get my best asset to work on the case." He winks at Meg. "I had to figure out what you knew and why you were here. And now, it doesn't matter because you're going to die and be out of my way once and for all." He shrugs.

My mind is quickly pulled off the fact that *he* had my parents killed. They were murdered...*because of me*. Because of some goddamned prophecy I don't even believe in. That *he* tried to have *me* killed. And the fact that he's planning on succeeding in doing so now. "You said that death was off the table in the fight."

"Nooo," he draws out. "I said that killing wasn't a *requirement.* It's very much still on the table if the fighter chooses to do it, and trust me, Tison has been *dying* to kill you."

"What the fuck are you talking about? I'm not fighting Tison tonight, I'm fighting Titus."

"Oh, did I not mention I made a fight card change? Oops, apologies."

All I can do is shake my head and laugh. I knew Chicago would be my downfall the first night I got to town. I should have left when I had the chance because this is what happens when I try to play hero. I fucking lose *everything.*

Because I'm not a hero.

Never have been.

Never will be.

I look at Meg, still sitting there, crying as if she fucking cares.

"Well, you must be pretty damn proud of yourself right now. You did exactly what you were supposed to do and now you're free. Your mom is free. Congratulations to The House, who always wins. Let's at least put on one final show, shall we?"

I turn to leave, ignoring Meg's cries as she calls out to me. Her hands pull on my arm before I get too far.

"Jett, please, don't walk away from me. Not like this. I—"

I yank my arm out of her hold. "You know, a firecracker is harmless if you don't let it near you, but set it off too close, or hold onto it when you shouldn't, and it can fucking destroy you. I should have never let you near me. I should have never held onto you."

I walk away with the feeling of her hands on my skin, lingering like never before, and my heart in shreds as the barbed wire successfully does its job. I've always wanted to feel the pain others feel, and now that I feel it, now that I feel my heart being ripped from my chest, I welcome the fight to come. I welcome the physical pain I'm about to feel. In fact, I pray that it's enough to make me forget this soul-crushing feeling I feel now.

I pray for death.

Chapter thirty-four

Worth The Fight by No Resolve

I'm left standing in Raymond's office, watching a weak and disoriented Jett head straight for his death. Even though Tison doesn't have magic like the twins or Titus, he is the strongest Titan by far. He doesn't need additional magic when his arms are made of solid fucking rock. Literally.

Once again, Ray's deal is twisted and one-sided. There can ever only be one winner when he makes a deal, and that winner is him. How many times did I try to warn Jett? He never believed me. Maybe that arrogance finally got the better of him, thinking he could win against the God of the Dead.

I turn my rage on Raymond. "You're a sick fucking bastard."

"Sticks and stones, Meg. A deal is a deal. You're free to go."

I narrow my eyes, watching him suspiciously as he takes the seat behind his desk. "You didn't include anything in the deal that made my freedom a mirage?"

"Nope. Your service to me is done. You can stay in The Underworld if you wish, but you'll need to find new lodgings. You will not remain in my building. I'll give you one week to figure it out."

He doesn't even look at me as he works at his desk, no doubt getting the books ready for bets on tonight's fight. The majority of the crowd will bet on Jett to win, not knowing that the fight has been rigged.

Ray will bet on Tison and will bring in hundreds of thousands of dollars. Just another day in the life of the God of the Dead.

I scoff. "You raised me. You're the only person I've ever known as a parent figure, and as evil as you are, a part of me always wanted to please you. To seek your approval and make you proud. And you don't give two shits about a girl you raised. You'll toss me out like a bag of trash. Just like that."

"Just like that," he says as he continues to work.

"You'll get what's coming to you, *Hades*. It may not be today or tomorrow, but you will."

He doesn't respond, thoroughly ignoring and dismissing me. I turn and leave his office for the last time, my mind quickly turning to Jett and what's about to happen in just a few hours. He's going to get in that ring and he's going to die.

I race to the elevator and up to my floor, barging in, yelling, "Peggy! Peggy where are you?"

She comes trotting out of the hallway. I've heard about the connections Pegasus' have with their bonded and I wonder if she feels what's happening to Jett right now.

"Listen, I know you don't really like me, but I need your help. We need to help Jett. I don't know if you can actually understand my words or not, but Jett's in trouble, and I don't know what to do. Can you take me to Phil?"

I'm not sure what I was expecting, but Peggy barks, the sound loud and quite vicious, with a low growl lingering at the end. I flinch as she launches toward me. This is it. This is how *I* die. But she darts around me and out the door. I'm dazed for a second before I charge after her.

Getting in the elevator, I hit the button for the main lobby floor. "I'm assuming Phil is topside?" Another bark of confirmation. "Ok." I nod my head and rub my sweaty hands against the material of my lavender dress. Shit. I should have at least changed into something I could move better in. No time.

We both rush out of the elevator as the doors slide open. The lobby is packed with people coming in for the fight and we push our way through the throng of people, finally getting some space once we're outside. We move quickly through the market and into the tunnels that lead to the subway and the entrance to The Underworld.

I've walked this path too many times to count, coming topside as often as possible, hoping and praying for a miracle to happen, something to set me free. And my prayers have finally been answered. Jett was sent and now I'm free. But the air has never felt more suffocating than it does now as I step out of the subway and onto the sidewalk.

I remove my heels that are slowing me down and nod to Peggy. "Fast," I say. "But don't lose me."

I hike up my dress around my thighs, holding my shoes in one hand, as we race through the city. I can't even imagine what a sight we must make, and I couldn't care less. This is the first time I'm not trying to hide topside, but I've never felt more trapped in my life. I don't want my freedom at the cost of Jett's life. I'd rather be a prisoner knowing he's alive than living every single free day with the knowledge that he died for it. That he died for me.

No. I refuse to let him die. This isn't how it ends. This isn't how *we* end. It can't be.

Peggy stops in front of a building that looks like it's under construction. I'm about to start fuming and yelling at the damn Pegasus for leading me on a wild goose chase when I look up at the broken sign.

Phil's Gym.

I let out a sigh of relief, trying to finally catch my breath, as I lunge for the door. We rush inside in such a whirlwind that the man in the office looks up from his desk.

"What is the meaning of..." He pushes up from his desk, walking around it and kneeling as Peggy dashes into his office. "Peggy." She starts barking furiously. "Whoa, it's ok, girl. You know I can't understand you like Jett can."

His eyes finally look up to me, where I'm standing in the doorway, chest heaving and feet throbbing from pounding on the cement the entire way here.

"I know who you are and who you work for. Where's Jett?" he asks accusingly, getting to his feet, eyeing me like I'm some sort of villain. I guess to him, I am.

"He's in trouble. We need your help," I say, still gasping for air. "I don't know what to do but you have to help him, Phil. He's going to die! They're going to kill him in the ring tonight! He made a deal with Hades and his strength is gone and he's fighting Tison and Tison will kill him if we don't—"

"Whoa, whoa, whoa, calm down. Take a breath. I can barely understand a word that's coming out of your mouth."

I close my eyes and take a couple of deep breaths, trying to steady my nerves and gain some semblance of control. When I open my eyes again, Phil is looking at me expectantly, but patiently.

"Alright, that's better. Now, tell me what's going on. Slowly, this time."

I do. I tell him everything that happened in Hades' office. About the prophecy and his parents. About the deal he made and why he made it.

Because of me. To save me.

"I don't know what to do but we have to try and stop this from happening. He can't die!"

"Let me think, let me think." Phil starts pacing his office. Peggy and I both watch, desperately waiting for him to say something.

Finally, he stops. "Did the deal mention anything about outside interference in the fight?"

I scrunch my eyebrows and close my eyes, thinking back to the exact words. "No, it just mentioned that Jett had to give up his strength and no magic would be used by Tison. There was nothing about anyone coming to his aid though. That's never happened in a title fight before."

"It's The Underworld, sweetheart, nothing is fair and the crowd lives for a little chaos. I need to make a phone call, and Peggy...," he turns to face her, "I know it's not in your nature, but you're gonna need to use them teeth tonight." She growls, pulling back her lips and showcasing just how dangerous those teeth really are. "Let's go," Phil says, grabbing his phone and keys from his desk.

We travel back to The Underworld in haste, but not quite as fast as Peggy and I did, which my lungs and feet are grateful for. We make our way quickly and silently to Raymond's building. I'm not sure what's going through Phil and Peggy's minds, but all I can think about is Jett in that ring with Tison, getting brutally beaten. Tison will end up killing him, but not before he makes Jett suffer.

Once we're back inside the building, my anxiety skyrockets. The crowd that was just in the main lobby, is gone. The fight must be about to start or has possibly already started.

"Oh gods, please don't let us be too late," I whisper.

The elevator takes us down. As soon as the doors open, the noise of the crowd hits me like a brick wall. The fight has definitely started. Instead of heading straight for the arena, Phil heads to the tunnel that leads to the locker rooms. The same tunnel the fighters come out of when they're announced to fight. I want to protest, to yell at Phil that we're wasting time, but I don't exactly have a plan. I went to him for a reason, I need to trust that he's thought of something.

A large form pushes off the wall as we approach. "Mordecai."

Phil's voice is full of relief. "Thank you for coming."

"Are you kidding? Happy to help, and happy to have a chance at Tison. What's the plan?"

"Other than making sure Jett doesn't die, there isn't one," Phil says. "Let's go. The fight has already started."

I trail behind them, still not exactly sure what's going to happen or what I can even do at this point other than watch like I always have. As we emerge from the tunnel, I immediately notice the ring. The fencing has been taken down and it's just an open dais, a raised stage with nothing to interfere from the crowd watching the slaughter. And in the middle stands Tison and an already bleeding Jett.

Tison backhands Jett, sending him flying across the dais like a ragdoll. The crowd *oohs* and *ahhs*, and Tison's deep laugh seems to echo through the arena. He walks over to where Jett is struggling to stand and yanks him to his feet before plowing his fist into his face, sending him to the mat again. It's exactly like what Tiberius did to Joey. Without his strength, Jett doesn't stand a chance.

Then there's a brilliant flash of white wings as Peggy launches into the air, headed straight for Tison. There's a brief silence as the crowd takes in what's going on before they explode in shouts.

Peggy lands on his back, her vicious teeth latching on to where his shoulder meets his neck. She shakes her head back and forth, ripping at the skin, but her attack is cut short as Tison latches onto her neck and pulls her off, sending her flying off the dais.

"Peggy!" I hear Jett's frantic cry as he watches her crash to the floor beyond the dais in a whimper of pain.

Mordecai jumps up onto the dais, stealing Tison's attention. My feet are moving again but I don't know what my intention is other than getting to Jett. Mordecai and Tison start to fight, I can hear the brutal hits, the grunts of pain, but they're nothing more than a blur in my peripheral, my main focus on Jett.

I climb onto the dais, thankful that Jett is on the edge, away from where the fight continues, but still too close for comfort. "Jett!" I cry as I kneel beside his broken and beaten body. All that glorious golden skin and muscle is covered in so much blood that I can't make out where he's actually hurt.

"What are you doing here, Firecracker?" His voice is strangled, filled with pain as he looks up at me with one bloodshot blue eye. The other is swollen shut, blood gushing from a cut above his eyebrow and another on his cheek. "You're free."

"Like it or not, I'm not leaving until I know you're safe. Can you get up?" I ask, looking down at his body. His legs don't appear to be broken, but his torso is already covered in bruises peeking through the blood. I'm sure he has broken ribs.

"Come on, kid." Phil's voice comes from where he's standing next to the dais, reaching for Jett. "I'll help you down."

"Phil?" Jett's one good eye searches for him.

"Yeah, kid, I'm here. Did you think I would just leave you to your death?"

"Yeah, actually." He tries to laugh but ends up coughing, blood spilling out of his mouth. *Oh gods, that's not good.*

Phil snorts. "Then you don't know me at all. Now come on, stop being a sissy and get your ass up."

I do my best to help get Jett moving, but he's easily three times my size and impossibly heavy. A loud, frantic bark from Peggy has me jolting. I look up and see Tison heading right for us. I don't even have time to think, or wonder where my burst of strength comes from, but I manage to push Jett over the dais edge toward Phil right before Tison's leg comes barreling toward us.

It connects with my stomach with so much force I hear the crack of bones and I'm sent spinning through the air, barely registering the impact of the floor as I land feet away from the dais. Somewhere far off, I hear Jett's scream, only this time, it's my name on his lips. Tison only kicked me in the stomach, but I swear I feel the pain radiate through my entire body. It's so intense that I can't even make a sound as black floods into my vision.

I blink, slowly seeing the world come back into focus, but as soon as I'm conscious, the pain rips through me. I gasp, trying to get air into my lungs, and I immediately regret the decision. My chest lights on fire and I start to cough uncontrollably.

"Meg!" Jett's hands are on me, pulling me into his lap, as his face hovers over mine.

"Wonderboy to the resc—" I try to speak but the words are cut off as I choke and spit up blood. *Oh gods, that's not good*, I repeat the thought.

"No, no, no." Jett's brushing at my hair, my face, his hands shaking furiously. "Why did you do that?"

"I know...you don't...believe me...." I speak slowly, trying to get the words out without choking on them. "But I love...you. I think...I loved you from—" It's no use. I can't get the words out. I can feel my heart slowing. I can feel the blood slowing as it flows through my veins.

"Shh." Jett's rocking me now, both of his blue eyes looking down at me with so much sadness it's almost too hard to hold his gaze. I watch as his injuries slowly heal right before my eyes. "Don't speak, we're going to get you to a doctor. You're going to be ok, just save your energy."

"The deal....." I close my eyes and try to swallow down some of the blood. I only end up coughing it back up. "Your strength...coming back...I'm hurt." I hope he can understand what I'm saying. His deal with Hades has been broken because one of the terms was that I wouldn't be hurt by him or anyone he commanded.

"No, no, no," he repeats frantically. "This isn't how it was supposed to end. You were never meant to be here. You were supposed to leave."

I manage to reach up, wiping the tears running down his cheek. "It's ok," I whisper. "I'm free now."

He tries to hold back a sob, but it rips up his throat. Then his gorgeous lips are on mine. I can taste the salt of his tears as it mingles with the copper of my blood. I'm overwhelmed with the scent of him, like fresh air and sunshine on a warm spring day. I smile, or at least try to, as the world fades, and my body goes cold.

Chapter thirty-five

Running Into The Fire by Simple Thieves, Sam Tinnesz

I feel her lips go cold against mine but I don't want to pull them away. I don't want to look down and see all the light gone from her beautiful eyes. I don't want to see her glowing skin dull and gray. I don't want to acknowledge that she's gone.

Or that she saved me.

Or that she loved me.

I was supposed to be the one saving her, not the other way around. I was the one who was always destined to die young. Not her. Not Meg.

"Come on, kid." I feel Phil's hand on my shoulder, gently pulling me back. "You've gotta let her go. She's gone."

I pull away from her, looking down at her dead body, limp in my arms, and that familiar anger starts to push to the surface. I welcome it. I relish the feel of it coursing through my veins, helping to clear my mind.

"No," I say again forcefully. "No, this isn't how it ends. Hades likes to make deals, so I'll give him one he can't refuse."

"Don't do this, kid. We've all lost people we love, and we all have to live through it. It's just part of life."

"I've lost enough, Phil. I won't lose her too."

"Think about this, kid," Phil says as he jogs beside me. "She wouldn't want this."

"I'm done caring about what other people want." I leave him as I work my way through the crowd carrying Meg's body, ignoring all the whispers and stares. I climb the stairs until I'm at the door to the glass suite that overlooks the ring. I know he's here, watching everything unfold.

I kick the door and it blows off the hinges. Hades is standing in the middle of the room, hands in his pockets in a casual stance, waiting for me. That stupid arrogant smirk is back on his face, and I grip Meg's body tighter, fighting the urge to set her down and destroy him, once and for all. But this isn't about him.

"I want to make a deal," I grit out through clenched teeth.

"I'm listening."

"My life for hers."

"Interesting." Hades takes his hand out of his pockets and rubs his chin in contemplation. "But I'm afraid this is out of my hands. Meg's soul is already in The Pit."

"Then I'll get it out," I say, more determined than ever.

Hades laughs. "You could certainly try, but the Fates hold the keys to the gates of The Pit. Any soul in or out is by their say alone. If you enter The Pit, the thread of your life will be in their hands, and the Fates don't take kindly to those who think they can manipulate them."

"Take me to The Pit," I order, already having made up my mind. I don't care what the odds are. I said it once and I'll say it again. "I'll save her, or I'll die trying."

Hades shrugs. "It's a win-win for me. You're willingly throwing yourself into The Pit. Why would I say no to that?"

He walks past me and out of the suite, down the hall to the elevator. I follow, clutching Meg's body in my arms, and call to Peggy through our bond. A few minutes later she's by my side, limping, but seems unhurt beyond that.

"You ok, girl?" She licks my hand. "Good, I need you to come with me."

We get in the elevator and Hades reveals the hidden console, hitting the button that will take us down to The Pit. I ignore him and the smug look on his face as we ride down in tension-filled silence.

Once I'm standing at the edge of the cliff, the eerie hum of voices surrounding me, I gently lay Meg's body on the ground. "I need you to watch over her body, Peg. Don't let anything happen to her, you understand?"

Peggy lays down next to Meg and covers her body with her wing. A low growl rumbles in her throat. "Thank you." I pet her head. "If I don't make it out of here, you go and you stay with Phil. Take care of the old man."

I feel her sadness through our bond, but I also feel her acceptance. She knows that I need to do this and she's going to be with me every step of the way.

I reluctantly stand and walk to the edge of the cliff. The last thing I want to do is leave them here with Hades, but I'm wasting time. I glance over the edge, and just like before, I can see clearly into The Pit. My eyes roam over the surface until I spot her. There. I see her soul slowly drifting further and further from the surface.

I have absolutely no fear and no hesitation as I launch myself over the edge, diving headfirst into The Pit. If I thought I felt pain before, when my strength was gone and Tison was beating the shit out of me, it's nothing compared to this. An intense, sharp pain slices through every inch of my skin. It feels like I'm being skinned alive and burned at the same time.

The pain halts me from moving for a few seconds as it's the only thing my mind can focus on, but something inside of me pushes through. Something inside of me allows me to somehow push through the pain and I remember why I'm here. I start to swim, aiming for Meg. I can see her soul floating below me. In fact, I'm surrounded by souls.

They don't seem to notice me though as I swim by their white, translucent forms, bumping into them as I move.

The lower and lower I get, the harder it is to swim. I feel the pressure of The Pit all around me. My chest is strains to hold onto the air in my lungs and my limbs suddenly feel too heavy. I'm just out of reach of Meg, I stretch my body, straining against the pressure that seems determined to hold me back. Bubbles escape my lips, and my lungs burn along with every inch of my skin.

Almost there. You're almost there.

White spots begin to blink in my vision. I blink furiously, trying to clear them as I continue to reach out to Meg. But it's no use. I feel my fingertips just graze against her soul before a blinding white light engulfs my vision and my body becomes weightless. The pressure is gone, and I find myself gasping for air. When no water fills my lungs, the realization hits me.

I'm dead.

"You're not dead." A booming voice echoes around me. I know I didn't say the words out loud, so how did he know what I was thinking?

I jolt. My eyes snap open and I find myself lying on a gleaming, white marble floor. A large man with blonde hair that flows around his shoulders, gleaming like the sun, is kneeling over me. His cerulean eyes as bright and clear as a perfect, cloudless summer sky.

"Who are you? And where am I if I'm not dead?"

"Let's get you to your feet. Let me get a good look at you," he says, grabbing my arm and helping me up.

Once I'm standing, I'm left to look up into the face of what must be God. "Are you?"

He chuckles. "A god? Yes. But not the God you grew up knowing." He sighs. "It was never meant to be this way."

"What way? Who are you? And where am I?" I repeat.

"You'll know me as Zeus, God of Olympus, and that's where you are. In my home to be exact. But another name I'd like you to know me by is Father."

I stare at him blankly. This stranger. This strange place I'm in and have never seen before. I'm dead. I have to be. There's no other explanation.

He sighs again. "I can see that it's going to take a little more convincing, but I'm afraid we don't have much time." He waves his hand, and an image appears in the air before me.

My memories are fuzzy, but I would recognize her face anywhere. "Mom," I whisper. I turn to face the stranger. "That's my mom. Where is she? Is she here?" I dart a look around, but the room is empty.

"No, Son." He shakes his head in defeat. "Your mother was human. Although my magic allowed her to live longer than she should have, in the end, she went to Heaven. Only gods can live in Olympus. But look." He points to the image.

I watch as memories and years unfold in seconds before my eyes. I see the beginning of time when Mageía roamed Earth along with the humans. I see my mother send her first prayer out into the universe. I see Zeus answer that prayer. I watch as their story, their love, unfolds before me. All the years they got to share before the prayers and the power of those prayers began to fade, leaving Zeus confined to Olympus once more. But not before I was born.

And the rest, I know.

I look up at Zeus, really look at him, and I see it. I see the resemblance in our eyes, our sharp jaws and straight noses, our builds. But my hair and lips. Those came from my mother.

"If you're my father then that means I'm..."

"You're a demi-god, Hercules, or at least you were until you willingly jumped into The Pit to save the woman you love."

"Hercules?" I ask, the name sounding vaguely familiar as if I've heard it before.

"That's your name, your true name. Your mother gave you a human name since you were forced to live amongst them, but your name is Hercules. And you, my boy, are no longer a demi-god. You are a god. You are my son." He smiles proudly. "And you can now come home and live here, where you've always been meant to be."

"A god," I say in awe, the shock of all this information sinking into my bones. It doesn't seem real, and yet, I think somewhere deep down inside, I've always known. The dreams I had as a kid, the snakes, the lion, and how they ended up on my skin, my strength, and my impenetrable skin. Somewhere deep inside, I always knew.

I laugh, a little at first, and then it bursts out of me all at once. But it dies just as quickly. "What about Meg?"

"I'm sorry, Son."

"No! No, I refuse to believe that's it. You're telling me I'm a god but I'm powerless to save her? I refuse to believe that!"

He sighs again. He opens his mouth to speak but no words come out.

"Tell me!"

"You can choose to save her but at an extremely high cost."

"Tell me," I repeat, softer this time but just as strongly.

"You can pull her soul out of that pit, but it will drain you. It will take everything you have to get her out. You'll no longer be this, a god. You will remain a demi-god, but you'll never get to come home. You'll never again get to step foot on Olympus, and I will never see you again."

I swallow. So much is being thrown at me in such a short period of time. It's hard to digest, but honestly, it's not even a question.

"My whole life I've been alone. I've struggled to understand why I am the way that I am, and why the world is so cruel. Just a few months ago, I would have jumped at the opportunity to live here. To get to know you and finally feel like the world made sense. Like I finally found where I belong. But I found it anyway, on my own. I finally found my home, and where I belong is not here, Dad. I'm sorry. I belong down there. I belong with Meg."

He frowns slightly but nods. "I know, Son. I know." He pulls me into a strong embrace, and I automatically hug him back. "Just know that you're loved. You've always been loved. And I will always be here, looking down on you, and I'm so incredibly proud of the man you're becoming."

I open my mouth to thank him, to tell him how much I love him, too, even though I never got the chance to know him, but a loud boom of thunder cuts off my words, followed by a bright crack of lightning. I close my eyes against the flash of light, and when I open them again, Meg's soul is in my arms and I'm swimming up toward the surface.

I gasp for air as I break through, feeling the air fill up my lungs in the sweetest breath I've ever taken. I call to Peggy through our bond and a flash of white dives over the side of the cliff. She hovers over the water, allowing me to pull myself over her back, then she carries us back to the cliff landing.

"This can't be real," Hades says, pure shock written all over his face. "You should be dead. Why aren't you dead?"

"Guess the Fates decided I was worth saving," I say as I carry Meg's soul to her body.

"No!" Hades shouts. He rushes over to intercept me, trying to grab Meg's soul and wrench it out of my hands. "If you live, she stays. That was the deal!"

I grab him around the throat, squeezing hard and lifting him off the ground. "We never actually made a deal. You left it to the Fates, so I'll do the same."

His eyes widen as understanding dawns on him. He tries to speak but can't, and instead desperately claws at my hand around his throat. I walk back over to the edge and dangle him off the side.

"I hope all the innocent souls you damned to this pit torture yours for eternity," I say as I let him go.

His scream is cut off as he falls beneath the surface of The Pit. The souls didn't seem to notice me, but now, they all come to life. They swarm around Hades' body, and I watch as they drag him into its depths until I can't see them anymore.

"Good luck getting out of there, you piece of shit." I spit over the edge before finally walking away.

I kneel next to Meg, Peggy eagerly waiting on the other side of her body, as I slowly lower her soul back into her body. When nothing happens, I pick her up, cradling her against my chest, and beg. "Come on, Firecracker. I need you to fight, one last time. Come back to me please."

Peggy whines as she waits next to me. It feels like eternity passes by as I wait for those beautiful eyes to open again. I'm beginning to doubt that this worked. After all, who the fuck do I think I am? I'm no hero. But I am a demi-god.

Then, her eyes flutter and slowly open. Her lips part, and she takes in a deep breath before letting it out on a shaky exhale.

"Those eyes," I whisper, gently stroking her cheek. "I thought I'd never see those eyes again."

"Wonderboy." Her voice is raspy. She clears her throat. "What happened? Did you beat Tison?"

I smile. "I have no fucking clue what happened with Tison," I admit. "But he won't be a problem anymore. None of them will be. We'll see to that."

"We?" she asks, pushing against me to sit up.

"Yes, Firecracker. You and me." Peggy barks, and I laugh.

"You and me and Peggy," I correct myself.

"I'm still not sure she likes me very much." Meg laughs nervously, and Peggy leans in and licks her on the face.

"I think you've earned her trust." I reach out and grab her chin, tilting her head back, forcing her to look at me. "And mine. You risked your life for me, and I've traded mine for yours."

Her eyebrows pull together. "What does that mean? What did you give up?"

"Nothing that matters. As long as I'm with you, that's enough. That's the only thing I want. I want you, Meg. I think I've loved you since the moment I saw you."

"Hey." She shoves playfully at my shoulder. "That's what I was trying to say! You can't steal my line!"

I laugh. "You're right. What am I thinking? I don't even like you."

She grins up at me, her beautiful eyes and skin glowing. I lean down, my lips hovering just over hers as she whispers, "Ditto."

I close the distance between us and fall helplessly into her kiss. I kiss her with every inch of my soul and every piece of my beating heart. Instead of saying goodbye, this kiss is saying hello. And there's not one single doubt in my mind.

This is where I belong.

Epilogue

"When you said you had a surprise for me, I have to admit, I thought it would be more along the lines of...."

"Of what?" I squeeze her hand tighter as we walk down the sidewalk in downtown Chicago.

A faint blush creeps into her beautiful cheeks as she glances up at me through thick lashes. "Of something that has to do with the bedroom."

I stop and pull her into me. "Being shy is cute, but I know you better than that, Firecracker. If you want me to find a dark corner to fuck you in, you know I'd be happy to," I offer, grabbing her hand and gliding it over my semi-hard cock. Just the thought of pulling her behind one of these buildings, lifting up that dress, and pushing inside of her has my cock twitching.

I slide my other hand down her back and firmly grip her ass. Neither one of us seems the slightest bit concerned that we're still in the middle of a busy sidewalk.

"Mm," she hums deep in her chest. "As much as that thought intrigues me, the surprise intrigues me more. Save this thought for after." She pulls away from me.

"As you wish." I take her hand in mine again and proceed down the sidewalk to our destination.

"Are you going to tell me where we're going at least?"

"We are going right here." I lead her to the side of the sidewalk where a set of stairs descends underground. At the bottom of the stairs is a small walkway that ends at a closed door.

"What is this place, Hercules?"

After the initial chaos of everything that unfolded once Hades was gone, I told Meg everything, and she filled me in on the pieces I didn't know. She knows my true identity, as well as everyone else in The Underworld. I'm no longer hiding from who I am.

"This is a speakeasy."

"Okayyy," she drags out the word. "But why are we here?"

"You'll see," I say as I knock on the door.

The small partition slides open and an unknown person behind the door asks, "Password?"

"Cherry Blossom."

The partition slides closed, and moments later, the locks click and the door swings open, allowing us entry.

I lead Meg through a dimly lit hallway until we come to a set of stairs and start climbing. The music slowly gets louder and clearer the higher we climb.

"That singer has a beautiful voice," Meg says in awe.

"That she does," I agree, a lilt of amusement in my voice.

At the top, the landing opens up to a wide balcony that overlooks a lower level. Tables line the railing on each side of the balcony, but the center has been left clear for people to stand. This is where I lead Meg. She grabs onto the railing, and I move to stand behind her, hands on the rail, pressing myself against her and leaning in.

Down below, the room is mostly lost to shadow, but the stage is lit up in a beautiful white glow. On the stage, a woman stands at the front behind a microphone stand, and a man playing the piano is slightly behind and to the side of her.

She is one of the most beautiful women I've ever seen. Her long, dark hair falls in waves around her shoulders and down her back. Her white dress flows against her curves, both flattering her figure but also not revealing too much. Her pearl skin is flawless and glimmers under the white light.

But her voice.

Her voice is the softest, smoothest, and most powerful voice I've ever heard. It's enchanting. Captivating. In Meg's own words, I lean down and whisper, "Isn't she hypnotizing?"

A small gasp escapes her, and she brings her hand up to cover her mouth, eyes wide and never once leaving the stage. "Is that...."

"Yes," I whisper, not wanting to break this spell.

I can see the tears shining in Meg's eyes as she continues to stare at the woman on stage. When the song comes to an end, the singer speaks to the crowd.

"As always, it is my absolute pleasure to sing for you tonight, but tonight, something a little different is going to happen. I hope you all wouldn't mind doing me a favor and indulging me briefly." The crowd murmurs their approval. "Tonight is a very, very special night. One that I only dreamed would ever come true. Tonight, I get to meet my daughter for the first time since she was taken from me."

Meg gasps again, the tears streaming down her face. "She didn't give you up," I whisper again. "That was just a lie Hades told you. He tricked her and took you from her. He threatened her with your life if she ever came looking for you, the same way he threatened you with hers. Don't hold it against her."

Her shoulders are shaking, but she isn't making a sound as her eyes stay glued on her mother.

"Ladies and Gentlemen, please let me introduce you to my daughter." Her eyes finally make their way up to the balcony, where a spotlight is shines on Meg. I've stepped back and out of sight, allowing her this moment. "Meghana Williams, my beautiful, beautiful daughter," Euterpe says, tears straining her own voice. "Come." She gestures to Meg.

Meg looks back at me, and I point to the stairs that lead down to the bottom floor. "Go," I encourage her.

The smile I'm rewarded with has me fighting my own damn tears. "Thank you," she says, and walks to the stairs.

The spotlight follows her, and I take her spot at the rail, watching along with the others as this beautiful moment unfolds. Meg slowly makes her way to the stage. She hesitates for just a second, but Euterpe never does. She embraces her daughter in the fiercest motherly hug I've ever seen.

I got all of my answers and am finally able to move on with my life, and now I get to see Meg and her mother get theirs. This is a moment of healing for everyone, and for once in my life, I'm excited about what the future holds.

Because as long as my future has Meg, as long as we're together, there's not a fight we can't win.

Author's Note & Acknowledgements

I know I always say this, but I can't believe I'm here again. It's always surreal to know that I'm doing this. Me. I'm writing books that people actually read and love. Please don't pinch me, because if this is a dream, I don't ever want to wake up!

As always, I have to thank my husband for being so incredibly patient and understanding that this is my passion. That the dream is to do this full time, and allowing me the opportunity to write, even when that means I neglect everything else. He is the real MVP.

My Alpha reader, Jenny. You always fly through my books and provide me with the BEST feedback. You really saved my butt on this one with that one sentence. Seriously, thank you for being conscious and also understanding what others might find offensive or insensitive. Thank you for always being so sweet! I adore you!

My Beta reader, Kara. You are the magic behind my books really coming together. You seriously saved me on this one. I can't believe how many filler words I used! And comas...SIGH. I tried to be proactive and get the right which I think just made this one worse haha Thank you for correcting my ass and always making me look good. I can't tell you how much I appreciate you!

I always need to thank my social media family. The handful of supporters that are fiercely loyal. You know who you are. I see you. I appreciate you. You make the hard days not so hard.

And to my readers, both old and new, I hope that I'm also inspiring your loyalty with every book I write, because I can't do this without you. Every single time you choose to pick up my book and give it a chance, you're giving ME a chance. You're giving me chance to live my dream, and I am forever grateful.

Please remember to leave those Goodreads and Amazon reviews. You don't even need to say anything, just a rating means the world and is so incredibly helpful. And, if you enjoyed this book, or any of my books, please help me spread the word! You will influence more people than I ever will with a genuine recommendation. Again, I can't do this without you.

Please don't be shy! Find me on social media, say hi, and stay tuned for all that the future holds.

XOXO,
Harmony

More From The Author

If you enjoyed this read, please check out my other retellings!
Unforgivable Sins
Beastly Lies & Beautiful Legends

Also, check out my complete urban/paranormal fantasy series, The Amarah Rey, Fey Warrior Series.
Awaken
Fey Blood
Dark Temptations
Divine Destiny

You can find them on Amazon here: Amazon Author page or the kindle version here: Amazon Ebooks/Kindle

Stay up to date on news and exclusive content and follow me on social media!

Instagram
TikTok
Newsletter

Thank you for being here and all of your support! Again, I could not do this without You. Leave those reviews 😊

www.ingramcontent.com/pod-product-compliance
Lightning Source LLC
Chambersburg PA
CBHW030649260626
47157CB00007B/2560